FIRE AND ICE

Gulliver set his hand over Maggie's mouth. "Do you ever stop talking? And most of it lies . . . or nonsense?"

She grabbed his arm and thrust his hand away, her fingers inadvertently closing over the knife slash. He winced with a swift intake of breath, and she instantly released him.

His pale eyes sparked, ice and fire both. "I should congratulate you. You're the first woman who's ever drawn blood." A slow smile drew up the edges of his mouth. "Though it seems to me you ought to pay a forfeit."

She scrambled back. "What?"

"A forfeit," he repeated as he reached for her.

He got her by the upper arms and dragged her across the bed, nearly up against his chest. She twisted in his hold and he shook her once. "Be still . . . this is going to hurt a lot less than what you did to me."

She had no idea what he intended, though any retribution was bound to be terrible. And he still had her knife—

When he kissed her, she was almost relieved. It was a brief, hard kiss, his mouth firm, his left hand steady behind her head. Not altogether unpleasant, though still an affront. When she opened her mouth to protest, he did it again. Slower, this time.

"That's better," he whispered against her lips, his fingers stroking her nape beneath the heavy spill of hair.

The Barkin Emeralds

Nancy Butler

A SIGNET BOOK

SIGNET
Published by New American Library, a division of
Penguin Group (USA) Inc., 375 Hudson Street,
New York, New York 10014, U.S.A.
Penguin Books Ltd, 80 Strand,
London WC2R 0RL, England
Penguin Books Australia Ltd, 250 Camberwell Road,
Camberwell, Victoria 3124, Australia
Penguin Books Canada Ltd, 10 Alcorn Avenue,
Toronto, Ontario, Canada M4V 3B2
Penguin Books (NZ), cnr Rosedale and Airborne Roads,
Albany, Auckland 1310, New Zealand

Penguin Books Ltd, Registered Offices:
80 Strand, London WC2R 0RL, England

First published by Signet, an imprint of New American Library,
a division of Penguin Group (USA) Inc.

First Printing, June 2004
10 9 8 7 6 5 4 3 2 1

For Hilary Ross—
Thank you for encouraging me, challenging me,
and, ultimately, letting me tell my own tales.

Take me back, O hills I love,
Lift me from this lonely bed,
Light my way with stars above,
Curl soft winds around my head.
Wash my feet with crystal streams,
Cradle my arms in boughs of oak,
Leave the scent of pine for dreams,
Wrap me tight in earthen cloak.

—Traditional Folksong

Chapter One

$\mathcal{T}$he sailboat slammed into an oncoming wave, its prow thrusting skyward like a grouse breaking cover. No sooner had the boat settled into a trough than it was heaved upward again by the churning water.

Maggie Bonner, windswept and a bit green about the face, held tight to her makeshift seat on a cargo crate and vowed she would not get seasick. It was bad enough that over the past three days she'd already endured a series of undeserved humiliations—she now refused to succumb to *that* final indignity.

Fighting down the queasiness, Maggie assured herself it was simply a case of mind over matter. Her stomach, however, which was pitching in time to the up-and-down motion of the boat, had other ideas. The clammy, bilious feeling was lowering a morale already at half-mast.

"I won't give in," she muttered, eyes firmly fastened on the horizon as the captain had advised. "It's bound to lessen in time." She purposely did not remind herself that the *Charles Stuart* had been on the water for nearly three hours.

Until today she'd considered herself a seasoned traveler—a youth spent on the road had seen to that—but this was the first time she'd ventured out to sea. It was not proving to be an auspicious maiden voyage.

"Captain Og," she called out to the gray-haired Scot at the ship's wheel, "is it possible you could take a smoother route to the island?"

"Take a route, is it?" he echoed, managing to express ed disdain around the stem of his unlit briar pipe. "Spoken like a true landsman, that were. 'Set a course' is what ye be meanin', lass."

He braced his legs even wider apart and, to Maggie's mind, intentionally aimed the ship into an oncoming swell. The stiff wind played havoc with the wispy strands that fell below his knit cap, reminding Maggie how much she wished she'd worn a warm bonnet—and a woolen vest under her pelisse. And as usual she'd left her gloves behind in Kilchoan. How could she have known it would be so cold out on the water? It was April, for heaven's sake.

The *Charles Stuart* did possess a cabin, but Captain Og had advised her that as a novice sailor she'd do better in the open air. She had settled in front of the mainmast on a battered crate, which had been lashed to the deck with thick cables. She suspected it had once held illicit cargo . . . French silk, perhaps, or tobacco.

Back at the posting house in Kilchoan she'd heard an earful about the men of these out-islands. Smugglers, the landlord labeled them, and worse than that, brigands and pirates. Captain Og appeared rather long in the tooth to be involved in anything so dangerous—or to be piloting his own boat, for that matter. Yet he had been recommended to her as the canniest captain in the Hebrides, and she'd hired him sight unseen.

It had been something of a shock when a man of sixty-odd years met her at the wharf and assured her with a broad wink that he was indeed the master of the *Charles Stuart*. He'd also expressed surprise that she was traveling alone to Quintay. She did not trouble him with the convoluted tale of how Lady Fescue's lone footman, who'd been ordered to accompany her, had that very morning been taken with a distressing flux. Sea travel was beyond him.

Beyond most sane people, Maggie reflected sourly, as her stomach performed another somersault.

The sky had been a watery blue-gray when they'd set out just before noon, the sun visible but veiled. Now the clouds overhead had thickened and the sun had taken its leave. All around the pitching boat the water was an inky black, relieved only by a tattered froth of whitecaps.

She lifted her carpetbag from the deck and clutched it to her chest, hoping to ward off the sharp sting of the west wind.

was the problem, she'd deduced, the reason it was taking so long to reach their destination. They were heading directly into the wind, and Captain Og was forced to sail in a complicated zigzag pattern to make any headway.

"How much longer will it take to reach the island?" she called out to him.

"Have urgent business with his lordship, do ye?" he called back. Captain Og was clearly an advocate of the "always answer a question with another question" school of conversation.

"Quite urgent," she responded, and then shivered as a wet tendril of hair wrapped itself around her throat like the slimy tentacle of some sea beast. Her chignon, always a challenge to keep neat even on the balmiest of days, was nearly undone. Her hair, damp with sea spray, would look like a nest of vipers by the time she reached his lordship's island. Not that it mattered what sort of impression she made; he was hardly likely to notice her person, not after she delivered her woeful message.

She squinted across the open water, trying to make out something distinct in the hazy distance. They had already bypassed Rum and Eigg, of the Inner Hebrides, plus a number of small, uninhabited islands, sitting like treacle-colored lumps of pudding in the midst of the sea.

Bleak, she thought, *bleak and uninviting.* It made her wonder why anyone would choose to live in such a remote, forbidding place. She was starting to commiserate with Alice Fescue on her decision to run away rather than wed a man, titled lord or not, who rarely left his island home. There were some things wealth and stature could not make up for, especially to a young lady with a taste for town life. Alice would have languished in such a place. And Maggie, as her hired companion, would have been forced to share her exile.

What had Lady Fescue been thinking, to affiance her daughter to a notorious recluse? It was all destined to come to a bad end, and so it had.

Maggie thanked Providence that at least she was no longer bound to remain on one of these godforsaken islands. She was merely the bearer of bad tidings—and the guardian of the betrothal gift, which as etiquette dictated must be returned to his lordship.

This duty was a small price to pay for having unwittingly let her charge slip away from the inn at Kilchoan—and into the arms of a chance-met militia officer. Lady Fescue had practically succumbed to an apoplexy upon discovering the elopement. Maggie, who often thought privately that the woman inclined toward melodrama worthy of Drury Lane, forgave her the outburst in this instance. Losing an earl as a son-in-law and gaining a captain of the militia, however charming and robust, was bound to shock any mother into severe spasms.

Maggie knew that Lady Fescue, widow of an impoverished baronet, had virtually beggared herself to present her daughter in London, hoping for a windfall match. That the reclusive earl had been visiting there on business and had come upon Alice feeding the swans in St. James's Park was a happy coincidence.

He had called upon Lady Fescue the very next day, declaring his intention to make Alice his wife. After a week-long courtship, he had departed for the Hebrides, assured by Lady Fescue that her daughter would be delighted to wed with him. All it required was a fortnight to order bride clothes, her ladyship insisted, and they would then follow him north to his castle on Quintay for the wedding.

Sadly, Maggie had missed the whole episode, having been called to attend her ailing father in Surrey. When she returned to her duties, it was to find Alice in alternating moods of excitation and despair. Maggie had duly admired the betrothal gift that his lordship had presented to Alice on the day of his departure, but she was concerned that the girl appeared so greatly enamored of her future husband's wealth and so little taken with his person.

"A washed-out stick of a fellow," Lady Fescue's footman had confided to Maggie. "And no more polish than a field hand."

Maggie wished she had met the earl; it would have made her mission a little less intimidating. Still, she would do what was required of her. It was that or face the prospect of finding new employment without a reference. Lady Fescue had been quite clear on that point. If Maggie was going to make her way in the world—and there was little hope that she would ever have anything to depend upon but her own wits—she needed that endorsement. Decent placements were hard enough to come by even with a sterling recommendation.

"Don't think about that now," she cautioned herself. "Time enough to fret when you are on the road back to England, sitting across from Lady Fescue, trying not to notice that her mouth has gone all pruney, knowing it's you she blames for her misfortune and not herself for forcing Alice into a distasteful marriage."

Maggie had become so lost in thought that she didn't notice the small, rocky island looming off to starboard . . . or the single-masted sloop racing toward them across the churning water.

"Heave to!" a voice called out in a commanding baritone.

Maggie's head shot up, and she leapt to her feet in alarm. She heard Captain Og mutter behind her, something about "blasted pirates," which certainly could not have been the case. The tales of pirates and brigands she'd heard at the inn were from the previous century, not this civilized age. Nevertheless, the tall, greatcoated man standing in the prow of the sloop definitely looked ominous—the more so since he was holding a pistol.

The sloop bore down relentlessly, sailing a course that would intercept the *Charles Stuart* in a matter of minutes. Maggie absently noted another figure seated at the tiller but couldn't seem to take her eyes off the man with the gun.

Captain Og cursed again, more colorfully than before, and the next instant abandoned the wheel and began lowering the ship's mainsail.

"You're not giving up?" she cried in disbelief.

"Sorry, lass," he said, and then by way of reassurance added, "I doubt you'll be harmed."

"What does he want?"

"Who can say?" He gave a shake of his grizzled head. "But ye be agreeable now, and give him nae trouble." He shot her a warning look.

"Couldn't we have at least tried to outrun him?"

"And where's the sense o' that?" he responded cryptically.

Maggie rolled her eyes while trying to contain her thicket of hair, whose wet tendrils were again flaying her cheeks. She managed to shove most of it under her bonnet just as the smaller ship came alongside. There was the hollow thud of wooden hulls engaging and then a rope came snaking over the side. The tall man swung himself over the gunwale, straddling it as he made the line fast on a cleat.

"What is the meaning of this?" Maggie called out boldly. From the corner of her eye, she saw Captain Og wince.

The man cocked his head as he regarded her, the fierce breeze whipping hair the color of a mink's pelt into a tangle over his forehead.

"Why, madam," he said smoothly, "I would think the meaning is quite clear." He nodded to the pistol in his hand. "I am robbing you."

She could have sworn there was humor in his tone. There was certainly amusement in his pale eyes, which danced wickedly behind a veil of thick black lashes.

A laughing brigand. Just her luck.

He motioned with the pistol. "Now, if you would ask the others in the cabin to come on deck . . ."

"I am the only passenger," she said.

He seemed momentarily perplexed by that statement.

"You will have very poor pickings, I'm afraid," she added. "I possess little of value save a cherished ring from my departed grandmother and a garnet brooch, which was given to me by my father. And if you are desperate enough to take those paltry items, which can mean little to you and are the whole world to me, why then, sir, you are worse than a robber, you are a complete rogue."

He thought this over a moment, then nodded. She hoped he was conceding to her argument, but then he said with a grin, "Rogue, it is. Now, hand over that carpetbag . . . if you please." He slid to the deck and came toward her.

She drew back until the opposite gunwale prevented any further retreat.

"Captain Og," she cried in desperation, "aren't you going to offer any resistance?"

"Appears to me you are doing a fine job of it by yourself, lass," he remarked from behind the ship's wheel, an expression of relish on his weathered face.

The tall brigand crossed the deck and tried to pry the carpetbag from her arms. Maggie held on tight. She heard his muttered oath before he finally ceased the tug of war and stepped back.

"Just how foolhardy are you, ma'am?" His eyes bored into hers. She got the distinct impression he was no longer amused.

"I mean to take what's in that bag and have no compunction about shooting you and throwing you over the side."

"If you take it," she said breathlessly, "you might as well throw me into the sea, because I will have no life worth living after that."

"I will leave you your baubles, if they mean that much to you. Just give me what's in the bag."

She clutched it even tighter. "I told you . . . I have nothing of any value in here."

"Oh, I think that's highly debatable."

Maggie's heart sank. The brigand knew about the betrothal gift. *How* he could know was beyond fathoming at this point. She'd told no one in Kilchoan of her errand.

"It's not mine to give," she said, since there was no point in prevaricating. "You must understand that. I'm honor-bound to see it safely delivered to Quintay."

"A pity, then, that you must fail," he said as he calmly thrust the pistol point against her throat.

She went instantly light-headed. No employment reference was worth dying over. Her stiffened fingers unclenched, and the carpetbag fell to the deck.

The man sketched a bow, a swift, graceful motion. "Thank you. It is always gratifying when prudence prevails."

He went down on one knee, opened the satchel and began to rifle through it, carelessly tossing her most intimate undergarments onto the deck. She gave a cry of dismay when the stiff wind buffeted them aloft and began darting awkwardly about to recapture shift and zona before they ended up in the water.

"Not a very enticing trousseau," the brigand observed, fingering one of her remaining petticoats, a plain muslin affair with a single limp ruffle. "I mean, for an earl's intended wife." He looked up at her, now clutching her wilted underclothes to her chest. "But then you're nothing like I expected. No entourage . . . no chaperone. His lordship must have kindled quite a fire in you, that you have ventured out to sea alone to reach him. What's the matter? Your mama have a touch of mal de mer?"

Maggie could voice no reply. The idiot thought she was

Alice Fescue. Whatever information had been passed to him about the betrothal gift, his spies were not aware that Alice had scarpered from the inn. Still, she wasn't sure it was wise to correct him; she assumed he was less likely to shoot a member of the gentry than a mere hired companion.

"Yes," she said at last, raising her chin in a parody of Lady Fescue at her most toplofty. "Mama suffers a great many ailments. And my companion hates the water."

"And so you rush to your lover's arms without heeding propriety. I didn't think you society misses had such grit. His lordship is to be congratulated on his choice." He went back to rooting around in the bag, his cheeks narrowing when he found the secret compartment at the bottom. "And I promise you," he said, looking up and meeting her eyes, "such devotion in a life's mate will compensate the earl for the loss of this."

He raised up the heavy tangle of gold filigree and glittering gemstones from the midst of her clothing. It uncoiled across his outspread palm, where it lay like shimmering green fire.

"The Barkin emeralds," he breathed. "Fifteen perfect stones set in yellow gold. Worth a king's ransom."

"Worth my whole future," Maggie moaned softly.

The brigand stashed the necklace in his waistcoat as he rose.

"Give my regards to Lord Barkin," he said with a bow. "I wish you joy of each other."

"He will find you," she said in a quaking voice, barely containing her outrage. "And see that you hang for this. Captain Og and I will describe you."

He narrowed one eye and looked across at the old sailor. "Would you do that?"

Captain Og shrugged. "And how could I be doin' such a thing? My eyesight's not what it once was, alas."

The brigand offered Maggie a smug smile. "I've been threatened with hanging before this. And here I am, still breathing." He chucked her once under the chin. She snarled as she jerked away from his touch. His eyes darkened then, and his hand slid purposefully past her throat to her loosened hair. His fingers corralled a handful and tightened, drawing her head back.

"Such black hair," he said softly, for her ears alone. "S

green, green eyes. I was wrong . . . you are *exactly* what I should have expected his lordship to choose."

She slapped his hand away and stepped back, fury simmering near the surface now. She was no longer playacting the affronted lady. "I gave you no leave to touch me."

His eyes lit up again. "Rogues never ask for leave, don't you know that?"

He sketched a quick salute to Captain Og and made for the opposite gunwale. He halted, half over the side, one booted leg dangling nearly down to the deck, and looked across to her.

"He'll give you other baubles, my lady. Be assured. His castle is full of pretty things. You'll just be another addition to his collection."

Then he released the line that tethered the boats together and slipped over the side.

Maggie raced after him, leaning out over the gunwale as he dropped down into the sloop.

"This is not the end!" she cried. "Not by any means. I *will* get that necklace back."

His eyes met hers and he sighed. "Such fire. A pity it's to be wasted on that puling whelp."

She watched in shocked disbelief as the sloop drew away from the *Charles Stuart*. In a matter of minutes all her prospects had disappeared. She could not sail on to Quintay and admit that she had lost the Barkin emeralds. His lordship would be beyond words—to have forfeited his betrothed *and* a prized family heirloom in one fell swoop. And she certainly could not go back to Kilchoan and tell Lady Fescue she had allowed a laughing pirate to purloin the betrothal necklace.

She paced the deck in agitation while Captain Og fiddled with the lines. She had a sneaking hunch he was in league with the pirate . . . or at the very least in sympathy with him. It was apparent he had no intention of laying evidence against him. Probably one of those masculine codes of ethics—men of the sea honoring each other or some similar nonsense. Good thing she had no such scruples.

"It appears yon ruffian mistook you for Lord Barkin's intended," said the captain, sidling up beside her. "I didn't think it timely to inform him otherwise."

"Thank you for that. I was sure he was going to shoot me in spite of it."

"You oughtn't to have resisted, lass. The men of these out-islands are a wild lot."

She motioned to the landmass half a mile away, where the sloop—and the earl's necklace—was just disappearing around a rocky headland. "It looks to me as though our brigand is heading for *that* island."

He shrugged. "Who can say? Though St. Columba's been home to cutthroats and scoundrels these many centuries. Few decent men venture there."

"Then that is assuredly where *he* is going."

"There's naught tae be done, lass. Ye best put it out of your mind."

"Who was that man?" she asked him doggedly, brushing away that eternally loose tendril with an impatient noise. "I got the impression you knew each other."

Captain Og was guileless enough to look caught out. Then his eyes narrowed. "Know him by repute, I do. They call him Black Collum."

"His hair was rather more brown than black," she observed.

"'Tis his heart they refer to. Blacker than pitch." He gave her a self-satisfied smile.

"So I gather you don't intend sailing after him so we can retrieve the necklace."

"Didn't ye hear what I just said? Cutthroats and scoundrels."

"Oh, bosh," said Maggie. "I know the accents of a gentleman when I hear them. That man is no more a pirate than you are, Captain Og."

He looked a little startled at that but then said reasonably, "There's many a highbred fellow takes to robbery when times are hard. And on these smaller islands that's the usual state of things."

"And so we will just blithely sail on and forget that I was assaulted and robbed?"

"His lordship is a wealthy man. He could replace that necklace a hundred times over and still be rolling in gelt."

"That is hardly the point. Justice needs to be served." She seated herself again on the crate and arranged her skirts. "And

I believe I've thought of a solution. We will sail back to the mainland, if you please—"

"But—"

"I recall there was an excise cutter in the harbor at Kilchoan. I will report the theft to the captain. I'm sure *he* won't shrink at retrieving Lord Barkin's necklace."

Captain Og scowled. "Ye've no call to be doing that, bringin' in the blasted navy. What's that necklace to ye anyway, that ye're so determined to get it back?"

"My future. If I don't return it to the earl, my employer will refuse to give me a reference. I doubt you've ever had to depend on the goodwill of others for your bread, but I assure you, that is what my life has become."

"And why would ye be returnin' the necklace to his lordship? What's wrong with the young lady he is to wed? She didna fancy it?"

"She fancied it just fine. It was his lordship she misliked . . . or rather, she preferred a strapping militia officer to a belted earl."

"Ran off, did she?" His voice held a note of wicked glee.

She nodded. Lady Fescue had ordered her not to speak of the affair, but Maggie had never actually agreed to the edict. After all, she was only nominally in the woman's employ. "Three days past she disappeared. Lady Fescue managed to avert a scandal by telling the innkeeper her daughter was suffering bridal nerves and had taken to her bed."

Captain Og rubbed his bristly chin several times and said half to himself, "So there's to be no wedding on Quintay. This certainly changes things."

"What it doesn't change is that *I* intend to get that necklace back. By whatever means."

"Oh, aye, lass. I doubt Black Collum's seen the last o' ye."

Captain Og stood lost in thought for a moment, gazing at the island in the distance, then he drew a small metal flask from the pocket of his oilskin.

"Whisky," he said, holding it out to her. "T'will calm yer stomach and warm yer toes. If we're to be headin' all the way back, ye'll need a bit of fortifyin'. The wind's come up somethin' fierce."

He had a point. She unscrewed the silver cap and wiped the

lip on her cuff before raising it to her mouth. The whisky tasted the way a peat fire smelled, earthy and pungent—and just as fiery. It fairly burned its way down her throat.

"Have another swallow," he advised. "As we say hereabouts, a drop o' good whisky will do ye nae harm."

Maggie did as he asked, feeling a suffusion of blessed warmth spread out from her middle. When she returned the flask, he tucked it into the pocket of his oilskin.

"Aren't you going to have any?"

"Used to the chill, I am. Been sailin' these waters nigh on fifty year, winter and summer and all the seasons in between."

Once he had raised the sails and brought the boat about, Maggie felt her tension begin to ease. She'd expected the captain to put up more of a fight. He clearly wanted no dealings with the authorities. But, oh, *she'd* have a fine tale to tell the captain of the excise cutter . . . of a laughing brigand with pale eyes and a black heart. She only prayed that Lady Fescue would be satisfied that she'd done her best to see justice carried out.

As they sailed eastward, Maggie peered over her shoulder, watching the rocky cliffs of St. Columba recede. The island began to take on an odd wavering quality . . . as though it were undulating in the sea. She blinked several times and looked again. No, it was still moving . . . up and down, side to side. She shifted around to ask the captain about this phenomenon, but he too had become wavery and indistinct.

Her heart began to race, even more rapidly than when the brigand came aboard.

Something was terribly wrong.

She tried to stand, but her legs were like rubber. She tried to call out to Captain Og, but she couldn't muster more than a strained whisper.

The darkness came closing in then, thrusting toward her like a great muffling blanket.

Help me! her mind screamed as she fought off the sensation of falling into oblivion. *Oh, God, please help me . . .*

Chapter Two

*T*he pounding surf awakened Maggie. She lay in her bed,
eyes closed, listening to the violent thudding of an angry
sea.

Boom . . . boom . . . boom . . .

It must be a gale, she thought blearily, that the waves are
breaking so hard against the wharf. But when she at last forced
her eyes open, she realized with horror that she was not at the
waterside inn in Kilchoan but lying on a rocky beach. And the
surf was not making that racket—the sea rose and fell with
only a soft splashing noise upon the shingle fifteen feet below
her. The pounding was coming from inside her head, where a
hellish headache had taken hold.

She closed her eyes again, willing the pain to subside, waiting for the shock to diminish. It was rapidly occurring to her
that the canniest captain in the Hebrides had given her drugged
whisky and marooned her on this remote beach. As for why he
would do such a thing . . . well, she'd need more of her wits
about her to sort that out. Right now she needed to get on her
feet and rub some feeling back into her limbs. They felt like ici-
cles.

She tried to boost herself up, but her arms were flaccid and
useless. Her legs, likewise, seemed to have no connection to her
brain.

At least Captain Og had had the forethought to wrap her in
his oilcloth cape so that her pelisse was still dry. And he'd
placed her carpetbag beneath her head as a pillow, so she was
not without some provisions. She always carried a tinderbox

and a small paring knife. There was half a scone left over from breakfast as well.

In spite of her supine position, she was able to take stock of her surroundings. The beach lay at the end of a small cove that was enclosed on three sides by granite cliffs. A few stunted bushes clung to the outcroppings of rock, but that was the only sign of life to be seen on the entire bleak expanse. One object of note stood in the water several yards out from shore—a wooden piling with a brass ring at the top. She could just picture Captain Og securing his vessel to the ring and then carting her onto the beach.

The treacherous old sea-devil.

She lay there in a sort of bemused stupor, imagining what it would be like to live on a deserted island. She could gather driftwood for a fire and find roots and berries to eat. It would not be so terrible. No Lady Fescue with her hysterical episodes and sour faces. No gullible young ladies to guard from scheming militia captains. You didn't need references to live on a deserted island. Perhaps she would tame a fox kit to be her companion . . . or a young badger. She would keep a diary in her sketchbook, and when she was rescued, she would be taken to London in great state and become all the rage. The intrepid Maggie Bonner they would call her and . . . and . . .

The tears started down her face in a slow trickle, but they soon turned into a deluge. She lay there sobbing and gulping, afraid and cold and so very alone. She tugged the oilskin closer around her with benumbed fingers, waiting for her spirits to revive. It was not her nature to succumb to tears, but then again, she'd never been stranded alone in the middle of nowhere.

It was true the acting troupe had had to camp out in remote places at times, but she'd had her parents close by, and the merry band of actors they traveled with always made it seem like an adventure. There would be boastful stories beside the campfire, and often singing and fiddle playing would ensue as they passed around a jug of ale. Those were some of her favorite memories of Harry Topping's Top-Rate Players. "Second-Rate Players," her mother used to call them in private, and though it was true they were mostly rather tarnished thespians, they were the kindest people imaginable. Just thinking about them began to cheer her up.

Maggie was lost in fond reminiscence when a scattering of small rocks came tumbling down from the top of the cliff. Alarmed by the unexpected noise, she scrambled to her feet — and was pleased to see her body was at last responding. Her head was still a problem, but the pounding had lessened to a dull, throbbing ache.

She found the place where the rocks had come down and scanned the top of the cliff, looking for signs of some person or animal. There was nothing up there but granite and sky, a sky heavy with threatening clouds. She'd be wise to get off the beach before the rain started up. The tide was coming in, and she had no way of knowing how high it would rise if a storm broke.

She hefted her carpetbag and headed toward the cliff at the back of the beach, praying there was a path of some kind. She hadn't had to scale a rock wall since she was ten, when the troupe summered in Cornwall. She and her father had spent an afternoon picnicking in a small cove and had nearly been trapped by the rising water. Papa had been an athletic, agile man back then and had had no trouble climbing to the coastal road above them. He had boosted her up onto each subsequent shelf of rock and then scrambled up behind her, making a game of it.

Captain Og apparently possessed a similar sense of whimsy — at the foot of the cliff lay a number of turnip-sized white rocks placed in the formation of an arrow, a clear beacon against the predominately gray stones of the shingle. The arrow pointed to the beginning of a path. Maggie fervently prayed it also indicated the way back to civilization.

Happily giving up her plans for life as a castaway — and subsequent public adulation — she set off up the narrow trail, carefully skirting the piles of loose shale that had accumulated there.

She took some small consolation in knowing that things couldn't possibly get worse.

Captain Og huffed and puffed his way up the cliff. He was closing in on seventy years and not quite the spry fellow he'd been a decade ago. Still, he needed to do this, had to make sure the young lady came to no harm.

After carrying his passenger onto the shingle of Withy Cove, he had sailed around to the next inlet, a place the locals called Craigleigh Beach. To reach it he'd had to circumnavigate rugged Craigleigh Point, the bane of sailors throughout the Hebrides. Any number of ships had foundered there, four in the past three years alone. But he'd been sailing these waters forever—he knew every treacherous rock that lay in wait below the surface and every snaking current that could haul a ship into the shallows and stave in her tender wooden belly on the tumbled granite blocks that made up the Point.

When he reached the summit, he went forward gingerly over the pitted ground and in minutes was looking down at the beach of Withy Cove. The young lady was directly below him, still laid out like a jug-bit parson.

He didn't even know her name, but that was immaterial. She was the tool that had been placed in his hands, and he was damn well going to use her. Oh, he could have let her sail on to Quintay, knowing she would tell his lordship that his intended bride had fled. But there was no guarantee such news would have brought the earl here. If anything, the man would hole up even deeper in his beautiful, soulless castle.

It needed a bold stroke to turn things about, and Og had seen the potential in that fiery young woman. If she were of a shrinking nature, he'd not have risked it. But he suspected she would hold her own with any of the islanders—and most especially with his master.

After ten minutes of lying on his cold stone eerie, Og scooped up a handful of small rocks and tossed them clattering down the face of the cliff.

The woman stirred and then rose to her feet in an attitude of alarm. When she approached the cliff and looked up, he ducked lower to the ground. He'd left a marker on the shingle for her—he didn't trust the English to find anything beyond their own backside without help—and he let out a sigh of relief when she started up the cliff right where he'd indicated.

"There's a good lass," he murmured.

He prayed his master would find her and hold fast to her, at least long enough for Og to tease his lordship into coming to the island. The happiness of any number of people depended on it, most especially his father and the young lady he served.

There would doubtless be hell to pay when Himself discovered Og's meddling. But it was long past time for the rift between the two islands to be healed, and as he knew from hard experience, fences rarely got mended without a few cuts and bruises along the way.

Maggie had a faint hope that Captain Og had brought her to Quintay, that she would reach the crest of the cliff and spy Lord Barkin's castle off in the distance. When she made the summit, however, and scanned the landscape, there was nothing that looked remotely like a human dwelling.

Directly below her lay a narrow glen, a shadowy world of moss and stunted trees. She went slowly down the descending path, stopping often to ease her aching head. When the path finally leveled off, the ground underfoot turned soggy; with each step brownish water seeped up around her half boots. She began looking for flat stones to step on, like a child crossing a stream.

At least there was some color here, the deep green moss and green-leafed alders, quite a contrast to the bleak gray monochrome of the beach. If the sun had been shining, this would have seemed an enchanted place, a haunt for fairy folk or pixies. In the waning, watery light, it was almost frightening. There was no sound of birdsong, no rustling of small ground-animals, just the occasional sodden squishing of her footsteps whenever there was no stepping-stone available.

The exertion of scaling the cliff had worsened her headache, so when she came across a small rill trickling through the moss, she knelt down to wet her handkerchief. She dabbed it over her brow, then cupped her palm in the stream and drank, hoping to clear the sour remains of the drugged whisky from her throat. The water tasted so refreshing that she scooped up several more handfuls and swallowed them almost greedily.

Below her silvery minnows darted past, and she smiled, relieved to see that there was some wildlife on this island after all. "Not much in the way of company," she remarked as another school flickered by, startled by the shadowy shape above them. Still, where there were minnows, there were kingfishers and herons. Furthermore, she'd yet to see a woodland where mice and voles did not dwell among the fallen leaves. She was not alone, she told herself, as she took up her carpetbag and headed for the end of the glen.

An overgrown meadow now spread out before her, a shallow bowl set between high, hilly embankments. Two black tors rose up, one on each side of the meadow, standing like ancient sentinels. There was heather in bloom here and rough-stalked broom to catch at her skirts as she went by. Tiny yellow stars of soapwort peeked up at her through the tangle of taller plants. She was bending down to admire a clump of them when the first raindrop splattered on her nose. A dozen more quickly followed, and thunder echoed off to the west.

She stood up with a groan. Her headache had miraculously disappeared, but now she was faced with finding shelter. She tugged the hood of the oilskin over her bonnet and moved away from the center of the meadow toward the pitted tor that rose up on her left. It might furnish a crevice where she could wait out the storm. The stream also ran here, in the shadow of the tor, wider than in the glen. She hurried alongside it, seeking a place to cross.

The rain was falling harder now, the light grown dim. She saw something keeping pace with her on the far bank, a small, sleek animal the size of a cat. An otter, she thought, though she'd only ever seen pictures of them in her mother's natural history books. She nearly laughed when it launched itself onto its belly and slid gracefully down the muddy bank into the stream. Here was a creature undismayed by a little rain.

When it became apparent there was no way to cross the stream without soaking her boots, Maggie turned and hurried across the meadow toward the opposite tor. Thunder sounded, much closer now, and she began to run. Her gaze was focused on the distance, so she didn't see the open pit that loomed in her path—not until she was teetering on the rim. For a horrified instant she stared down at the dark hole, then tried to spin away from the edge. But her boots could find no purchase on the wet turf, and with a sharp cry she pitched backwards, arms flailing. Her body hit the bottom with a resonating thud that knocked the wind out of her. A low groan welled up in her throat, but she didn't have the strength to expel it.

She lay there looking up at the grim sky, rain dashing down on her face, and wondered how things could get any worse.

She'd lost her post, been robbed at pistol point, been marooned on a bleak, inhospitable island—and now she had fallen into a hole.

It was difficult to decide who deserved more of her anger: that dashed militia officer for running off with Alice or Captain Og for drugging her and leaving her here. No, it was that laughing brigand she felt the greatest fury toward. If she ever saw him again there would be such a reckoning. Hanging was too good for the rogue. A pity the old custom of drawing and quartering had gone out of fashion. Or pressing . . . now, there was proper retribution, the victim slowly crushed under the weight of a large rock.

She savored this delightful image for a few moments, waiting to get her breath back. When the rainwater started sluicing down her neck and soaking the collar of her pelisse, she realized it was time to get on with things. She climbed gingerly to her feet and assessed her prison.

It had been neatly excavated, a crisp, mattress-sized rectangle carved out of the turf, with a level dirt floor and squared-off walls, which clearly spoke of some human presence on the island. And it wasn't very deep—if she stretched up, she was able to place her elbows on the rim. She tried leaping up and grabbing at the wet weeds that edged the pit, but they were too weak to hold her weight. What she needed was something to stand on to boost herself out.

She thought for a moment, then fished around in her bag for her paring knife. The dirt walls were relatively compacted, and the small knife hacked away good-sized chunks of soil. In a matter of minutes she had created an indent two feet off the floor.

The rain had nearly let up by the time she heaved her carpetbag over the edge and stepped onto the narrow shelf. Her head and shoulders now rose above the pit. She dragged herself slowly forward, fingers digging into the turf, until her feet were dangling free. Just another few inches and her hips would clear the rim.

Maggie was prematurely congratulating herself for being so clever, when a loud barking erupted from the end of the meadow. Her head shot up. An enormous dog was bounding toward her, baying like a hound on the scent of its prey.

She had a startled notion she might be that prey, and in that instant of inattention, she lost her finger hold. Her body slipped inexorably back, pulled down by the weight of her lower limbs. She slid over the lip and slithered facedown along the dirt wall to land in a huddle on the floor.

It took every ounce of determination not to weep.

A large, ragged head appeared above her, mouth open, bared teeth gleaming. Her only weapon, the paring knife, was again inside her carpetbag, which lay beside the ravening beast. She began frantically undoing the laces of her half boot, thinking that at the very least she could defend herself with her shoe, meanwhile casting anxious looks up at the dog, expecting him to launch himself upon her at any moment. She nearly cried out when another form appeared above her, a human form.

"What the devil are you doing in Fingal MacNeill's grave?" a male voice inquired irately.

Maggie gasped and leapt to her feet.

Oh God, a grave! She had fallen into a grave!

"Please . . . please help me out!" Raising her arms entreatingly, she flung her head back—and met the amused gray eyes of the laughing brigand.

Oh, sweet Jesus, she thought as she reeled back, her arms falling limp at her sides. *This tears it!*

She was on St. Columba, of all wretched things. Captain Og had delivered her right into the hands of Black Collum.

"Lost your way, have you?" he asked, taking a step closer and peering down.

She steeled herself and darted a glance up at him. Even though he'd exchanged his greatcoat for a stained sheepskin jacket and covered his dark hair with a wide-brimmed felt hat, she was certain he was her pirate. Although at present he looked more like a mountain bandit. The shotgun resting in the crook of his arm only added to the raffish effect.

Not that her own appearance—engulfed in an oilskin and begrimed with mud—was anything to boast about. She had a thought that the voluminous cape, which covered her from head to foot, might keep him from recognizing her.

His next words dashed her hopes.

"Looks like we've trapped ourselves Lord Barkin's intended

bride," he remarked to the dog. He prodded her carpetbag with one boot. "*And* all her dainty furbelows."

Maggie cursed the wretched bag that had given her away. It was clear the time for playacting was over. "I'm not anyone's intended bride," she said in a crisp, clear voice.

"Oh," he asked urbanely, "have you called it off, then?"

"Alice Fescue called it off."

He knelt down, setting the butt of the shotgun on the ground. "And who might you be?"

"Maggie Bonner, Miss Fescue's hired companion."

"Pull the other one, ma'am. I hardly think Lady Fescue sent a servant alone to Quintay carrying a fortune in jewels."

"I don't care what you think," she snapped. "It happens to be the truth."

"You didn't bother to correct me on the ship," he pointed out. "And neither did Og MacNeill."

"So you *do* know him!"

"Of course I know him. He was born on this island."

"He left me here," she cried with some heat. "Put me on the beach and sailed off."

He rubbed at his chin. "Why on earth would he do that?"

"I haven't a clue. Now, if you would just help me out of this *grave*—"

But the man was no longer attending. He was staring off in the direction of the cove where she'd been put ashore. Then he frowned down at her and murmured, "If I had half a brain, I would leave you where you are. You've a look of trouble about you."

Maggie fumed silently. He didn't know the half of it.

"Just help me out and I will be on my way. We can both forget this unfortunate meeting."

"So, you haven't come here to fetch back your necklace?"

"I wanted to, but Captain Og warned me the island was full of cutthroats and scoundrels."

His eyes crinkled appreciatively. "*And* holes in the ground." With that he set down his gun and slid feet-first into the pit. "Now, come here and let me have a look at you."

She stood rigid but unresisting while he thumped his hands dispassionately over her shoulders and along her arms. "Anything damaged when you fell?"

"Only my pride," she muttered.

He turned her about once, then tugged back the oilcloth hood and fingered a lock of her hair. "Not bad," he said under his breath. "Not bad at all."

"Stop that! You're not buying a horse, you know."

He grinned, a swift flash of even, white teeth. "I'm thinking the old rascal left me a rather valuable gift. His lordship should pay handsomely to have such a pretty . . . filly restored to him."

Maggie's head started to spin. This couldn't be happening. She was unaware of backing into a corner but became very aware of it when he stalked up to her, caught her about the waist and boosted her effortlessly up onto the grass. She scrambled to her feet as he clambered up beside her. Her breath was coming in fits and starts, as though she had just finished a footrace.

"You can't mean this. . . . It's ridiculous. I am *not* Alice Fescue."

He cocked his head and crossed his arms over his chest. "You'd better be Alice Fescue. You're no use to me if you're only her hired companion." He leaned in closer and whispered confidingly, "You know, I've never had to *hire* a female companion in my entire life."

Maggie nearly rolled her eyes. "I doubt there is enough gold in the kingdom to make you palatable to a woman."

He winced theatrically. "Slings and arrows, Miss Fescue, sound and fury. I am unscathed."

"And what will you do to me if I am not who you think?"

He hitched one shoulder. "Hard to say. Though it's never difficult to dispose of bodies here on St. Columba—the place is full of bogs."

Maggie gritted her teeth. For all her dismay, she surprisingly felt little sense of peril. The wretch was just trying to intimidate her. And he was dashed well not going to succeed.

"Surely there is some manner of law on this island."

"There is . . . a rough sort, but law for all that."

"Then the authorities will get wind of this soon enough. If you let me go, however, I will promise not to lay evidence against you. For this outrage or for stealing the necklace."

He tsked softly. "You can't bargain with a rogue, Miss Fescue. You really need to learn that. No, you're my gift from Og, most happily accepted. It's a wonder I didn't think of it myself."

"It's a wonder no one's put a bullet through your black heart," she grumbled under her breath.

"I heard that. And I'd be careful of what I said within earshot of Fabian." He stroked the dog's ragged head. "He doesn't take kindly to anyone threatening me."

Maggie's gaze swung wildly across the meadow as she gauged the odds of getting away from him. She'd always been fleet of foot, and if she could just put enough distance between them—

He immediately clamped a hand over her wrist. "Don't even think about it. Fabian's favorite sport is chasing down runaways. And I can't answer for how much damage he might do before I pulled him off you. An arm . . . a leg . . ." He shrugged meaningfully.

The dog took a step closer to Maggie, looking up at her with an eager expression in his eyes, as though he was daring her to flee. She tugged her hand away from the man, then set both hands behind her back and out of gnawing range.

"You're making a terrible mistake," she said. "The real Alice Fescue ran off from Kilchoan. Her mother sent me to return the necklace to Lord Barkin. Can you comprehend that simple progression of events . . . or are your wits too meager?"

He was scowling again. "You *are* going to be trouble. I see that plainly now. But if you're wise, my lady, you won't rile me."

"Or else what?" she asked, her irritation outstripping her prudence.

He smiled slowly. "I can gag you, for a start." His gaze moved to her mouth. "Although I fancy a man could think of an even more effective way of stopping that shrew's tongue."

She was about to ask him to elaborate, when an image flashed into her head—of this man swooping down and taking her mouth. Taking it hard and fast and with certain heat.

Maggie's whole body tensed. Surely that was not what he meant. She eyed him cautiously, but he wasn't regarding her with anything approaching lust. Distaste was more like it.

"Now, move along," he said as he bent to retrieve the shotgun. "I'd like to get home before dark."

Since nightfall was hours away, Maggie wondered how far they would have to walk. The island, as she'd seen from the boat, was not that large.

He's being facetious, she told herself. Wonderful. A laughing, *snide* brigand.

She set off toward the end of the meadow, then immediately doubled back for her carpetbag, sitting waterlogged beside the grave. Her paring knife was in there, some minor protection if it ever came to defending her honor. The first time her captor was distracted, she would slip it into the pocket of her pelisse.

Unfortunately, he took the bag from her as she came even with him, observing that she looked at the end of her rope. "And, God, you are filthy," he added over his shoulder as he set off. "A pity his lordship can't see you now. He'd be the one to call off the wedding."

"He wouldn't know me from Eve," she said as she trudged along beside him, "since Lord Barkin and I have never met."

"Ah, so it was an arranged marriage. I'd heard he courted you in London. Just goes to show a man shouldn't listen to village gossip."

Maggie spun to him. "It wasn't an arranged *anything*! I've never met the earl because l was attending my father during the time he was paying suit to Miss Fescue."

His eyes danced. "I believe you ought to take up writing novels. You've quite a fertile imagination. Lord knows you'll need some pastime to keep you entertained after you're wed. From what I hear, things are fairly dull on Quintay."

"Oh, and St. Columba is such a hotbed of activity?"

He laughed at her barb, a warm, engaging chortle. "Not where you're going, it isn't." He prodded her with the side of the shotgun barrel. "If we ever get there. Bless me, but I never yet met a woman who didn't dawdle."

She made no answer but started walking again, determined to keep up with him. It was not easy. His legs were long, hardly surprising since he stood well over six feet, and he moved across the turf with awesome sides.

At the end of the meadow, a trail angled sharply upward to run along the side of a craggy, bracken-covered hill, the first in a range that straggled away to the north like the unearthed teeth of a great dragon. Her captor started up this trail, and after a few minutes of walking, Maggie looked back to the cliff above the cove. They were level with its summit and still climbing.

"Where are you taking me?" she huffed. "To some mountain hideaway?"

"I'm taking you to the cottage where I live. We're using this route to avoid the marsh."

He motioned to their left, where the ground fell sharply away. A hundred feet below them lay a large patch of swamp, dotted with hillocks and partially obscured by mist.

"Fabian and I know our way through it, but I don't want to have to pull you out of a bog. Though I doubt you could get any dirtier."

Maggie forced herself not to respond. A gentleman would have offered her his handkerchief to wipe the mud from her face. This creature found it a source of amusement. But thinking of handkerchiefs gave her an idea.

She purposely stumbled forward on the path and fell to her knees, catching herself with one hand.

"Ouch!"

He stopped and turned. "Oh, what is it now?"

"I've scraped my palm." She whimpered as she pushed herself upright.

"Let me see."

Maggie promptly cradled her arm against her chest. "I need my bag. I've some clean handkerchiefs in there."

He set it down before her. She crouched over the opening and quickly searched through her jumbled garments, feeling for the handle of the knife.

"What's taking so long?" he asked, moving closer.

"Everything was neatly packed," she said, looking up with an arch smile, "until some rogue got his hands on it."

He tugged the bag away from her just as her fingers grasped the knife. Fortunately his head was down as she slipped it into her sleeve.

"Here," he said, plucking up two folded linen squares. "You must be blind. They were right on top."

She didn't thank him as she wrapped one around her imaginary injury and used the other to scrub at her face. "You might have offered me your own, you know."

In response, he dug into his pocket and drew out a large white handkerchief. It was covered with dried blood.

Maggie let out a yelp.

He grinned. "No, it's not from one of my human victims. I was out hunting, and I gutted a hare."

She'd been too distracted earlier to note the canvas game pouch slung over his shoulder. It explained the presence of the shotgun and served to reassure her—a little.

They continued on in single file, her captor in the lead, the dog trotting behind her. Maggie carefully transferred the knife to her pocket, hoping the dog wouldn't growl or bark to give her away. It seemed to her those amber eyes missed nothing.

Every so often, the man would turn and ask her how she was faring. Maggie was sure she had never felt so weary in her life, but for some reason she wanted him to think of her as stalwart and hardy. "Fine," she'd answer. "Perfectly fine."

The trail finally leveled off as they crossed a narrow alpine valley hammocked between two hills. When they emerged on the other side, a wide vista opened up before them.

The terrain below had changed from marsh to rough pastureland, where shaggy reddish brown cattle and black-faced sheep grazed in small groups, interspersed with bands of dun ponies. In the distance lay a sizable bay with a village clinging to its right-hand shore. At the far end of the village, on a slight promontory, sat a castle as gray and rugged as the open sea behind it. It looked desolate, likely abandoned, and Maggie gave up any hope of finding an ally there.

Once they began their descent, Maggie felt only relief—until her legs started to tremble from the exertion. She'd thought herself fairly fit until she came to this wretched place. She stumbled in earnest while going down a steep patch and was surprised when the dog put his shoulder against her thigh as if to steady her. Tentatively she laid her hand upon his back, wondering how many fingers she could afford to lose. The beast turned his head to look at her, his ancient eyes calm and unthreatening.

She'd never seen a dog so large or so unkempt, like an oversized greyhound who'd been battered with wood shavings. But his tawny coat was soft to the touch, soft and warm.

Her captor stopped when they reached level ground, scanning the landscape in all directions. She immediately sat on a nearby rock, relieved to get off her aching feet. Denim half boots might be just the thing for a stroll in the park, but they were hardly adequate for trekking over rough ground. Not to mention they were soaked through to her stockings.

Finally, the man signalled her to follow him. He veered away from the direction of the village, setting off across the grass toward the bay. She rose and went after him, again trying to keep up with his ground-eating strides.

"How did you know?" she called out, hoping to slow him down.

"Know what?" he said without turning or halting.

"About the necklace."

"That hardly matters," he said gruffly.

"But we told no one in Kilchoan about it."

"You didn't have to," he said. "Everyone there assumed Lord Barkin's bride would be traveling to Quintay. And that she would have kept such a valuable gift close by her."

"So you merely had to wait for Og's ship to pass by and hope that Alice Fescue was on it."

"That was the general plan. Although it occurred to me that his lordship might have sent an emissary to see the ladies safely to his home."

"He did, a rather insinuating fellow named Edward Matchem."

The earl's steward had arrived in Kilchoan the morning after Alice fled. Maggie recalled how desperate Lady Fescue had been to keep the news from the man. As if there was still hope of a wedding. She'd told Mr. Matchem they'd left a piece of luggage behind in Fort William and asked him if he wouldn't mind fetching it. Her ladyship had already sent her two coachmen after the girl, but Maggie knew that even if they did manage to find her, Lord Barkin would consider Alice soiled goods. After two days passed with no word from the coachmen, her employer finally admitted defeat and grudgingly ordered Maggie to return the betrothal gift. Of Mr. Matchem there had been no further sightings.

"Lady Fescue sent him away from Kilchoan on some trumped-up errand after her daughter ran away," she explained. "Which is how I came to be transporting the necklace alone."

"Ah, I see you are still sticking to the story of the hired companion. I must tell you, it's losing its appeal by the minute."

She disregarded this. "I'm curious. What would you have done if there had been an armed man aboard the *Charles Stuart*?"

"I made a contingency plan for that. Captain Og was to ply him with drugged whisky. There's barely a Scotsman born who'll say no to a free tot. Especially Neddie Matchem."

"Unfortunately, the captain saw to it that *I* drank the whisky."

He *did* stop at that, stopped and turned to her with an incredulous grin. "He never did! I wondered how he got a little pepper pot like you onto the island without risking life and limb. Leave it to Og to come up with a solution." He looked at her through his dark brows. "How's your head? Og's concoctions could fell a steer."

She put her chin up. "I'm none the worse for it."

"My bet is you cast up your accounts on the beach."

"No such thing," she protested. "My head throbbed a bit when I awoke, bit I drank from the stream in the glen and it cleared up."

"That stream runs from St. Columba's spring," he told her, pointing to the hills behind them. "It's the only natural water source on the island. It starts up there and runs down in a number of separate branches, one toward the village, another through the meadow where I found you. The old ones here say it can cure almost anything." He added in a low voice, "Anything but poverty and despair."

Maggie heard the pain in his voice but did not remark on it.

He started walking again, her bag swinging at his side. She stuck close behind him as they traversed another boggy area, watching her footing as they passed beside still, scum-covered pools. Her already poor opinion of St. Columba was rapidly worsening.

The ground underfoot turned to sandy shingle as they neared the bay and made their way along a strip of land that jutted out into the water. A gray stone cottage with a chimney at each end sat at the tip, facing the bay. A few rickety outbuildings were scattered around it, screened from the wind by stunted trees.

So this was to be her prison, she thought, a remote dwelling separated from the village by an expanse of water, guarded at the landward end by a treacherous bog. She didn't bother to ask if he was going to leave her here alone or stay with her. Either possibility was equally disturbing.

The dog raced ahead of them as they neared the cottage, sending the chickens in the yard scattering.

"Fabian!" he called out, then muttered in irritation, "They won't lay for days now."

"So much for my breakfast," she sighed.

"Don't worry, you won't starve. I'll bring some provisions over first thing tomorrow."

"So you're leaving me here alone?"

He gave her a mocking leer. "I could stay with you, Miss Fescue, but his lordship might hear of it. Your value goes down radically if he thinks you compromised."

She sniffed. "And can you vouch for the other men on this island of cutthroats and scoundrels? I imagine not all of them have your sense of the . . . niceties."

"No one will molest you. Not if you are under my protection."

"Protection," she echoed sourly as he moved away. "That's rare."

She trailed him around to the front of the cottage, where a sailing skiff was beached on the shingle ten yards from the stone wall of a weed-infested garden. Gray water, gray shingle, gray stone . . . the whole place had a bleak, uncared-for aspect that depressed her even further.

He left his shotgun and game pouch on the narrow porch and entered the cottage after her, going forward to light a lantern. The ceiling was low and beamed, the crosshatch of hewn timbers nearly brushing his crown as he moved about.

When he crouched down to light a fire, she thought of sneaking up behind him and stabbing him with her knife. But he was so large and her knife was so small; she imagined it would do very little damage. Even if it did, then what? She'd never rowed a boat on anything wider than a village pond, and she doubted she could safely negotiate the bog in the waning light.

He rose and turned to her. "You'll want to wash up. There's

a cistern outside full of rainwater. This bucket on the sideboard is from the stream . . . for drinking."

He raised a dipperful of water and offered it to her. "Here," he said. "I promise it's not drugged."

She shook her head, then said in a low, urgent voice, "I don't know what I can say to make you believe me. I am not Alice Fescue. You saw for yourself that my clothing is old and worn. Would the earl's intended own such shabby garments?"

He drank deeply from the dipper, then tossed it back into the bucket. "I assumed you were traveling incognito. Perhaps you took your companion's, this Maggie Bonner's, clothing to complete the ruse." He fingered a fold of her sleeve. "Though this pelisse is rather fine. Finer than anything I own."

"Lady Fescue bought it for me, for the journey. She didn't want me to shame Alice in front of Lord Barkin."

"Very convincing, but it won't wash. You see, I know something about his lordship that points to you being the exact woman he would choose."

"You mentioned something similar on the ship . . . about my hair and eyes."

"Let's just say the earl has a fondness for tall, slender women with your coloring."

That made no sense to Maggie. Alice had reddish hair and blue eyes. Furthermore, she barely topped five feet—and was the slightest bit plump.

"Couldn't you just be satisfied with the necklace? You said yourself it's worth a king's ransom. Why do you need *my* ransom, as well? I think you're being excessively greedy."

"The money the necklace will fetch is not for me, if you must know."

"Then who?"

"I don't think that's any of your concern."

He shifted her about to face the kitchen. "That cabinet is the larder. There's oatmeal and treacle and tea. With any luck, you'll find a few eggs in the henhouse come morning. You'll have to make do without bacon—I'm fresh out."

This talk of food made Maggie realize she was famished. That half-eaten scone wasn't going to do much to dent her hunger.

"You could leave me the hare you shot."

"And what would a lady know about dressing a hare?"

Plenty, she almost said. When they were on the road, the actors often resorted to snaring small game. She'd dressed hare and woodcock, even the occasional stolen chicken. But there was no point in telling him; he was not inclined to believe anything she said.

"There's a bedroom beyond that door and plenty of peat for the fire. Sorry if the place is not up to your standards. I . . . I wasn't expecting a houseguest."

"Hardly a guest," she grumbled.

He thrust his hands into his coat pockets and stood looking about the room as if there was something he'd forgotten to tell her, and she found herself observing him in the lantern light. As on board the ship, she was struck by the power of his presence, the natural air of confidence. But he'd seemed relaxed, almost swaggeringly casual during the robbery. Now he appeared more wary.

In other circumstances she would have deemed him an admirable figure of a man—broad-shouldered, well-muscled, with a determined jaw and intelligent eyes. Right now, however, that strength, determination and intelligence were all aligned against her.

She also had to admit he was strikingly good-looking. Not that looks were proof of anything.

While traveling with the Players, she had known any number of handsome leading men, and she'd soon concluded that a fine face was no guarantee of fine character. Percival Lancaster, of the twinkling blue eyes, had been an habitual sot. Valerian Valmont, velvet-voiced and a wonder with a sword, spent every free minute at dice. Clive Oakley, who had stolen her heart when she was ten, had also stolen the receipts from a prosperous engagement in Chester and disappeared on the night mail.

No, he might be fair to look upon, but she had little reason to doubt the man's heart was black as the muck that oozed up from the bog.

"I'll be off now," he said.

Maggie hadn't expected to feel so panicked by those words. The complete reality of her situation swept over her—she was without allies in a hostile, frightening landscape. Even the company of this man might be preferable to being left alone in an isolated cottage.

Who knew how long she might be stranded here? What if Edward Matchem discovered that Alice had fled and relayed the information to Lord Barkin? In that case, his lordship would not even bother responding to the ransom note. He'd likely laugh it off as a prank.

She stood there trembling with exhaustion and delayed shock, forcing herself to remain upright as he went past her. It was as though she were drugged again, drugged by weariness and hopelessness. And hunger.

It all came crashing down on her—the defeats of the past three days, the tongue-lashings and threats from Lady Fescue, the treachery of Captain Og, the pure pigheadedness of this man called Black Collum, and most of all the fear of being held prisoner.

She barely gave a sigh as her knees buckled, and the floor rushed up.

"Damn!" The man crossed from the door in one great stride and caught her just before her head bounced against the flagstones. He scooped her up, barely conscious, and carried her to the bedroom.

She had the sensation of being laid on a featherbed—it felt like heaven—and of hands tugging off the oilcloth cape and then fiddling with the frogs on her pelisse. She felt herself being raised up, fingers coaxing the fitted gabardine sleeves down along her arms. Then she was facedown on the comforter, with more fiddling at the back of her gown.

"Wh-what are you doing?" she managed to whimper raggedly.

"I'm undoing your tabs," he said. "So you can breathe. Damned women go about all corseted and bound and then wonder why they faint."

Alarm at his words brought her back to full consciousness. "You're not going to loosen my corset—"

She swore she heard him chuckle. "It won't be the first time I've had to wrestle with one of those infernal contraptions. But, no, I think this will do the trick."

She *was* breathing easier, she had to acknowledge. The

gown she'd worn under her pelisse was one of her best, but it had always been a trifle tight in the bodice.

He slipped one arm beneath her and turned her again on her back. His face was very close to hers now as he knelt beside the bed. There was some emotion flickering in his pale eyes, regret or sympathy, she wasn't sure which. Then she recalled that this was the same man who had threatened to shoot her and throw her into the sea. What her addled mind had read as kindness was probably nothing more than avaricious calculation, her captor gauging what she was worth.

She stiffened as he removed her bonnet and stroked a lock of hair back from her brow.

"I'm thinking his lordship will have his hands full," he said, leaning one elbow on the pillow beside her head. "A peppery swooner . . . now, that's a rare and difficult combination."

"I am neither," she declared. "This is the first time I've ever swooned. And I am not peppery, not unless someone is robbing me at pistol point."

He tapped the tip of her nose. "Now, *that's* the time to swoon."

He got up then, removed his weight from the mattress beside her and left the room. When he returned, he was carrying a crockery mug.

"Drink," he said, his voice brooking no argument.

He held the mug as she sipped at the cool water, which quickly soothed her parched throat. St. Columba's spring, he'd said, could cure most ailments. She wondered how effective it was against fear and frustration.

"Hasn't it sunk in that Lord Barkin will have you imprisoned, or at the very least horsewhipped, for this?"

"He can try."

"Captain Og warned me that you were a desperate man, but surely there are less hazardous ways to get money." She added tartly, "You might try toiling for your bread as most people do."

His face darkened as he slammed the mug onto the night table. Maggie's eyes widened. This was the first show of real temper she'd seen from him.

"Toiling, is it?" he seethed, looming over the bed. "Bloody lot you know about toiling, my lady." He jerked her upright. "Look," he ordered. "Is this the hand of an idle fellow?"

He grasped her neck, forcing her head down. She had no choice but to observe the hand spread before her, to note the scars and calluses that marked his palm and outspread fingers.

"I doubt you've done an honest day's work in your entire life," he snarled. "Underlings to fetch and carry for you, servants to cook your meals . . ."

"Th-that's not true," she gasped. "You know nothing about me."

He snatched up her own hand, pried the fingers open. "Then why is your hand unmarked, madam? So soft and white?"

His touch was like a burning brand against her skin. "Let me go!" she cried, trying to tug away from him. He held fast.

"I may not toil in the fields," she cried softly, "but I have been earning my own keep since I was sixteen. True, it's been genteel work—"

"Genteel," he echoed, making it sound like a curse. "What's that, stitching a sampler? Painting in water colors?"

"I was a French tutor, a governess, and then a hired companion."

His cheeks narrowed. "More lies," he muttered, casting her hand away from him.

It fell to the comforter beside her discarded pelisse—six inches from where the bone handle of her knife jutted from the pocket. Without thinking, she wrapped her fingers around it, obscuring it from view

"Look in my carpetbag," she said. "I've two books with me, both of them inscribed with my own name, Maggie Bonner."

He shrugged. "Easy enough to have borrowed them from your companion."

She scrambled to her knees, the better to face him, now holding the knife among the folds of her skirt. "You are the most stubborn, the most pigheaded individual it's been my misfortune to meet. If you'd ever in your life been in the company of a *real* lady, it would be very clear to you that I am nothing more than an upper servant. I told Captain Og you spoke like a gentleman, but a real gentleman would have instantly known me for what I am."

For the first time, an expression of doubt crossed his face—followed rapidly by a sly smile. He shook his head slowly. "You really ought to be on the stage. That was nearly convincing.

And as for my being a gentleman"—he caught her chin in his hand—"you seem to forget that I am merely one of the . . . what did you call us? . . . the cutthroats and scoundrels who live on this island."

"Let me go," she said between her teeth as he knelt on the bed beside her. She was sure he could feel her trembling.

"No," he said. "I want you afraid. Fear breeds obedience, and I don't want you trying anything foolish."

He was keeping her immobile, his fingers clasped hard on her jaw, his pale eyes holding her captive, bending her to his will as a snake beguiles its prey.

Yet it was she who lashed out, slashing with her knife at the arm that held her, cutting through fabric and flesh.

He started back with a cry and in the next instant disarmed her, easily twisting the knife from her fingers. He held it up, his gaze moving from the small blade to the seeping cut on his forearm. He tsked softly. "Lucky for me no one's ever showed you how to use a knife."

Maggie was breathless, canted back on the bed, awaiting some retaliation. He leaned in closer, balancing the blade on his hand. "I could show you," he said softly, and she swore the amusement was back in his eyes. "I could show you a lot of things a fine lady never learns."

"I *know* how to use a knife," she said in a quavery voice and then recited, "strike at a man's throat or his belly. But, I wasn't trying to kill you. I lashed out because you were frightening me."

"Good."

"You still are."

"Even better."

"Do you enjoy intimidating helpless women?" she said, rallying a bit. "I'm curious how brave Black Collum would be facing an armed man."

His brows meshed. "Black Collum?"

"Captain Og said that's what you were called. And I must say, it doesn't surprise me a—"

He set his hand over her mouth. "Do you ever stop talking? And most of it lies . . . or nonsense."

She grabbed his arm and thrust his hand away, her fingers

inadvertently closing over the knife slash. He winced with a swift intake of breath, and she instantly released him.

His pale eyes sparked, ice and fire both. "I should congratulate you. You're the first woman who's ever drawn blood." A slow smile drew up the edges of his mouth. "Though it seems to me you ought to pay a forfeit."

She scrambled back. "What?"

"A forfeit," he repeated as he reached for her.

He got her by the upper arms and dragged her across the bed, nearly up against his chest. She twisted in his hold and he shook her once. "Be still . . . this is going to hurt a lot less than what you did to me."

She had no idea what he intended, though any retribution was bound to be terrible. And he still had her knife—

When he kissed her, she was almost relieved. It was a brief, hard kiss, his mouth firm, his left hand steady behind her head. Not altogether unpleasant, though still an affront. When she opened her mouth to protest, he did it again. Slower, this time.

"That's better," he whispered against her lips, his fingers stroking her nape beneath the heavy spill of hair.

His mouth was warm, warmer than the drugged whisky and just as potent. His hand moved to her back, sliding inside the opening of her gown, pressing the bare skin above the edge of her shift. She shivered, and he tightened his hold. His lips moved over hers, coaxing some response. When she opened her mouth wider beneath his, his drawn-out sigh set her heart racing. She was just getting the right of things, when he pulled back abruptly.

"This isn't fair," he muttered. "I may be a rogue, but it's hardly sporting to seduce a woman who's been drugged and kidnapped and dragged half across an island."

His words shook Maggie back to reality. Whatever had she been thinking, to let this man, this *stranger,* take such liberties? This was exactly the sort of thing she'd been warning Alice about for ages . . . cozening men with wickedly attractive smiles who dallied and then fled.

"You weren't seducing me," she managed to gasp out, still a bit breathless. "I was merely incapacitated by fear."

"Ha! There's a ripe one." He shifted back onto his elbow.

"I've ravished enough women to know the difference between complicity and incapacitation."

"It's hardly ravishment if there's complicity involved," she pointed out.

"That's splitting hairs," he said as he plucked her knife up from the mattress and pocketed it. "Anyway, I'm done arguing with you. Lord Barkin will need a hogshead of headache powder to live with such a shrew."

"Yes, what of Lord Barkin?" she said as he rose from the bed. "You vowed he would not find me compromised."

He regarded her coolly, through the tangle of hair at his brow. "You can tell his blasted lordship that his lady is none the worse for being kissed by an honest laborer." He added with a studied drawl, "He should thank me for schooling you."

That last comment, dripping with masculine smugness, set her off again. She cast about for something to hurl at him, but he was through the door before she got her hand around the vase on the night table.

"You puffed-up buffoon!" she called out.

She heard him rattling about in the other room, probably removing any object she might use as a weapon against him, and then the final thud of the front door closing. She climbed from the bed, still a bit tottery, and went to the bedroom window, watching surreptitiously from behind the tatty lace curtain. At his whistle, the dog came bounding up to him and was motioned into the boat. He cast off with an oar, not raising the sail until he had cleared the shallows.

The evening sky was now free of clouds, the newly risen moon almost full, so she was able to follow his progress across the bay. A battery of thoughts and sensations tumbled inside her head as she watched him sail away. She didn't want him to leave her . . . she never wanted to see him again. She fervently wished he was safe on Quintay, asleep in Lord Barkin's castle . . . and yet she couldn't help feeling as though this strange, arduous day had brought her to some place quite outside her own experience. A place she needed to explore.

"You're daft, Maggie," she told herself as she abandoned her post by the window. She was the prisoner of a dangerous, desperate man, and there was no veneer of glamour or adventure to be drawn over that fact.

In spite of her hunger and the turmoil inside her, she fell back onto the bed, still wearing her loosened gown, and was asleep almost immediately. And if she dreamed, those phantoms of the night were as fleeting and insubstantial as the ghostly image of a sailboat crossing a moonlit bay.

Chapter Three

"*T*his is rich," Dorcas said as she tended his arm. "You've turned robber and kidnapper all within the space of one day. I don't dare wonder what's next." She added with an arch little smile, "Are you feeling the urge to set fire to something, perhaps?"

They were in his cousin's parlor, Gulliver sprawled in an armchair near the hearth with Fabian asleep at his boots. Dorcas was seated on a footstool beside him, a basket of medical supplies on her knee. He kept reminding himself—a lesson learned in childhood—that when a woman nursed your wounds, she invariably thought she had the right to criticize you.

Gulliver explained patiently for the second time that he'd done it all for the greater good.

"I saw the opportunity to take the necklace and seized it. And as for kidnapping the lady, Og was the one who put her ashore. I am merely offering her the hospitality of the island—and expecting his lordship to pay her shot."

Dorcas rolled her eyes as she dabbed ointment over the knife wound. "That's a convenient rationalization. You'd best memorize it for the baile."

He tactfully did not point out to her that *he* was the baile—by default. "You don't honestly think the earl will press charges, do you?"

"Maybe not for stealing back the necklace. But this other matter . . . the lady herself could see you put behind bars."

"Oh, she'd enjoy that," he said under his breath.

"So what is she like, Lord Barkin's future wife?" Her light tone was a little too calculated.

Gulliver had known the question would crop up, and he'd toyed with a number of replies while crossing Whitesands Bay. He eventually decided it didn't matter what he told her, that Dorcas would be disposed to dislike the woman regardless of what he said. It would only add fuel to the fire if he shared his own reaction to his captive—that he found Miss Alice Fescue irritating and infuriating. Made him wonder why he'd kissed her.

"She's rather commonplace," he ended up saying. "Just another of those frail society misses, all chatter and no bottom. She even swooned at one paint."

"A wilting lily, hmmm? I'd hoped Guy would find someone to stir him up a bit."

Gulliver thought the woman was more likely to drive his lordship into the grave. Not than he'd ever been very far from that ultimate destination.

"I want you to stay clear of her, Dorcas," he said. "The fewer people who know about her presence here, the less chance of anyone risking prison if Guy does decide to make trouble."

"Anyone but you, you mean," she pointed out. "Do you really believe Miss Fescue won't identify you, Gull?"

He laughed softly. "She thinks I am called Black Collum. One of Og's little fibs."

"But that's what they called your father."

"Mmm . . . as opposed to Red Collum, our grandfather."

Her brows meshed reflectively. "Have you noticed there are not nearly enough Christian names in Scotland to go around? Bad enough everyone on this island has the same surname."

"Almost everyone," he reminded her. "So we MacGuigans have to stick together."

"You're on your own if the authorities from the mainland show up here," she teased. "I've a very pretty neck and I don't fancy having it stretched."

"Speaking of necks, what's that under your tucker?"

Dorcas grinned as she loosened the muslin kerchief. A fortune in emeralds gleamed back at him. "I found it in the inside pocket when I hung up your coat. I recall the time your mother wore this necklace to a masquerade ball at the castle—I coveted it desperately."

"I remember that night," he said softly. "We hid in the minstrel's gallery to watch the dancing. My father knew we were up there and he sent Fingal to bring us cake and punch. It was the first time I'd tasted spirits—"

"You fell asleep, and Guy was so proud the next day that he outlasted you."

They lapsed into silence, and Gulliver knew they were both thinking back to a happier time in their lives—and all that had been lost to them since then.

"I miss the parties," she lamented. "And all the visitors. Boats coming and going in the harbor. St. Columba's like a ghost island now, Gull."

"It won't be after I mortgage the Barkin emeralds."

"You're not going to sell them?" She placed her hand over the largest stone, a full twenty carats, which formed the centerpiece of the necklace.

"I can't. I still have some sense of family obligation. But the necklace will furnish enough collateral for me to buy seed corn and new farm machinery—"

"And a decent bull?" she asked anxiously.

Dorcas's father had maintained a flourishing herd of Highland cattle as far back as Gulliver could recall. But the stud bull had died over the winter and there were only yearling calves left from last spring's crop.

"Yes," he conceded. "A fine bull . . . unless you'd rather keep the necklace."

"I hate to give it up." She sighed. "It matches my eyes."

And another pair of eyes as well, he couldn't help thinking, greener even than his cousin's. And although Dorcas was an acknowledged toast—at least here on the island—hers was a more traditional sort of beauty. Miss Alice Fescue, an the other hand, possessed something of the wild gypsy in her looks. It could have been the high cheekbones or that mass of coiling hair. Or perhaps, he thought with a grin, it was all the grime she'd managed to cover herself with. Whatever it was, it lent her a distinct appeal—if one could overlook her uncertain temperament.

Dorcas touched his hand. "What is it, Gull? You've got such a bemused look."

"I was just thinking about my prisoner. She kept insisting she was Alice Fescue's hired companion. . . . It got rather tiresome eventually, but it was entertaining at first."

A tiny crease of worry showed on her forehead as she tied off the bandage on his arm. "Is it possible you took the wrong woman?"

"Only woman on the *Charles Stuart*," he said simply. "Og vouched for her while I was taking the necklace. And why else would he have left her for me on Withy Beach?"

"Og MacNeill would as soon lie as look at you," she said with some force. "It still breaks his old father's heart."

"Trust me, Dorcas. This woman is Alice Fescue."

"It would be awful if you were mistaken—"

"I am not mistaken."

"But—"

"Confound you, Dorcas!"

Fabian started up at once, roused by his master's voice. Gulliver smoothed a hand over the dog's head and continued in a more even tone. "Look, I didn't want to tell you this, but you always have to prod at me. The reason I am certain she's Lord Barkin's future bride is because she . . . she looks enough like you to be your sister."

Dorcas winced. He cursed himself for hurting her.

"That's lowering," she said. "You just told me she was commonplace."

"I didn't want to tell you the truth. And if you could see your face right now, you'd know why." He reached out to her. "Ach, don't cry . . ."

"I'm not," she protested, muffling a sniffle behind her hand. "Anyway, I suppose I should be flattered. He didn't want me, yet he chose a woman who reminded him of me."

"If that's any consolation."

"And is she a wilting lily, as you described?"

He knew he ought to say yes, to let her think the other woman lacked courage. That was one thing, however, for which he couldn't fault the lady.

Dorcas forestalled him. "She isn't, is she? Oh, I swear you

are as bad as Og when it comes to telling tales. I bet she's fine
and brave and has dozens of pretty gowns and kidskin slippers."

"On that last I can answer with some accuracy, since I had
occasion to look through her carpetbag. Her clothing was quite
plain. Although I suspect she was carrying her companion's
bag."

"She must care for Guy very much if she was traveling alone
to be with him."

"And that doesn't bother you?"

"Of course not. Guy needs someone who'll look after
him . . . he always has. Someone more trustworthy than that
odious Neddie Matchem."

"Lady Fescue sent Neddie packing, according to her daughter."

"I give her points for that." She bundled up her lint and
basilicum ointment and placed them in the basket. "So, what
now? I don't suppose it's occurred to you that the earl will have
a pretty fair idea of who took Miss Fescue."

"I want him to know—or at least guess."

"Are you mad?"

"Not a bit. Guy's family instigated the decline of St.
Columba. He needs to start making some restitution. I'm
merely forcing his hand."

She sighed wearily. "Gulliver, what makes you think you
can force anything? He knows you too well to believe the lady
is in any danger. Unless she forms a *tendre* for you . . . women
seem to do that as easily as breathing."

Gulliver pointed to the bandage on his arm. "I don't think
you need worry about that happening."

Dorcas cocked her head. "I don't understand. You told me it
was an accident."

"Miss Fescue 'accidentally' attacked me with a paring knife.
She didn't like it that I was trying to intimidate her."

She set her hands over her face. "This keeps getting worse
and worse." She looked up. "I think you'd best bring her here
in the morning—"

"It's not an option. Half the island would know about it before noon. Trust me, she's fine where she is. Not much trouble
she can get up to out there."

Suddenly her expression darkened, and she exclaimed, "I

know what this is. You're playing at hideaway again, aren't you?"

"Hideaway?" he repeated blankly.

"That idiotic game you and Guy always played, stealing each other's possessions and hiding them."

"You know, I'd forgotten about that. Though I don't know how—it seems we were at it for years." His eyes brightened. "Remember when I carried off the microscope Guy's father gave him for his thirteenth birthday? You and I spent a week looking at seashells and birds' eggs and bits of fern. We were both utterly cast down when he finally found it hidden under one of your bonnets."

Dorcas sniffed. "See? Even then you were involving me in your larcenies. I *also* remember the time Guy stole your volume of Plato from the schoolroom. It took you a month to find it . . . which might explain your present difficulties with *logic*."

"This isn't about logic. It's more a matter of expedience." He slid down in the chair until his chin was nearly on his chest and then added in a low, weary voice, "Truth is, I've run out of ideas, Dorcas. I can't make up for all the young men who've left here looking for work. I can't bring the fishing back. I certainly can't make crops grow or cattle flourish. Not alone."

She knelt down and clasped his hands between her own. "I know, Gull."

"The emeralds still won't be enough. We need loans, mortgages, money to get commerce started here again. Most of all we need to get the earl's damned embargo against us lifted. St. Columba won't survive much longer without trade from her sister island."

Dorcas shook her head. "The old earl couldn't know what a thorough leveler that embargo turned out to be."

"Well, I promise you the current earl is going to rethink things a mite. Look, I know kidnapping his bride is not exactly the best way to win him over to our cause, but all I want right now is to get his attention."

Dorcas gazed at him warily for a moment. "You've never asked it of me, but I would go there and talk to him myself . . . if you thought it would help."

He shook his head adamantly. "No, not after what he's already put you through."

He pushed up from his chair and went to his late uncle's elegant writing desk. After lifting a stack of notepaper from the drawer, he uncapped the inkwell and took up a quill pen. "Now to business. What shall we demand of the earl?"

"Money would be nice . . . and food."

"That reminds me. I told Miss Fescue I was fresh out of bacon,"—he gave a humorless laugh—"as though we've had salt back here in a twelvemonth."

"At least you're able to keep us supplied with game. Though I am heartily sick of rabbit stew."

"Ah," he said, "I don't suppose you looked in my game bag while you were rifling through my coat pockets."

She wrinkled her nose. "Another rabbit?"

He nodded. "You can console yourself with the knowledge that, unlike you, the accomplished Miss Fescue does not know how to dress a hare."

"Thank you, Gulliver," she said with a tight smile. "My consequence is quite restored."

Once his cousin had gone off to see to their dinner, Gulliver applied himself to writing out the ransom note. In truth, beyond the Barkin emeralds, Guy owed them nothing. Nevertheless, he was rolling in the ready, as Gulliver's university friends used to say, and he spent it on fribbles—moldering maps and medieval texts and bits of broken statuary.

Meanwhile, the people on this island were facing starvation. During the past few years it had been one disaster after another. When the stud bull died, it seemed to take the last bit of heart out of everyone.

Gulliver had sold or mortgaged nearly everything he owned to help the people of St. Columba. They were more than neighbors; they were his family. And if he ended up in prison for abducting Miss Fescue, well, it would be worth it if it brought the island's plight to the attention of the earl.

He jotted down a few tentative lines.

I will restore someone who is dear to you, if in return you help restore something that is dear to me.

That sounded like a lot of piffle.

He tried again.

If you have a shred of conscience over the fate of these islanders, whom you once esteemed, you will seek to remedy their dire situation.

No, too melodramatic.

He set his chin on his fist, wondering if it would be bad protocol to ask the clever Miss Fescue to compose her own ransom note.

Truth was, this was not the first time he'd written to Guy asking for aid. Dorcas didn't know that, how he'd swallowed his pride and overlooked a nine-year-long feud, only to be met by total silence. The whelp hadn't even had the courtesy to offer him a proper refusal.

It occurred to him now that instead of stealing the necklace or holding Guy's intended for ransom, he ought to have sailed over to Quintay and asked for aid in person. The earl could easily ignore letters of supplication, but it would be a deal harder to overlook six and a half feet of determined Scotsman in his front hall.

Too late for that, he thought wearily. He'd committed himself to this course the instant he took Miss Fescue prisoner.

When Dorcas called him into the kitchen for supper, the only thing he'd accomplished was the ruination of six harmless sheets of paper. He told himself he'd write the blasted thing tomorrow morning, when his head was clearer.

It was early evening by the time Og finished unloading his cargo in Luray harbor and made his way through the town to the castle beyond it. The place was hard to miss. Lit torches burned at the entrance and high upon the battlements, making it a bright beacon against the gray gloom of the dusk sky. He went through the ornate iron gate that guarded the earl's domain, nodding to the gatekeeper. There were several watchmen out on patrol, but they paid him no heed. He was a familiar sight in this town, even to the earl's flunkies. In fact he was the only inhabitant of St. Columba—with one notable exception— who had ventured onto Quintay in nearly a decade. He'd been sailing to this island his whole life and was not about to let some ridiculous embargo keep him from his business. Furthermore, the islanders welcomed his visits. He charged less for the supplies he carried from the mainland, legitimate and otherwise, than any captain plying the Western Sea.

Og climbed nimbly up the wide entrance steps—unlike Whitesands, Luray Castle boasted no portcullis or moat—and gave several thunderous knocks upon the massive oak door. Within seconds a liveried footman drew it open.

"I need to see his lordship at once," Og said, striding into the hall.

The footman, who had moved quickly to bar his path, was regarding him as though he were something nasty the tide had cast up on the beach.

"Now," said Og, in case the fellow was a dullard.

"It's out of the question," said the footman, tight-lipped and oozing condescension. "His lordship is not receiving callers."

Og stuck out his chin. "I mean to see him, with or without your leave."

"The earl is just sitting down to supper, and I am not about to disturb him for the likes of you." He glared at Og over the tip of his long, ratlike nose. "Not if I value my position."

Og could think of a fitting position for the preening weasel—something to do with an anchor chain and fifty fathoms of water—but he kept this thought to himself.

"Ye'll suffer for it if you don't heed me. I bring urgent news from St. Columba."

The man drew himself up to his full height—he was nearly a head taller than Og—and hissed, "Suffer? It's you who will suffer if you don't take yourself off."

Og reached out and gathered a handful of the man's starched cravat, tugging him close as though he were a cherished confidant. "Now, ye be a good lad and run and fetch the earl. That way I won't be forced to separate yer inflated head from your puir wee body." Og gave him a twinkling smile. "Are we of a like mind, then?"

"I will do no such thing," the footman huffed.

Og got a firmer grip on his throat and lifted him right off his feet.

The footman's eyes goggled as he sputtered, "Yes, sir. I will see to it immediately, sir."

"Festering rodent," Og muttered as he watched the man scurry off. What was the earl about these days, to surround himself with such scabby servants?

He wondered if the fair-minded lad he'd once known could have altered so much. He'd heard rumors in the town that his lordship had lately become fretful over his safety, setting a gang of rowdies to guard his castle, keeping the torches burning day and night—and then there was that infernal gunship he now had patrolling the coast. Well, Og thought, why shouldn't a man sitting on a mountain of gelt take the trouble to safeguard it? Not that twenty gunships could keep away the dark specter that had trailed after the earl these many years.

Still, the rumors puzzled him, though not enough to pass them along to his master. A pity he couldn't walk right up to the earl and ask him outright if he had turned into a lily-livered poltroon. While Og sometimes spied his lordship in the town, the man never acknowledged him beyond the barest nod of his head.

He gazed around the vast chamber where he waited, noting every detail with the canny eye of a born appraiser. This was the first time he'd been inside the castle in nine years, and it had been embellished almost beyond recognition. The stone walls were covered with layers of intricate tapestries, while the flagstone floor boasted not one but three patterned carpets. Towering marble statues and delicate inlaid tables bearing bronze candelabra and Oriental vases lined the room. Og reckoned the price of any one of those dust collectors could have fed his village for a month.

The earl finally appeared at the top of the staircase, and Og watched him descend, noting his pallor, his stilted posture, the careful way he held onto the banister, like a doddering old man. His brown hair was neatly barbered but appeared lank and lackluster—clearly beyond the skill of any valet to brush it to a sheen. His eyes, once so blue they stole your breath, had a dull, rheumy aspect that bespoke extreme fatigue.

Not a well man, Og thought. But this diagnosis had more to do with the state of the earl's soul than with his frail body. The lad had always thrived on St. Columba; a pity he'd forgotten that for nine years.

As the earl reached the bottom step and moved to cross the

hall, Og hurried to meet him halfway. He hadn't come here to tax the lad, only to pique his interest.

His lordship didn't bother with a greeting but immediately pressed him. "They tell me you've urgent news from St. Columba."

Og nodded. "I do."

"Is it Miss MacGuigan?" It was hard to miss the anxiety that pinched his thin face.

Og nearly snorted. "Now, why would ye be concernin' yourself with my young mistress?"

The earl's brow creased. And when he spoke, it was in the autocratic tones of a man who had complete expectation of being heeded. "I want none of your roundabouts, Og MacNeill. Now, tell me, how is Miss MacGuigan faring?"

"How do ye think she is faring?"

The earl's mouth tightened. "How can I answer that? I've had no word of her for more than two years."

"Ye might have broached the matter with me earlier, as I am a regular visitor to your island. But I will tell ye now—Miss Dorcas is hale and full of high spirits, as usual."

Og watched with some satisfaction as the earl's hands fisted and his cheeks narrowed.

Ye don't like that, do ye laddie? Hearin' she's doin' fine without ye, believin' she's got on with her life. Well, so have you by all appearances. Off to London courting young ladies, plannin' a grand wedding here in your fine castle. Seekin' after yer own happiness, I warrant, and yet you don't like it one bit, thinkin' my Dorcas is happy too.

"But 'tis of another I have come to speak," he said after he'd let the earl stew a while. "Your intended bride, as it were."

The earl's head jolted back. "Miss Fescue? What about her? It's obvious she did not travel with you to Quintay." His voice lowered slightly. "I . . . don't suppose she's changed her mind about the wedding."

"Quite the opposite. She was so fretful to be with ye that she begged me to bring her here, in spite of her mother being laid low with a terrible case o' the grippe."

His lordship did not appear overjoyed at this news. "Then where the devil is she?"

"Ah, now there's the problem." He motioned with his chin

to the footman who was at present hovering near the staircase. Og swore he could see the man's nose twitching. "But perhaps we'd best discuss this in private."

The earl nodded and led him to an anteroom that was as opulently furnished as the hall. Og settled in a leather chair near the hearth, stretching out his boots to the fire. After he'd cast several pointed looks at the drinks tray, the earl sighed and poured him a healthy tot. He handed off the drink and then took up a position before the fire.

"Let's hope the brandy loosens your tongue," his lordship grumbled. "I'd forgotten that talking to you is akin to pulling teeth."

"The thing of it is, I took yer Miss Fescue aboard the *Charles Stuart* in Kilchoan. But as we were sailin' past St. Columba, who should I spy but Gulliver MacGuigan in his sloop. He came right up alongside my ship and boarded her." He paused to take a long, slow sip from his glass.

"And what happened then?" the earl prodded.

Og barely repressed a smug grin. His lordship was well hooked now. "Why, what would you think? Gulliver had the emeralds off her. Ach, but she set up such a squawking, worse than a Glasgow fishwife. I nearly had to stopper up my ears. Though that's a canny lady you've chosen, my lord, to know the value of a gemstone—or fifteen."

Lord Barkin frowned. "I'm sure Miss Fescue was merely overset. Gently bred young women are not accustomed to being accosted by robbers."

Og smiled for an instant, thinking back to the way his real passenger had held off Gulliver with only the sharp edge of her tongue.

"But MacGuigan was nae satisfied with the necklace. No, the rascal hoisted yer lady over his shoulder—like she were a drunken doxy—and carried her off."

Lord Barkin assimilated this in a matter of seconds. "Your entire story is quite absurd," he said calmly. "For one thing, I seriously doubt Miss Fescue would have embarked for Quintay without a chaperone. Lord knows I was never allowed a moment alone with her in London. For another, how would MacGuigan even know she was on board your ship?" He paused and gave Og a speaking look. "Unless, of course, you'd sent word to him."

Og leapt to his feet, making sure not to spill a drop of his brandy. "On my dear mother's grave, I did no such thing."

The earl tapped the fingers of one hand upon the marble mantel. "This is getting tiresome, Og. Do you have any proof of this infamy? Proof that Miss Fescue was even on your ship? A handkerchief the lady left behind, perhaps, or a fallen bottle of scent."

"Not one thing. MacGuigan swept her up, carpetbag and all."

"Carpetbag? I somehow can't picture Miss Fescue toting a seedy carpetbag."

Og thought furiously, then smiled slowly. "The lady was traveling light."

"Worse and worse," the earl muttered. "Not one word that rings true."

Og's white brows flew up. "Don't ye be hintin' such things about me. Me, who was like a father to ye."

"I am not hinting. I am coming right out and calling you a liar. And your *father* was like a father to me," the earl amended stonily, though Og thought he could detect a glint of humor in his eyes. "You were rather more the ne'er-do-well uncle whom no one invited to dinner for fear he would filch the silverware."

"But why would I lie about such a thing?"

"You lie for the pure pleasure of duping people."

Og took a moment to savor this. It would have made a decent epitaph.

The earl continued, "If MacGuigan did take Miss Fescue, then he will send a ransom note. I believe I will wait until then to act."

Rushing to strengthen his case, Og cried, "He knew I'd come to ye with the story. Why, just before he left me, he called back, 'The earl will know what to do.' Now, I'm thinkin' we should head out for St. Columba right now—"

Leaning forward from the waist, Lord Barkin inquired severely, "What, and walk into a trap of MacGuigan's setting? Do you think I don't know about the plans he's making with his islanders to raid Quintay?"

Og's brows shot up even farther than before. Now, here was

an untruth even *he* could barely encompass. "Excuse me for sayin' this, yer lordship, but whatever it is that ails ye must have crept into your brainbox. There's no plan for a raid. Not even the whisper of one. The MacGuigan bears ye no ill will."

"Except that he's abducted my fiancée, or so you say."

"P'raps he has no wish for ye to wed this woman. Ye can't be arguin' the logic of that considerin' how close he is to Miss Dorcas." He paused to let this sink in. "And as for plots, well, my guess is that yer pet jackal Neddie Matchem's been fillin' yer head with hobgoblins. And there's puir Miss Fescue, waitin' on ye to save her, while ye sit here startin' at shadows."

The earl stared down at the fire for a moment; Og prayed he was beginning to waver. When he looked up, however, there was firm conviction in his eyes. "I'm not setting foot off this island until I hear from Gulliver. If I do, then naturally I will sail over to St. Columba in my gunship—"

"Ach, ye shall not!" Og cried. "This is a matter between you and MacGuigan, not somethin' ye want half the Hebrides to know about. Just think of yer lady's reputation. Why be bringin' that wicked ship into the harbor and scarin' the villagers like to death—not to mention distressing Miss Dorcas—when we can slip into the bay unannounced?"

"We're not 'slipping' anywhere," the earl said implacably. "Not until I have reason to believe Miss Fescue is in peril. Right now my only concern is that she is a trifle overdue."

"But doesna that add weight to my story?" Og said with a hopeful leer.

The earl shrugged. "It's a wearying journey up from London. I expect the ladies required a few days in Kilchoan to recover their looks. Besides, Ned Matchem is there with them. So you see it's most unlikely Miss Fescue set out alone."

Og put up his chin and looked the earl square in the eyes. "All I know is, there was a young lady on my ship and now she's on St. Columba. I swear that on the sainted soul of my Granny Adelaide."

"Spare me," said the earl with a flick of his hand. "According to local tattle, your Granny Adelaide was a worse scoundrel than you are. But I will give you this much—if I do hear from MacGuigan, I will sail with you on the *Charles Stuart*. Meantime, I'd prefer it if you stayed here on Quintay." His words were only notches away from an edict. "I've some pine seedlings that need to be carried to the west side of the island. The work is yours if you want it."

It was time to strike his colors, Og realized dejectedly. His ruse to lure the earl to St. Columba was not going to work. He might just as well take up the man's offer, transporting those blasted twigs, and relinquish his hopes of staging a reunion. For now.

Playing matchmaker was clearly not his best role.

Chapter Four

*M*aggie awoke at dawn, her stomach rumbling and grumbling for food.

She thrust up from under the comforter, amazed that she was still fully dressed. At some point she must have removed her half boots, which were sitting by the cold hearth. She hoped the fire had burned long enough to dry them out.

She climbed from the bed and came face to face with herself in the mirror of the shaving stand. Hair corkscrewed away from her head in every direction, and there were smudges of mud along her cheek and jaw.

"Lord Barkin's bride, indeed," she muttered to her reflection. "Black Collum is a nodcock."

She went into the main room of the cottage, intent on foraging for food. She wasn't going to think about her situation until she'd had a cup of tea and some oatmeal to fortify her. Then she remembered the chickens in the yard. An egg or two would be even better.

Still barefoot, she went out the door—and stopped dead on the threshold.

The bay before her was awash with light, glorious trails of pink and gold shimmering on impossibly blue water. The sun was rising behind her, just climbing above the ragged, rocky spine of the island, and its rays were magically captured by the azure sea. To her right, the village had taken on a halo of rosy hues, as though the sandy shingle was a peat fire casting up its warm glow.

It struck her that this island could have been the first place on earth. Not some temperate, exotic Eden, but a more rugged paradise—primitive and challenging—yet just as freshly created and pristine.

She breathed in the sea air, feeling revitalized. The breeze that stroked along her cheeks was balmy as she ventured forward to the edge of the bay. The surf lapped gently at the shore, the water beyond it nearly clear. She could see the pebbled bottom and the random sprays of seaweed flowing with the motion of the waves.

In less than a minute she had tugged out of her gown and was striding into the water. It was cold, bracing. She dashed handfuls over her limbs, and then boldly dunked her head. She came up sputtering and laughing, dancing along the shallows, spinning and whirling with her arms outspread.

Something surged inside her, a sense of freedom, almost abandon. For eight years, circumstances had forced her to tamp down her true nature. It now came flowing forth, refreshed and hungry for life. Her body tingled, awakening to every new sensation. She was a pagan creature, rising from a golden sea . . . reveling in all the possibilities before her.

She didn't need to wonder who this strange incarnation might be. She knew. She was Marguerite Bonheur, child of earth and air . . . and sea, reborn on this bright spring morning. The revelation stunned her.

Not that she was lost to the irony of suddenly feeling so unbound when she was in truth a prisoner. Yet there was something about being pulled from one's normal sphere that swept away the minutiae of daily life and left in their stead a broad, vivid panorama. And here she was, right in the midst of it.

She waded out of the water, now sopping wet, and recrossed the shingle, hugging herself against the breeze. The cistern at the back of the cottage was full to overflowing after all the rain. More splashing and dunking, and she finally felt truly clean. After drying herself with her discarded muslin gown, she went in search of breakfast. Three hens were sitting in the henhouse, two of them on actual eggs. She gently filched them, another skill she'd acquired at the hands of the Players.

It was only when she was returning to the house that she noticed the sailboat on the bay. It wasn't close enough for her to see who was aboard, but it looked suspiciously like Black Collum's skiff. Only it was heading away from the cottage.

Probably just a fisherman, she told herself.

Gulliver couldn't believe it.

He'd seen her walking along the shingle from his skiff and hadn't thought anything of it. But once she went into the water, he'd quickly opened his brass spyglass. He feared the wench might be trying to drown herself or attempting to swim across the bay, which was tantamount to the same thing.

Oh, he'd got an eyeful—his captive capering in the water like a sea sprite, half out of her shift, with the part she'd managed to keep on soaking wet. He didn't need to see that. Or to watch as she left the water and continued her bath at the cistern. Twice he put the spyglass down to tend to his sailing, twice he picked it up again.

Finally, he turned the boat about. There was no way he could face her now with any composure. Bad enough he was still thinking about kissing her last night. Worse yet, he was also thinking about kissing her today. Right now. This minute. Kissing the sea spray off her cheek and throat, letting his tongue taste the salty droplets on her shoulders and breasts.

What madness had consumed him? He wasn't sure he even liked her. It was true that he'd lately been avoiding the company of women . . . a self-imposed penance, perhaps, for leaving the island and leading a life of dubious merit in London. But it was ludicrous to be panting over Barkin's intended like a callow schoolboy. The woman was starchy and headstrong, not remotely seductive. She was doubtless one of those bookish virgins who talked her suitors into a stupor.

So, why was his resolve to stay away from anything in petticoats suddenly eroding like a sand dune in a spring gale?

He knew himself well enough to form a reasonable answer. She belonged to Guy, and so he wanted her. It was that basic. Blame it on the long-standing competition between the two of them . . . to be smarter or quicker, to have the faster boat, to be the better shot.

When they were young it had been a friendly rivalry, but after the rift occurred between the two families, it became a bitter test. Gulliver studied at Edinburgh University; Guy was tutored at home. Gulliver moved to London; Guy remained sequestered on Quintay.

Oh, but Guy was winning hands down now. He possessed a title and great wealth, while Gulliver's only asset was vigorous good health. Guy had never laid claim to that; he'd been a sickly boy who rallied only when he came to visit the MacGuigans on St. Columba.

Yet somehow the invalid earl, the notable recluse, had found and won a woman of spirit and intelligence. One brief trip to London and it was accomplished. Gulliver had spent years in that city without once meeting a woman who stirred his heart. Dorcas wasn't even sure he had one where the fair sex was concerned.

He docked the boat at the stone wharf that ran below the village. He'd find someone else to take the provisions over to the cottage. Since the fishing offshore had virtually disappeared, there were plenty of men willing to earn a few shillings. He'd have him leave the wooden box on the shingle, so that there was no chance of the fellow encountering his houseguest. Unless she was again cavorting in the sea.

No, he decided, he'd better rethink that idea.

He tried unsuccessfully to banish her image as he went up the stone steps to the High Street. If he was smart, he'd have as little to do with the woman as possible.

It was market day, and the High Street should have been bustling. But the stalls with their meager collection of produce, baked goods and household implements were nearly empty of customers. It brought home to him that he was fighting a losing battle.

The Trident Tavern, situated directly above the wharf, was open for business in spite of the early hour. When men had no gainful work, they found occupation in the bottom of a bottle. A group of fishermen had already gathered at the oak bar when Gulliver came through the open door. He'd offered to help Barry MacNeill with his plowing, but he felt the urgent need for a drink first.

He ordered whisky and knocked it back with one long swallow. The men in the tavern raised their eyebrows. It wasn't like the MacGuigan to be tippling so early in the day—he was certain that's what they were thinking. Sure enough, they gathered around him, waiting to hear the latest in his long list of troubles.

Shandy Taybeck, a wizened captain who claimed to be even

older than Fingal MacNeill, sidled up close to his ear. "We're
thinkin' o' takin' the boats over to Quintay. . . . There's been
schools of pilchard sighted there accordin' to Og. We ha'nt seen
a pilchard off this island since ought-nine."

Gulliver shook his head. "I hear the waters off Quintay are
patrolled by the earl's new gunboat."

"'Tis all the same ocean to us, laddie."

He sighed. Fishing rights had been causing friction between
these out-islanders for centuries.

"What does Fingal say about all this? After all, he's the harbormaster."

"Fingal says we must go where the fish are."

Gulliver didn't like that one bit, the old man encouraging the
fishermen to sail into potential danger. He'd thought Fingal
wiser than that.

He clasped the captain's forearm, amazed at the strength remaining in those aged muscles. "I've something brewing,
Shandy. Bide your time until I see how it plays out."

"Oh, aye, as ye say, MacGuigan. We'll bide. But not for
long."

After a satisfying breakfast of oatmeal and eggs—she'd do-
nated the stale scone to the chickens—Maggie explored the
cottage. She doubted her captor had carelessly left the necklace
lying about but decided it wouldn't hurt to search the place. The
furnishings were spare: a wooden settle, a pine table with two
wooden chairs, and an upholstered chair near the fire. A book-
case held fat volumes on agriculture, husbandry, natural history
and astronomy, several treatises on navigation and a collection
of atlases. Not exactly ideal bedtime reading.

There was also a slant-top desk beside the front door, set directly beneath one of the windows that looked out over the bay.
She settled there and began to go through his papers. She knew
she ought to feel guilty about this invasion of his privacy, but the
man had robbed and abducted her. Surely snooping was the far
lesser crime.

At least she had a name to put to him now—she'd found a
stack of invoices with "C. MacGuigan" written at the top. There
were bills for seed corn and feed, many of them dated from the
previous year, and more overdue bills for sugar and flour and

treacle. Not just a household's worth, but hogsheads' full. She had a startling thought that her captor was provisioning the entire island. Or perhaps he had an interest in the local mercantile and these were bills for his inventory. That made more sense. Except she couldn't picture Black Collum in a clerk's apron waiting on customers.

There were a number of personal notes crammed into a cubbyhole, reminders to attend meetings of the fisherman's guild or farm auctions. They were signed with a feminine flourish by someone named Dorcas.

Maggie wondered if this was his sweetheart. The notes had a wifely tone, though she assumed he was unmarried. This cottage bore nothing of a woman's touch. Even the French vase beside his bed held clay pipes instead of flowers.

In the center drawer she found an etching of the castle, buried beneath a bound sheaf of legal papers, which she didn't risk opening. WHITESANDS CASTLE, ST. COLUMBA, was printed across the bottom, with the date 1792. Pennants flew from the battlements in the etching as two carriages drove single file toward the portcullis gate. She looked out the window to the derelict edifice across the bay. No pennants, no carriages, just a flock of gulls riding the air currents above the stone towers.

What a shame the place had been left to molder. It appeared stately, almost majestic, in the etching. There had been life in those old stones . . . perhaps because there had been life within the castle walls. She'd have to ask MacGuigan about the place. *If* he ever returned. He'd said he would bring provisions over first thing in the morning, but his mantel clock was already showing half past ten.

She moved her search to the bedroom, quickly going through the tall armoire that was home to the man's meager wardrobe—and not a single purloined jewel. The drawer of his night table gave up only a worn copy of Swift. And then she saw the trunk in the corner; a tin military trunk with a broken lock covered with a knitted throw. Careful not to disturb the neat piles of clothing inside, she searched it thoroughly.

No necklace, alas, but true bounty for a woman who had traveled with an acting troupe—a patterned woolen square, an old hunting jacket, a small linen tablecloth . . . and at the very bottom a briar walking stick with a dolphin-shaped brass knob.

St. Columba might have been a pretty prison, she reflected as she gathered up her finds, but it was a prison just the same. She'd made up her mind as soon as she saw what was in the trunk—she was going to escape.

Half an hour later she emerged from the cottage unrecognizable as the woman who'd set sail from Kilchoan. Her hair was bound up, gypsy-fashion, in the patterned scarf. The tweed hunting jacket obscured much of her gown, which was a soft gray and quite unremarkable. She had further pinned the tablecloth below her bodice to mimic an apron. With a basket over her arm and the walking stick in her hand, she was sure she would pass for a local farmwife.

She scanned the bay once to make sure MacGuigan wasn't about to come ashore and spoil her plan, then went briskly along the path behind the cottage until she got to the bog. Some of their footprints from yesterday remained in the moist soil, and this gave her a starting point. Each time she came to a questionable bit of path, she prodded the ground with her walking stick. Only twice did it sink down into the black muck, and then she cast about with the tip until she found solid footing again.

Once she was past the bog, she fairly flew around the perimeter of the bay. It was a glorious day and she had thwarted her gaoler. All that remained was for her to find a boat to take her to Quintay. There were coins in her pocket, money Lady Fescue had given her for transport back to the mainland. It was more than enough to get her to Lord Barkin.

She passed a number of stone cottages similar to Collum's and then came to a small sandstone church with a graveyard beside it. A gallant rector would have been just the ticket right about now, but the church appeared shut up. A few cottages down, she came to a fine brick house set back from the road and shadowed by tall trees. She had a thought to go up the walk and ask for aid, the place looked that reassuring. But she had no way of knowing where his nibs had spent the night, and wouldn't it be her luck to knock on the door only to have it answered by a tall, pale-eyed Scot! It wasn't worth taking a chance.

The low cottages soon gave way to multistoried shops, and the dirt lane changed to cobblestones as she entered the village proper. Most of the shops ahead of her had been whitewashed over the native stone and one was a striking shade of blue. But as she drew closer, she saw the paint was flaking off the facades—a number of the shops were even boarded up. In spite of that, the place had a definite charm, the sun gleaming warmly off the bits of mica in the stonework.

Opposite the shops, a street market sprawled beside the seawall above the wharf. She leaned over the granite parapet and counted five small boats tethered there—the larger fishing craft were moored a way offshore—and was not surprised to see MacGuigan's skiff. Since he'd probably berthed it here last night, its presence didn't mean he was nearby. As a precaution, however, she pulled the front edge of her kerchief forward to shadow her face.

Vendors called out to her as she passed by in a language she could not understand. Gaelic, she thought. Captain Og had warned her that some of the islanders still used the old tongue of Scotland. She was intrigued by the melodic, singsong cadences but then felt a ripple of anxiety. What if none of the boatmen spoke English?

No, even if that was true, she merely had to show them her coins and say, "Quintay."

She relaxed again as she hurried past booths offering meat pies and wildflower honey, whisk brooms and horse liniment, although she couldn't help noting that most of the stalls held very few items. Also, the people, both vendors and shoppers, appeared to be quite poor, their clothing worn and patched. St. Columba was apparently not a prosperous island.

She was scanning the street for a possible boatman when a tiny woven basket caught her eye. She stopped to admire it, and the ruddy-faced woman behind the stall spoke to her.

"Pardon," said Maggie. "I'm afraid I cannot understand you."

"Don't have the Gaelic, then?" the woman responded with an easy grin. "No harm. We dinna get many strangers here on market day."

Maggie swallowed stiffly. Five minutes in the village, and she had already been pegged as an outsider. "I'm staying with someone on the island."

The woman's eyes brightened. "Ach, you mun be Iona Mac-Neill's niece come tae visit from Edinburgh."

Maggie said a silent prayer of thanks for this neatly offered reprieve. "'Tis good tae get away from th' big city," she said, aping Percival Lancaster's theatrical burr from the Players' rendition of *Macbeth*.

"I've a mind to take a sail about the island," she said to the woman, then motioned to the wharf. "And was wonderin' where I might find the captain of one of those boats."

"They're mostly whilin' away their time in the Trident Tavern," she told Maggie. "'Tis a little ways down the High Street."

With a quick smile of thanks, she headed toward the tavern, thinking she'd linger nearby until a suitably nautical-looking person appeared. Just before she reached the Trident, a tall man in a tan buckskin coat came out of the shop next door, nearly colliding with her. Maggie looked up to excuse herself, then promptly shut her mouth and lowered her head. His pale eyes barely flicked over her as he turned toward the market stalls.

She sidled away, praying MacGuigan hadn't recognized her.

After ducking into an alley, she leaned back against the wall to catch her breath. This certainly complicated things. What was he doing hanging about in the village, when he was supposed to be sailing across the bay with her provisions? Though maybe this would work out better. If he had brought the supplies over and found her gone from the cottage, he'd have raced back here and likely thwarted her escape. She'd completely overlooked that scenario when she set off. Now, at least, she could keep an eye on him from a distance and make her escape after he left the vicinity of the wharf.

She peeked out from her hiding place and spied him talking to a white-haired man. When a group of children came down the street toward him, she heard him snarl, "Be off wi' ye, ye young scoundrels."

Maggie recoiled, but the children flocked around him, undismayed, tugging at his pockets. He went down on one knee among them, laughing as he handed out pennies. When he rose, he'd scooped up the smallest of them—a black-haired girl in a darned pinafore—and tucked her into the crook of his arm. The other children danced around him, clamoring to be carried.

What a great canard! Maggie thought, nearly grinning. All that talk of shooting her and throwing her into the sea. All that threatening and posturing. He wasn't a rogue at all; he couldn't be, not when children treated him like Father Christmas. The worst she could say of him, after seeing the accounts in his desk, was that he was truly and deeply in debt. No, not a rogue perhaps, but a troubled, burdened man.

.What had Captain Og said to her . . . that many's a fine fellow takes to robbery when times are hard. Wise words, but then he'd also told her that St. Columba was home to cutthroats and scoundrels. Since she hadn't seen anyone even remotely resembling a ruffian in the village, she wondered if the good captain hadn't spent too many years boiling his brain in the sun.

When MacGuigan came strolling back in her direction, Maggie slipped out the other end of the alley and made her way toward Whitesands Castle. She had to hide somewhere while he was still at large in the village. The castle would be perfect.

"Met Iona MacNeill's niece just now, I did," Laurie Mac-Neill was telling him from behind her stall of woven baskets and wooden trugs. "A pretty lass, though dressed verra, verra plain. An old brown coat and a threadbare paisley kerchief. Ye know those Northland MacNeills," she confided, "pinch a penny, pinch a pound. Though I will say, with such green eyes, the lass doesna need much in the way o' finery."

Gulliver was starting to get an odd feeling in his stomach. He'd met Iona's niece a week ago at Northland Farm, where he'd gone to help repair the barn roof. The Edinburgh lass was a buxom blonde with cornflower eyes. He ought to know; she'd certainly batted them at him enough times.

"Green eyes, you say?"

"Aye, greener than a field of clover. Noticed them as she was looking at that basket. There, the wee one with the acorn top."

Gulliver fingered it absently, then reached into his pocket for a coin. Informants, even unwitting ones, needed to be paid.

"I'll take it," he said.

Laurie's eyes danced. "Ah, and is it romance I smell in the air this fine mornin'?"

Gulliver maintained his sangfroid. "You never know. Did you happen to see which way she went?"

Her face screwed up comically. "She was inquirin' about a

boat to take her around the island, but bless me if I didna see her walkin' up the path to th' castle not five minutes past. You might show the lass around the old place, MacGuigan—a man couldna ask for a more secluded spot."

Gulliver was gone before she could make any more teasing comments. At this moment romance was the farthest thing from his mind.

Whitesands Castle was not overpowering, Maggie decided once she'd seen it up close. Not like some she'd visited while traveling the byways of rural England. It wasn't a patch on Warwick or Leeds. What *was* apparent was its air of neglect— lichen and trellises of ivy covered the outer walls, and the hinges of the weathered wooden shutters were eaten with rust.

To keep out of sight, she was walking the perimeter in the moat, which had long ago gone to grass. When she reached the safe seaward side of the castle, however, she climbed up from the moat. Here, the grassy surround gave way to a granite cliff, which led down to a pale sand beach.

It would have made a splendid hotel, she decided, if the Hebrides were not so remote from the centers of English and Scottish society. The gentry needed a reason other than a charming village and breathtaking vistas to travel so far. And then there were all those bogs. People liked to walk about when they stayed in the country; there would have to be a constabulary solely dedicated to pulling unwary hikers out of quagmires.

No, Whitesands Castle was not going to get refurbished or reoccupied anytime soon, not as long as the rest of the island remained so impoverished. She recalled what MacGuigan had said about St. Columba's spring, that the water could cure anything . . . except poverty and despair.

In her experience those were two things only gold could cure.

And she knew then, without a doubt, why MacGuigan had taken the necklace—he was planning to give the money it fetched to the islanders. In a bizarre way, it made her proud to be playing some small part in bringing relief to these people. Yesterday she'd fought to keep the necklace; today she'd likely have handed it over without protest.

"The noble abductee," she said aloud, and then chuckled. "How about the escaped abductee?"

He was leaning against the wall of the west tower, not twenty feet from where she stood, the breeze tossing his hair and buffeting the skirts of his buckskin coat. Maggie found herself trapped between his scowling form and the cliff. She began edging toward the north tower, keeping as close to the rim of the drop-off as she dared. If she could only get away from the castle grounds, she was sure she could lose him in the village below.

He saw where she was heading. "I'm not going to play race-around-the-castle with you." He nodded to the cliff. "And if you're thinking of jumping to your death in maidenly protest, I should warn you, you're more likely to break your leg. It's only a twenty-foot drop."

In response, she plucked up a walnut-size stone and skimmed it at his head. When he ducked away, she ran. Ran like all the demons of Hades were after her.

She managed to get past the north tower before he tackled her, rolling with her several times before they came to rest on the grass.

"Where in blazes did you think you were going?" he growled, holding her down by the shoulders. "Do you imagine anyone in the village would have aided you?"

"I have money," she said through her teeth, struggling to get up. "That's usually persuasive."

He glared at her. "Yes, it persuaded Og MacNeill to strand you on this island."

"Og is a fool if he thought I had *that* much money."

"No, but your future husband does."

She finally succeeded in loosening his hold and sat up. "I'm not going to explain all that to you again," she said, trying to get the skewed kerchief around her hair. "You've a brain like a sieve. Hard facts go in . . . and trickle right out again."

He surprised her by laughing. "You know, I doubt I've taken so much abuse from one person since I suffered my first tutor as a lad."

"He has my belated sympathy. It's never pleasant to instruct a sieve-brain."

"Here, stop that." He reached out impatiently and snatched

the kerchief from her hands. "There's no point in covering your hair . . . since I've found you out."

She frowned. "I can't just leave it undone. It's a dreadful mop at the best of times."

He cocked his head and stared at her. "I think it's quite fetching."

Maggie nearly blushed.

He reached forward to drape the cloth around her shoulders. "Why do women think there's any allure in having their hair scraped back and pinned in place? You ask a man, he'll tell you it's much more effective when it's down."

"Yes, but well-bred ladies must wear their hair up."

He fingered the hem of her aged hunting jacket. "And is this sort of garment all the crack among well-bred ladies these days?"

"It's part of my disguise," she huffed.

"Then you can leave your hair as it is. No one would ever take you for Lord Barkin's bride."

"Least of all Lord Barkin," she murmured.

He rose then and reached a hand down to her. She came up from the grass in one fluid motion; he gave an extra tug and she found herself trapped in the crook of his arm.

He studied her intently for a moment, as if gauging her resistance, and she felt her breath catch. He was so stirring up close, his skin tanned and fine-grained, that mink-brown hair gleaming in the sunlight. His dark coloring made a perfect counterpoint to his pale eyes, which were by turns an icy blue or an intriguing wood-smoke gray. Just now they'd gone almost silver.

Maggie was observing his mouth, wide, mobile and at present curled into a half-smile—when he lowered his head and kissed her. The lips that had been so hard last night were all suppleness now. He held her lightly, keeping her close but not constraining her in any way.

His eager mouth sought hers from a variety of angles, as if trying to find the perfect one. She thought they were all splendid. Yet she hesitated to respond, fearful of lowering her considerable guard even a notch. She might have danced in the surf as a free soul, but she wasn't sure she had the wherewithal to dance with this particular devil.

Still, it was very nice, standing in the warm sun, caressed by a balmy breeze, being kissed by a man who smelled of sea air and tasted like wild honey.

Eventually, with a low, drawn-out sigh, he raised his head. For an instant she saw something in his eyes that might have been confusion before they reverted to their usual cool appraisal.

"Was that another forfeit?" she asked as she backed away from him.

He nodded once. "So mind you, don't cause me any more trouble."

"You make very free with a woman you believe is promised to someone else," she said as she headed back to where she'd left her basket and stick. He stayed right beside her.

"You weren't exactly beating me off with a cudgel. In fact, I'd almost think you enjoyed it."

She put her chin up. "I wouldn't know, having no point of comparison."

"What's the matter, his lordship never try to steal a kiss while he was courting?"

"I can't answer that, since it wasn't me he was courting. I would certainly hope Alice allowed him no such liberties."

He did not respond, but it was clear he still wasn't buying her story.

"I've been wondering about one thing," he said as they made their way around the castle. "How did you get to the village?"

"I crossed the bog." When his expression darkened, she added quickly, "It wasn't so dangerous. I used my walking stick to check for oozy places."

"You might be interested to learn that four people have been caught in that bog in the past year. And any number of sheep."

"Did they die?"

"No, but—"

She poked him playfully in the ribs with the dolphin end of her stick. "I see what you are. You are a worrier. It's no surprise you always look so grim."

"Me? I am the soul of levity."

Maggie nearly snorted.

As they came even with the castle's front entrance, she

stopped walking and turned to look up at the impressive stonework. "Who owns this place?"

"The laird of St. Columba."

"Why doesn't he live here then?"

"He's dead."

"And did no one inherit the title?"

"You are a regular question mill today. Why are you so interested in the old ruin?"

"It's lovely," she said.

He recoiled slightly. "That's the daftest thing I ever heard."

"No, truly," she said. "It's got wonderful presence and a sense of timelessness. Furthermore, whoever built it had an eye for design; he created an intriguing perspective by making the two back towers shorter than the front two."

"You sound like a guide at Blenheim."

"Don't you like it?"

"It's a draughty, damp eyesore. If I could sell the stones for ship's ballast, I'd jump at the chance."

"But they're not yours to sell—and a good thing too. Whitesands needs someone who appreciates it. And you didn't answer my question. Where is the laird's heir?"

"He wanted nothing to do with St. Columba. He left here years ago."

"Maybe if you wrote to him . . ."

He grumbled something under his breath and refused to answer any more questions as he hurried her through the village. Most of the market had dispersed, but the basket seller was still there; she waved to Maggie as they passed by and gave her a broad wink.

MacGuigan manhandled her down the steps to the wharf and prodded her into the skiff.

"You don't need to be so rough," she said. "And you can stop trying to prove how dangerous you are. Because I've seen through *your* disguise, as well."

He climbed in after her and took up an oar to cast off. "I have no idea what you are talking about. As usual."

"I saw you at the market . . . with the children."

"And?"

"You were laughing with them, passing out pennies for sweetmeats. You even carried one little girl in your arms."

"So you believe a rogue can't be kind or generous on occasion?" he asked as he stood to hoist the sail.

She replied primly, "I am rethinking the whole rogue issue."

"Jesus preserve me," he muttered.

They were in the middle of the bay when Gulliver brought up the matter that was foremost on his mind. "I've been meaning to warn you . . . the cottage is visible from the village."

"Really?" She squinted across the expanse of water. "We're halfway there and I can only just make out the front door."

Somehow he wasn't conveying things to her properly. "There are plenty of fishermen who own spyglasses, fishermen not at sea, because there are no fish."

"And you're saying they can see the cottage?"

"Precisely. So you don't want to be doing anything outdoors . . . to call attention to yourself."

She gave him a long, calculating look. "That *was* you out here earlier this morning. I thought I recognized your skiff."

"I was coming over with these provisions." He nudged the wooden box beneath her seat with the toe of his boot. "I saw you go into the water and was afraid you were going to drown yourself, so I took out my own glass."

Indignation suffused her face as she leapt up. "You . . . you were watching me through a spyglass?"

"Sit down!" he barked as the boat began to heel over.

"But I was bathing!"

He shrugged. "Nothing I haven't seen before. Now, sit down before you fall in."

She did sit and crossed her arms over her chest. "I had a particularly nice morning, in spite of everything, and now you've ruined it. I can't believe you were spying on me."

"Yes, well, it's all part of the job. Goes with being a kidnapper and a rogue. Just try and stay out of sight, will you? I don't want every young bantam in St. Columba sailing over to visit the local mermaid."

Chapter Five

*M*acGuigan carried the provisions into the cottage while Maggie sat and fumed on the garden wall. She'd been a fool not to hide properly until she was sure he was gone from the village. But the castle had caught her imagination and her caution had evaporated. *And* her chance to escape, it now appeared. Her captor was going to be extra vigilant after this.

"Don't you want to see what I've brought you?" he called from the doorway.

She slid down and trudged dutifully into the house.

He had spread the food across the pine table. "Cheese and sausages," he said. "A sack of potatoes, a bag of onions, a crock of fresh cider and some strawberries."

"Wonderful," she said in a dull voice. "Where's the gall and wormwood?"

"What?"

"Isn't that what penitents are supposed to eat?"

He set his fingers beneath her chin. "What's wrong, Alice? Feeling guilty over your attempt to escape?"

"Not guilty, frustrated. And embarrassed."

His eyes narrowed. "Because of what I saw this morning?"

She nodded. "It was such a pure moment. You can't imagine. I've never danced in the sea before. Now you've made me feel soiled."

"I never said I was leering at you. It was . . . you were . . . to use your own word, lovely."

Her expression softened. "Then why did you turn back?"

He cleared his throat. "Because I didn't want to intrude on you. I knew you were enjoying a . . . a private moment."

"Oh."

He began to put the food in the larder, purposely avoiding her eyes. "But I'm afraid I'm going to have to intrude on you now. It's clear I can't leave you here alone."

"What if I promise not to run off again?"

He tsked. "I can hardly trust a woman who spouts lies and fabrications with every breath."

Maggie did not rise to the bait this time. "Aren't you afraid that will give rise to gossip?" She added dryly, "Especially with all those spyglasses trained on us."

"Not if I sleep out on the shingle. It won't be the first time, by the way. There's a cool sea breeze there on warm summer nights."

"It appears I have no say in the matter."

"No, you don't," he declared. "And I'm relieved you've finally realized that."

They managed to keep out of each other's way for most of the afternoon, Gulliver busy at his desk, his guest weeding the bedraggled garden.

"I think you should water these plants from the stream," she called in to him through the open window. "The one that runs from St. Columba's spring. You said it has curative powers."

"I was just relaying an old wives' tale."

He bent his head over his ledger and she went back to her spade. Every so often he would sneak a look out the window. She'd rolled up the sleeves of her gray gown but left the makeshift apron pinned to her skirt while she chopped and hacked at the nettles and dandelions.

It was distracting, having a woman about the place. He could hear her singing under her breath, little snatches of French ballads and English folk songs. She occasionally passed by his window, carrying armfuls of garden debris to the wheelbarrow she'd unearthed in the shed. Her soft, white hands weren't going to remain in that condition for long if she kept working without gloves.

Finally he pushed away from his desk and went to the door.

"You don't need to do that, you know. I hardly expect you to work for your keep."

She looked up from pruning a straggling rosebush. "I've

never had a garden of my own," she said. "This is actually a treat for me."

"I suppose you've always had gardeners to look after your family's property."

She shook her head. "No gardeners, no property. My parents traveled a great deal, so I never had a real home."

"Your father was a baronet. He surely had an estate of some sort."

She sighed. "My father was a librarian for a wealthy widow in Surrey."

Gulliver found himself frowning. Why on earth did she persist in spinning him these ludicrous tales? Maybe Og's concoction had made her delusional.

She read the annoyance in his face and turned away, her attention once again on the rosebush.

Damn, he hadn't meant to rebuff her that way.

He came down the steps and took up the basket on the ground beside her. "You can look forward to having a fine home on Quintay," he said. "You've doubtless seen pictures of Luray Castle."

"No, not a one."

"You must know its history."

She tapped the blade of her secateurs on her chin. "Tell me."

He settled against the stone wall and crossed his long legs. "There was once a brother and sister, the children of an English earl. The sister met and married a gentleman from St. Columba who was visiting London. And since the siblings were close, her brother often stayed with her here and soon grew to love these islands. Eventually he brought his own English bride here and built her a castle on Quintay."

"Built?"

"Mmm . . . he bought a ruin in Ireland and had it shipped, every last stone, to the island."

"And that was the current Lord Barkin's father? His son must like Luray Castle a great deal; they say in London that he rarely leaves the place."

"His constitution is frail. But surely you were aware of that. You have only to look at him to know he is not robust."

Of course Maggie did not know anything of the kind. And she further doubted that Alice had been informed of her intended's poor health. That scheming Lady Fescue had bartered her daughter to a man who was likely to leave her a widow within a year or two. Then again, what better way than through her daughter to get her grasping hands on his lordship's gold? Widows were allowed to manage their own finances; married ladies were not.

No wonder this man mistrusted her, Maggie thought. He saw her as an avaricious harpy, eager to wed an ailing aristocrat who would soon die and leave her set for life.

"And do the earl's daughter and her husband still live here?" she asked, trying to get him to continue with his tale.

"No," he said. "They are long gone."

Maggie knew enough to back off from the subject. His eyes had gone flinty, his mouth hard.

"Here," she said, laying her secateurs in the basket he held. "I've done as much as I can with the garden. You've let the weeds run riot, I'm afraid."

"I have little time for gardening."

"That's true," she said thoughtfully. "You're too busy taking to the high seas and carrying off women."

His cheeks narrowed. "You were left here, if I recall correctly. If I had a choice, I'd certainly not have carried *you* off."

She watched him stalk away toward the cottage and mouthed to his departing back, "Ah, but you certainly choose to kiss me whenever you please."

He turned and gave her a long, probing took.

She smiled sweetly, then went off to deal with the wheelbarrow.

At dusk, he built a peat fire on the shingle, near where the skiff was grounded. He didn't invite her to partake of his dinner of roasted sausages and potatoes, but the campfire drew her like a night moth, harking as it did back to her youth on the road.

She slipped on the hunting jacket against the evening breeze and made her way along the garden path to the stone wall, lingering there, watching him grill sausages on a stick.

"Have you had supper?" he asked without looking at her.

"Not yet . . . I took a short nap while you were building the fire. The sea air is invigorating but it's also very sleep inducing."

"I've enough for two if you'd like to join me."

"I'll need a stick."

He got up. "Here, take mine. These sausages are almost cooked through."

He met her at the garden gate, handing off his own stick, and went to find a replacement. She settled down facing the bay on the blanket he'd spread beside the fire and lowered the two sausages again over the flames. He came back and sat beside her, taking two more sausages from the basket he'd carried from the cottage and spearing them on a slender branch.

"That is a very paltry stick," she remarked as he held it out over the flames. No sooner had she spoken, than one of the links slipped off.

"Fat's in the fire now," she said, trying not to grin.

"I'm beginning to appreciate that," he muttered as he snatched at the sausage and burned the tips of his fingers for his trouble.

Maggie transferred her sausages to the plate where the roasted potatoes lay, crisp in their jackets, and handed him her stick. "Try this one."

He was toasting his supper one-handed—and sucking on his blistered fingers—when Maggie lifted a small jug from the basket.

"Here," she said, coaxing his hand from his mouth. She held his arm away from his body and trickled a stream of spring water over his fingers. "Better now?"

"Mmm." He still didn't look very happy.

"You know, you really can't blame this new injury on me."

His eyes flashed. "I'll find a way."

They shared the single plate, eating with their fingers like South Sea savages or Turkish pashas. When they were finished, he passed over his handkerchief, freshly laundered this time.

She glanced at him as she wiped away the remains of the grease from her hands. "What did you mean just now, when you said you knew the fat was in the fire?"

"I wasn't being facetious," he said, stretching out alongside her. "Trouble's been brewing between St. Columba and Quintay for nearly a decade . . . and I think I might just have forced a confrontation."

"You mean by stealing the necklace and holding me hostage, you're going to bring the wrath of Lord Barkin down on the islanders?"

He chuckled. "*The Wrath of Lord Barkin.* Sounds like the title of a lurid novel."

"So you don't think he will retaliate?"

"Not against the islanders themselves. But the local fishermen want to try their luck off Quintay. In the normal way of things, his lordship might overlook this sort of poaching. But lately he's got an armed cutter cruising the waters around Luray Castle—God only knows why. And he'll have his dander up, once he gets the ransom note—"

She scrambled to her knees. "You still haven't sent it?"

"Hush! I'm deliberating over what to say."

"I'd think the solution was obvious. If you want to help the fishermen and restore the earl's goodwill, let me go and return the necklace."

"The earl's goodwill is long lost, Miss Fescue. That had nothing to do with you."

"Just how well do you know him?"

"Well enough. He was often here as a boy, visiting the laird's family at the castle. St. Columba was like a second home to him. That's why it infuriates me that he's turned his back on the island."

She laid a hand on his arm. "Has it occurred to you that you ought to be more angry at the laird's son, who is actually *from* here, than his lordship, who lives across the water?"

"Yes," he said. "It occurs to me every damn day. But there's no point in expecting aid from that quarter; he's virtually penniless."

"Ah, but you know how people rally when the master comes home. If you could entreat him to return here, it might put some heart and grit back into the islanders."

He was looking at her with an odd expression. "They have plenty of grit," he said in a low, rasping voice. "It's gold they require."

"Well, I hope these people appreciate what you're doing for

them. Maybe they'll put up a statue of you in the town square—*after you've been arrested and hanged.*"

Her harsh words hovered in the air, and then he was on his feet, hands fisted. Without a word he spun away from her to where the skiff was beached. He fiddled with the mooring line, then lit his pipe and perched on the gunwale, watching the moon rise over the bay.

Maggie thought this would be a good time to slip back to the cottage; it was obvious he didn't want her company. Still, she couldn't leave him in such a sour mood.

"I'm sorry I let my tongue run away with me," she called out.

He made no response, and she feared he was going to keep ignoring her. Finally he pushed away from the boat and approached the fire again.

"No," he countered. "That might be the first true thing you've said to me. I knew the penalty I could face when I sailed out after the *Charles Stuart.*"

"I don't wish that end for you. I honestly don't."

"Why should you care?"

Maggie couldn't even answer that question for herself. All she knew was that it got harder and harder to keep any emotional distance from him. And it wasn't just those stirring kisses that drew her. She'd never met a man with such a variegated nature . . . kindly, yet harsh when provoked, with a questionable conscience, but a streak of morality a mile wide when it came to the welfare of his people.

His people. That was clearly how he viewed them. A pity *he* wasn't the laird's son.

"I was imagining how much it would hurt your family," she said at last. "I assume you have one, though you never speak of them."

He shrugged. "There's not much to tell. My father's ancestors lived on St. Columba for centuries. He and his brother raised cattle, farmed, invested in local shipping. I suspect there were smugglers somewhere in the family tree, maybe a pirate or two." He gave her a swift wink. "Just so we don't sound too prosy. And I've a cousin who lives here. Her parents are dead . . . as are mine."

"Is that her house, the pretty brick one in the village?"

"Mmm."

She had a strong inkling he'd spent the previous night there. Good thing she hadn't knocked on the door.

"And where is your home, MacGuigan?"

He sketched a motion behind them. She frowned. He'd painted a picture of a fairly prosperous family—not one that dwelled in a two-room cottage.

"You're being purposely obtuse."

He gave her a crooked smile. "It's one of my better qualities."

"Was your family home outside the village . . . to the north, perhaps?"

She felt his withdrawal like the curtain going down on a play.

"You ask too many damn questions." He turned away from her, his gaze again on the bay.

Maggie sighed. "What's the point of all this secrecy? It's not as though Lord Barkin won't figure out who sent the ransom note. Especially if the two of you were friends once."

"That was not precisely our relationship," he said.

"Still, he's bound to remember you. You make rather a . . . strong impression." She poked at the fire with her stick, watching the tip start to glow. "I don't suppose it's occurred to you that kidnappers need somewhere safe to run off to once they've got the ransom. There aren't many places to hide on an island this small . . . unless you plan to spend the next few years living in a cave."

"I'll go away if it comes to that. The money will stay here; that's all that matters."

She threw the stick down and scrambled to her feet to face him. "But what if there is no money!" she cried, needing to make him see the truth. "Listen to me . . . *please*. Before long word will reach the earl that Alice Fescue has jilted him. It will come from Edward Matchem or Captain Og or from one of his servants with family in Kilchoan. Lady Fescue can't keep it a secret forever."

She gripped his sleeve. "And what do you think his lordship will do when he gets a ransom note for a woman he knows is an imposter? He will cast it into the fire—and then, make no

mistake, he will send the authorities after you. For having the
temerity to even *think* of abducting his future wife."

She stopped to take a breath.

"Go on," he said lightly. "These tales of yours get better and
better." But his expression was now wary.

"You haven't sent the ransom note yet . . . I beg you, please
don't go forward with this course. Even if you send it tomorrow, it might be too late. He could already know of Alice's defection. You'll be risking prison, or risking exile from this place
you love. And you're not likely to get a ha'penny in the end."

He absorbed this, his mouth tight, his eyes hooded. "There's
still the necklace. It should get us through the summer, maybe
even the autumn."

"Good," she said. "Keep the necklace with my blessing.
I'll . . . I'll tell the earl it fell into the sea. Og won't say anything about the theft, you know that. Just let me go. Let me
carry on with my duty to Lady Fescue, and I will never set foot
in Scotland again."

He pushed away from her, muttering that he needed to think,
and went striding off along the shingle.

She plumped down by the fire again, wrapping her arms
around her knees. All she could do now was wait . . . to see if
he finally believed her, to discover whether or not he was going
to continue with this mad and dangerous plan.

She wanted him to set her free, though now more in consid-
eration of his safety than her own comfort. She no longer
minded being on the island. In one short day she had gone from
loathing the place to finding it intriguing. It was a land of con-
trasts, stormy and bright, bleak and beautiful. Its varied moods
mirrored her own inner complexities—and perhaps those of
the man pacing along the shore.

He had to believe her now, she told herself. He had to have
heard the honest entreaty ringing in her voice.

Damn and blast the chit! What concern of hers was it
whether or not he was in danger from the earl? He didn't want
the woman wringing her hands over him. Still, he had no intention of telling her the truth of the matter—that he was not
likely facing any personal risk. The worst that could happen
would be a widening of the rift between himself and Barkin.

Gulliver was beginning to suspect he was indeed holding the wrong woman. Surely Alice Fescue, a pampered daughter of the gentry, wouldn't have given a fig for *his* safety. But a hired companion, someone only notches above a servant, might have developed a smattering of compassion for others.

If she really was this Maggie Bonner, however, then he had lost his bargaining chip with the earl. The man was unlikely to hand over a large sum of money to redeem a woman he'd never met—chivalry went only so far.

Perhaps he'd believed more of her story than he realized. It could explain why he'd balked at writing the ransom note. And there was another reason for his hesitation—Og had told him recently that Guy's health was worsening. The fact that he had risked the long journey to London—possibly to put the affairs of his English estates in order—and courted a woman in a week's time, seemed to bear this out. If it were true, if Guy was failing, then news of Miss Fescue's abduction might send him into a rapid and permanent decline. The last thing Gulliver wanted was the man's death on his conscience. Especially after his own part in the wretched events that had transpired nine years ago.

He ought to let her go, he told himself. Before he got attached to her. In spite of the frequent friction between them, he was beginning to enjoy her company. And it had been oddly comforting to hear her express concern over his situation here. Dorcas often tried to reassure him, but that was to be expected from one's cousin. Not from one's captive.

Maggie watched him cautiously as he hunkered down beside her and threw a few more peat bricks into the fire.

"I've thought about what you said," he told her. "And so I'm going to hold off on sending the ransom note . . . if only because I don't want to incite his lordship against the fishermen."

Her eyes brightened. "Then am I free to leave St. Columba? If you believe my story, you know I'm not worth anything as a hostage."

"I'm still not sure I can credit any of it, especially the part about Alice running off. Why would a baronet's daughter whistle away a chance at becoming a countess? For another thing, you've more than once expressed concern that his lordship might consider you compromised. You've got to admit, that sounds more like Alice's voice than that of her hired companion."

Maggie bristled. "I am a woman alone in the company of a strange man, so you will have to forgive me if out of fear I occasionally take shelter behind my mistress's rank. If you recall, I did the same thing aboard the *Charles Stuart*—when you were threatening me with a pistol."

"Yes, you conveniently put on, then take off, the trappings of Miss Fescue. So don't blame me for being confused or mistrustful."

"But even if I were Alice, there's no point in keeping me here if you're not going to send a ransom note."

"Ah, but I can't have you running to Lord Barkin with tales of my misdeeds. As you pointed out, his lordship might become angry on principle, and I can't risk that, not with the fishermen so keen to set sail for Quintay."

Maggie scowled. It appeared she'd been hoist with her own petard.

"What if I promise not to say anything to the earl?"

She swore she could feel him wavering, weighing the odds of her keeping silent against the possible repercussions to the islanders if she implicated him.

"No," he said finally. "I've no surety that you'll keep quiet."

"You have my *word*," she said indignantly.

He shot her a cockeyed look. "In my experience, a woman's word is about as reliable as quicksand. It shifts out from under you at the least provocation. Besides, I'm only holding off on sending the note to his lordship. Once I've talked the captains out of their foolhardy quest, I can set my plan back in motion."

Maggie wanted to growl; she settled for a ladylike sigh. "I see we are going round in circles, you and I. And the worst of it is, I must find a new post as soon as may be. Like you, sir, I have people depending on me. My father is crippled by arthritis, and my wages go to pay for his caretaker."

He set his chin on his hand and stared into the fire. "Well, if that's true, then aren't we a fine pair? Not a groat to our names and each of us with more responsibility than any person should have to carry."

"I was doing very well until Alice ran off with that militia captain and you stole the Barkin emeralds. I'll never get my reference from Lady Fescue now." She added quickly, "Not that I am asking for them back, mind."

He surprised her by taking up her hand. "I have a duty to the islanders. Otherwise, I'd give them back, mignonne, truly I would."

In spite of her irritation at him, Maggie was charmed by the endearment. Her father had called her that as a child. It felt like decades since anyone besides Papa had addressed her with fondness. It was definitely time to go inside, before he crept any further under her defenses. She gently disengaged her hand and rose, uttering a soft good night.

She was at the gate when he called her back.

"I forgot . . . I bought this for you at the market. Laurie said you'd been admiring it."

He stood and held out the small trinket basket. Maggie came forward and took it with a sort of awe. In addition to endearments, presents had been singularly absent from her adult life.

"I don't know what to say," she whispered. She put her head back and smiled up at him. "You must be the first kidnapper in history to be offering gifts to his prisoner."

He shoved his hands into his pockets. "Take it as a token of truce. I honestly mean you no harm."

I only wish that were true, she thought, as she walked back through the garden, holding the delicate basket cupped in her palms. He'd already done a great deal of harm to her equilibrium.

For years she'd wondered if she would ever meet someone who could overshadow all those dashing—but flawed—leading men who'd inflamed her girlish imagination. Now here was a man as handsome as any actor, who was intelligent and amusing and so compelling—and he was more flawed than all her childhood crushes put together. No matter that he saw himself as some sort of out-island Robin Hood, the fact remained that he was a thief. In a world where a child could hang for stealing an apple, Black Collum's potential as a suitor was not great.

Not that he'd ever given her any indication of aspiring to that role. The kissing didn't signify. Men kissed willing women as a matter of course, and Maggie had to admit she'd been more or less willing both times.

If she flattered herself, she could believe that he wanted to keep her here because he was growing to like her. If she was being more realistic, she'd take him at his word—that he didn't want her running off to the earl with an incriminating story.

After she changed for bed, she stretched out on the counterpane, listening to the waves lapping on the shore and picturing her captor rolled in a blanket beside the fire. There were so many mysteries surrounding him, she didn't know where to begin untangling them.

He was a vigorous, rugged man, who did not shy away from hard work—the state of his hands bore that out—and yet she sensed so much of the gentleman about him. There was his cultured voice, with only a smattering of Scotland in it, and his general manner toward her, which was highly considerate, at least when she wasn't riling him over something. There was also his enormous concern for the people of the island. That would have made more sense if he'd been a landowner or a member of the gentry, the men who normally took responsibility for the welfare of the locals. But he'd said himself that he didn't have a groat. No money and no home, beyond this humble cottage. It made no sense that his cousin lived in a fine, big house, while he lived—

Maggie sat up suddenly, recalling something he'd said at the castle. *"If I could sell the stones for ship's ballast, I'd jump at the chance."* As if Whitesands belonged to him, as if he had the right to dispose of it.

Great heavens, could it be true? Was MacGuigan the old laird's son?

No, she told herself, settling again on the bed. It was ludicrous. It didn't prove anything, just because he'd avoided answering her questions about his family home. He'd said his parents were dead, so perhaps the place had a bad association for him. She still got a twinge whenever anyone mentioned York, which was where her mother had succumbed to a wasting fever.

No, if he was the present laird, he wouldn't be living here, not when he had a perfectly wonderful castle across the bay. But that brought her right back to the question of his family. Someone had reared him properly, seen him educated, given him a certain level of refinement—and she doubted they had accomplished all that in a tiny cottage.

"How ironic," she murmured, just before she drifted off to sleep, "that he thinks I'm the one chock-full of secrets."

Gulliver refilled his pipe from the tobacco pouch in his pocket and lay back on one elbow, sending fragrant clouds swirling up to mingle with the smoke from the peat fire. It was a pity his guest had gone inside. . . . She was always stimulating company. It felt a lot less lonely having her here with him. Nothing like a pretty woman bustling about the place.

He inhaled sharply—and choked on the harsh tobacco.

"Damn," he muttered as he reached for the water jug. Where the devil had that thought come from? He *wasn't* lonely. He didn't want a woman here prying into his life and invading his home. Oh, he understood himself well enough to know that she attracted him. There was that kissing business to start with. He could barely keep his hands off her when they were together. She was slender to look at, but surprisingly sturdy to hold. He liked that. Not a wilting lily, to use his cousin's expression.

And beyond the physical pull, there was the pleasure of engaging her verbally. He enjoyed taunting her just to watch the sparks fire up in those bright green eyes.

All right, so maybe he wanted her, but to what end and for how long remained to be seen. He certainly wasn't in the market for a bride; he already had a crushing amount of responsibility. And ladies of his guest's ilk did not idly dally with men. More's the pity.

Besides, he reminded himself sternly, it was all moot if she really was Alice Fescue.

He gazed up at the night sky, now a swath of ebony velvet, and wondered whether it was wiser to believe her story or to discount it. If she truly was destined for Guy, then that set her firmly out of his reach. If, as she claimed, she'd never even met the earl, he was free to pursue her if he chose. Then again, if Guy wasn't clamoring for her, Gulliver might just end up losing interest himself.

"Lord, you're a shallow wretch," he murmured miserably. "Still battling him to see who comes out on top."

He knew that was often the way with boys, but he was

nearly eight and twenty. Surely time to put such childish—and petty—competition behind him.

The more he thought about it, the more he realized he no longer wanted to best Guy, he simply wanted him back in his life. Seducing the man's intended bride, however, was hardly likely to accomplish that. They were more apt to end up with pistols at twenty paces. And for all his frailty, Guy had always been a damned fine shot.

Gulliver smiled, remembering the time they had stolen his father's dueling pistols and sneaked off to the beach below the castle to practice shooting at pieces of driftwood. Old Fingal had caught them at it, and instead of tarring their respective hides, he'd taken the time to show them how to shoot properly. Fingal, on other occasions, had also demonstrated how to land a punch, cast for trout and break a green colt. Gulliver swore that the old man had been more of a father to Guy than his own sire, however much that illustrious gentleman loved his son.

And yet Guy had turned his back on Fingal, on all of them, for nine long years.

Gulliver calculated all those dear to him whom he'd lost in that span of time: parents, aunts and uncles—and his best friend. If he were truly wise, he'd not risk his feelings any further by forming an attachment to the lady who currently slept in his bed.

There was only so much loss a man should have to weather.

Chapter Six

*T*he next morning, Maggie heard her host moving about in the parlor. She dressed quickly and emerged from the bedroom to find him making buttered eggs over the fire.

"I need to go to the north end of the island today," he told her. "I promised to help one of the farmers with his plowing." He set a plate of eggs on the table. "Here, eat while I get cleaned up."

"Would you like oatmeal? Or some pancakes?"

He scowled and banged the plate against the tabletop. "No. Now, eat!"

Goodness, he was certainly being abrupt this morning. Especially since she thought they'd smoothed things out between them last night.

"What's the matter with you?" she called out as he crossed the room.

He stopped and turned, framed in the bedroom door. "I have no choice but to take you with me—and I'm not happy about it."

"Oh."

"Now, if I could trust you not to run off . . ."

Maggie didn't want to be left alone all day, even though she had no intention of trying another flight for freedom.

"I'm not making any promises," she declared. "I consider myself rather like a prisoner of war—it's my duty to escape."

She ate quickly, listening to him moving about in the bedroom, her gaze darting to the door when she heard him utter a swift oath. When he emerged, she was not surprised to observe a seeping nick on his chin.

"Not my fault," she said at once.

"Don't bet on it," he growled. "Now, are you ready?"

"One minute." She got up, wet her napkin thoroughly from the water bucket and handed it to him. He stood looking at it blankly.

"Oh, for heaven's sake." She took it back and dabbed gently at his chin. "The miraculous water of St. Columba's spring, remember? Here, let me see your fingers." She took up the hand he had burned last night and was thrilled to see there was no longer any sign of blistering. "It really is amazing."

His fingers tightened over hers. "Yes," he said gruffly, looking deep into her eyes. "I believe amazing just about covers it."

Maggie had the distinct impression he was going to kiss her again, especially when he pulled her a bit closer and lowered his head.

But then he seemed to recover his senses; he blinked several times, released her hand and stepped back. "Get your things," he said, again in that odd, gruff voice.

She ran to fetch shawl and bonnet, then followed him out to the beach. He helped her into the boat and pushed off, leaping into the stern as it drew away from shore.

Maggie sat facing him just behind the single mast, trying to muster a stalwart, adventurous expression, but the first time the boat capped a swell, she felt her nerve shrink. When MacGuigan remarked on her expression of anxiety, she said, "I don't think I've the makings of a sailor. I felt wretchedly seasick coming over from the mainland."

"That's because you were on the open sea. Our bay is usually quite calm."

Small consolation when the boat kept rising and falling. At least it was another fair, cloudless day, the water around them gleaming with pinpoints of gilded light. Maggie distracted herself by watching him man the tiller. The wind ruffled his hair back from his forehead and she spent some time admiring his high, intelligent brow.

"Where are we going?" she asked as they rounded the headland where the castle sat, solitary and majestic, like a neglected dowager duchess at a garden party.

"To a farming village, Cranlochie. You'll get to meet some

of the crofters. I . . . I suppose I'd better think of an explanation for why you're trailing after me."

She nearly smiled. "I'd hate for you to lie. Why not tell them I'm Maggie Bonner from Surrey? Come up to Scotland on holiday."

"That'll do. Though whether it's a lie or not remains to be seen."

He hugged the coast once they were outside the bay, sailing along sheer cliffs and rolling downs that plunged, like a green carpet, right into the sea. Maggie put her head back, glad for the sun on her face, and breathed in the sea air. So far, her stomach was only mildly troubled and she had hopes of making a sailor yet.

As they passed a scattering of flat rocks jutting above the surf, he pointed out a group of basking seals. The sun struck beads of light off damp pelts the color of MacGuigan's hair.

"The females come here in the spring to bear their young," he said. "For centuries the islanders hunted them for their fur, but Fingal put a stop to that when I was a lad. He told everyone they were selkies."

"Selkies?" She leaned toward him eagerly.

"Seals that take on human form. If a man weds with a selkie, he has to find her shed seal skin and hide it . . . to keep her from returning to the sea."

"It appears you island men have trouble holding on to your women."

His mouth twisted. "Only the wild, untamed ones. And who'd want a woman like that?"

Maggie suspected that was exactly the sort of woman MacGuigan needed. Not a mealymouthed drudge but someone who could give as good as she got. Someone, she thought wistfully, exactly like her.

He had brought the skiff in closer to the rocks, and one venturesome cub shied away from his mother's side to observe them over the edge of his perch. His dark, liquid eyes, now large with curiosity, had an almost human aspect.

"I'm glad you no longer hunt them," she said. "They're quite beautiful. Though I'm surprised a superstition would keep your people from pursuing something so valuable. Especially now."

"Value is relative. The seals left here a number of years ago and shortly afterward, the schools of fish offshore disappeared. This year the seals came back, and the fishermen have taken it as an omen that the fishing will pick up again. No, no one from St. Columba is going to bother them."

"But you told me there were still no fish."

"Hope springs eternal, ma'am. At times I think it's all they have left."

Not long after, MacGuigan put into a small cove. The village of Cranlochie sat at the far end, its shops and cottages rising up a steep, tree-filled slope, stacked like cracker boxes in a shop.

People hailed her companion as he and Maggie passed along the waterfront. "G'day tae ye, MacGuigan." "'Tis is a fine mornin', MacGuigan." "MacGuigan, come for supper if ye've time . . ."

He returned their greetings, smiling, shaking hands, slapping one old fellow on the back.

Maggie was surprised by this reception. She didn't question that he was regarded with favor in the village of St. Columba, but he seemed just as well liked in this village.

They hiked up through the maze of narrow streets, with not a straight passage to be found anywhere, and Maggie was quite winded by the time they reached the summit. Here the cottages and trees gave way to an open heath bisected by a dirt lane. MacGuigan pointed out a farm in the distance, a single-story house with several barns and a patchwork of fields surrounding it.

"That's Finbar MacNeill's place," he explained. "Both his sons left for the mainland two winters ago. They're working in the shipyards of Clyde, sending money home. But old Barry is a farmer to his bones. If he couldn't work the earth, I think he would die. So I lend a hand when planting time comes around."

"Can I help?"

He sniffed. "I doubt that plowing is part of the curriculum at a lady's finishing academy. Not something a pampered princess is ever asked to do."

Maggie nearly snorted. "You just put me to work, and you'll

see how much of a pampered princèss I am. Who knows, you
might even begin to believe my story."

His jaw clenched, as though he was about to say something
weighty, then his face relaxed. "We'll see," he murmured.

As they passed the first of the fields, a weathered, wiry man
with a shock of grizzled hair called out to them. They both
halted, and MacGuigan approached the stone wall.

"Been picking rocks," the man said as he came toward them,
wiping his hands on the seat of his canvas breeches. "If rocks
was a crop, by God I'd be rolling in it, eh, MacGuigan?"

"We'd all be, Barry, every last one of us."

The farmer was staring at her now, and MacGuigan quickly
said, "This is Miss Bonner, a distant connection of my
mother's. From Surrey. She wanted to see a real crofter's farm."

He smiled and touched his forelock to her. "Oh, aye, that it
is."

The old man walked with them to the house, still on his side
of the wall, the two men discussing the state of the weather.
Maggie, meanwhile, took in the stone farmhouse and the low-
lying barns. As in the village of St Columba, the buildings appeared weathered and in need of paint. When the farmer's wife
came out onto the porch to greet them, Maggie noticed the
patched, faded apron she wore over her threadbare dress. Lean
times had truly hit the island if a woman of property didn't even
own a decent day gown.

MacGuigan again introduced Maggie.

"Ye must call me Cora," she said with a smile. "There's a
mite too many Mrs. MacNeills on this island to suit me."

MacGuigan motioned Maggie into the house, then took the
farmer's wife aside. Maggie watched through the window
while he spoke to the woman, obviously giving her some kind
of instructions.

When she returned, her expression was wary, and Maggie
wondered what that annoying man had told her. The answer
came soon enough.

"I'm tae find ye something tae do," she said, her bright blue
eyes full of concern. "But not too taxing, what with ye being on
the island for a rest cure."

Maggie blinked. "A what?"

Cora touched her hand. "I'm nae surprised the life in London's worn ye down, body and soul."

Maggie's eyes narrowed. "What exactly did he tell you?"

"That I'm to pay ye no mind if ye start spinnin' me tales. The MacGuigan says ye're prone to all sorts o' odd starts."

"Oh, he did, did he?" Maggie was definitely going to eviscerate him.

The woman studied her closely. "But ye look hale enough to me. Was himself havin' a wee jest at yer expense?"

"Yes," Maggie said with a tight smile. "A very wee jest."

The woman shot her a look of commiseration. "Still, he said I should find something tae keep ye out o' trouble. Now what sort o' things are ye clever with?"

Maggie thought a moment. She doubted Cora MacNeill was in the market for French lessons. "I like gardening," she said at last.

"Then come along and I'll put you to work thinning seedlings in the vegetable garden."

She found Maggie an apron and a large straw basket and walked her out to the back of the house where a sizable garden lay, surrounded by a woven wicker fence.

"The new plants come up all in a bunch," she explained, "and ye need to be spreadin' them out." She spread the fingers of both hands and held them up. "This far apart will do. Throw the ones ye pick into the basket. I'm makin' soup, and the greens will go into the pot."

Maggie made her way along the rows of baby plants thinning them carefully, stopping occasionally to admire a butterfly or ladybird or to listen to the trill of a skylark. It was tiring work, requiring a deal of bending and stooping, but she knew it wasn't a patch on the rigors of real farmwork. Fields had to be cleared of stones, then plowed, sown, weeded, watered and harvested. Crops had to be made into ricks or packed in sacks or crates, stored or siloed or shipped off to market. And that did not even address the needs of livestock, which required feeding, breeding, doctoring and dipping. It was thankless work, often with little profit at the end of the growing season.

Her mother had regularly pressed her father to buy a small holding somewhere and set up as a farmer, and those were the arguments he had set before her. Maggie could still recite them by heart. Her father used to say that a man either had soil under his fingernails and in his blood, or he did not. Papa, on the other hand, had performing in his blood. Noble gestures and eloquent speeches were the fruits of his own personal garden.

By the time the sun was directly overhead, Maggie had finished her chore. She wandered out of the enclosure and went to investigate the barn. A small herd of milk cows were lounging in the paddock beside it; every one hollow-faced and bony, though scrupulously clean.

The barn's interior was shadowy and still, dust motes thick in the air. Maggie found a rush broom and began to sweep up the bits of straw and dried manure that littered the central aisle. As she scooped them up into an old sack, she had a thought that this was exactly what MacGuigan's garden needed—some nice rich mulch.

Mrs. MacNeill found her hanging over one of the stall doors, admiring a black-and-white cow with a newborn calf at her side.

"Not sure the bairn will make it," the woman said with a sigh. "The puir mother either. The birthin' took too much out of her, with her bein' sae thin. We've little feed left over from th' winter and th' spring crops will nae be ready for months yet."

Maggie turned to her. "What about the pasturage beyond the village of St. Columba?"

"'Tis too far away. And this part of the island is too rocky for wild grass tae take root. I'll be sorry to lose my Rosie. Raised her myself, I did, after she lost her mama. Fed her from a bottle, right in ma own kitchen."

Maggie didn't hesitate; she undid the brooch at her throat and held it out. "You must send to the mainland for feed," she said. "This should help."

The woman made as if to refuse the gift.

"Please," Maggie said. "I would like to do something. I promise you this is not an odd start."

Cora MacNeill slipped the brooch into her apron pocket. "Bless ye, lass." She reached out to scratch the cow between her ears. "'Twould break my old heart to lose her."

Once they were back in the kitchen, Mrs. MacNeill poured Maggie a mug of water, apologizing that she had nothing finer to offer. Maggie did not complain. She drank the water slowly, savoring the cool, silvery taste, feeling the stiff ache in her neck and shoulders begin to ease almost at once.

Cora collected the greens from the basket and replaced them with a meat pie and a half dozen scones. She held it out to Maggie. "The men will be gettin' peckish about now. How'd ye like tae take them their lunch?"

Maggie nodded. She wanted MacGuigan to see that she'd been carrying her weight.

Mrs. MacNeill took her onto the porch and pointed out the distant plot where the two men were plowing. Maggie set off briskly, keeping on the verge between the fields, where tender green shoots were already showing above the surface. As she drew closer, she saw MacGuigan manning the plow behind a team of gaunt chestnut horses. Mr. MacNeill was following a few paces back, spreading seed from a sack over his shoulder. They'd both rolled their shirtsleeves above their elbows, and Maggie couldn't help admiring the taut sinews in MacGuigan's forearms as he wrestled the plow along the row. For all their fine faces, there hadn't been one leading man in the acting troupe who could boast such a rugged physique.

Both men caught sight of her and waved. When she reached the edge of the field, MacGuigan came toward her while the farmer unhitched his team and led them toward a distant stand of trees.

"Been keeping busy?" MacGuigan asked, as he swiped his handkerchief over his face.

She narrowed her eyes. "It was difficult, what with all my . . . odd starts."

MacGuigan laughed. "I had to think of some reasonable explanation, in case you told Cora about being my prisoner."

"Well, this is hardly a rest cure. I thinned the entire vegetable garden *and* swept out the cow barn."

"Byre," he said, taking the basket from her as they headed toward the trees.

"Byre, then," she repeated. "And I collected a sack of manure and hay bits to bring home."

He raised one brow. "Back to England? That should make an interesting memento."

Maggie ginned up at him. "No, dunderhead. Back to Bay Cottage. For your garden."

Gulliver didn't point out to her that she'd called his cottage home. Not just his cottage, he mused, but *Bay* Cottage. For centuries the windswept stone dwelling had had no name, and now this woman who'd been on the island a scant three days had christened it. And gathered manure for his garden.

If he wasn't careful, he told himself, she was going to domesticate him, She'd have him planting and painting and God knew what else.

She settled in the shade and began cutting the meat pie into slices, placing them on threadbare napkins. Barry came over from tending his horses, easing himself down against the trunk of an alder with a heavy sigh. Gulliver took his portion from her and also leaned back against a tree. He tucked into his lunch, taking time to admire her profile as she plied Barry with questions about his sons in Clyde. The sun had left a soft blush upon her skin and he couldn't take his eyes off one peach-tinted cheek; it had to feel—and taste—as soft as it looked.

Why now, he wondered, when he was beset with a thousand worries, did he have to become smitten with a gently bred off-islander? Oh, she might brag of her accomplishments in garden and byre, but one morning of hard work was a lark compared to the drudgery most of the islanders faced day in and out. Aside from the fact that he had nothing material to offer her— and that she *might* be affianced to Guy, no woman would willingly take on the burdens he carried. Those soft, white hands of hers bore mute testimony to the easy life she'd been leading. Whether she was lady or lady's companion, she was hardly the sort of woman who would forsake comfort and security for this rugged, uncertain life.

Eventually they all lapsed into silence as weariness caught up with them. Barry was soon asleep, his straw hat dipped low over his brow. His captive was facing away from Gulliver now, looking out over the newly turned field.

He wasn't sure what possessed him, but he whispered softly, "Miss Fescue . . ."

She didn't make any sign that she had heard.

He tried again, this time even softer. "Maggie?"

She turned almost immediately, her eyes puzzled. "Yes?"

He kept his expression purposely bland in spite of having made a momentous discovery. "Just how tired are you?"

"Why do you ask?"

"I was wondering if you'd like to help me finish up the field." He motioned to the dozing farmer with his chin. "Let the old fellow rest a while longer."

She nodded. "Just tell me what to do."

Maggie thought her arm was going to fall right off. It hadn't seemed that difficult at first, sowing the seeds with a flinging motion as she walked behind the plow. Now, an hour later, she could barely raise her arm above her waist. And her shoulders felt as though she'd been pummeled by a prizefighter.

MacGuigan soldiered on ahead of her, keeping the plow straight and true, as it sliced through the crusted soil. She understood now why he'd grown so angry when she'd taunted him for not toiling. He toiled harder than anyone she'd ever met.

Only a few more rows to go, Maggie thought with relief, as they neared the edge of the field.

But Farmer MacNeill had apparently awakened from his nap; he came trotting across to them, chiding MacGuigan for treating her like a field hand.

"'Tisn't fittin' work for a woman. What were ye thinkin', man?"

MacGuigan twisted around and gave her an assessing look. "She appears fine to me."

"Go rest, lass," MacNeill said, patting her on one shoulder. "This brute will have ye pullin' the plow next, mark my words."

Maggie gladly relinquished the seed sack and staggered off toward the trees. She could still hear the farmer protesting to MacGuigan as she curled up under an alder and closed her eyes.

"Maggie . . . Maggie Bonner."

Someone was shaking her awake, a hand insistent on her shoulder. Maggie didn't want to open her eyes. It was lovely to lie drowsing on the cool grass, pretending that when she got up every joint and muscle wasn't going to ache like the dickens.

"Maggie!" The shaking grew rougher. "Wake up. It's time to go."

"Ye've kilt her," Farmer MacNeill pronounced dourly.

"My luck's never been that good," MacGuigan grumbled.

He returned to pestering her. "Come on, lazybones. We've brought a cart around. You won't have far to walk."

She finally did open her eyes. Her tormenter was crouched on the grass beside her, the farmer a few feet behind him, wearing a puckered frown of concern.

MacGuigan leaned down and said softly, "I'm sorry. I didn't mean to wear you out."

"Yes, you did," she said, drawing herself up on one elbow and stoppering a yawn with her hand. "I think you were testing the pampered princess."

If tossing his own words back at him had any effect, she couldn't see it. He looked neither abashed nor contrite, merely annoyed.

"Are you going to get up?"

"In a minute," she answered peevishly.

She gave a little squawk as he scooped her off the grass and rose with her in his arms. He carried her to the back of a dog-cart, which was waiting beyond the trees. She no sooner felt the hard seat beneath her bottom than he climbed in and sat down opposite her. The farmer eased himself into the driver's seat and set the spindly horse in motion.

"This was Barry's idea," MacGuigan told her. "He's going to take us down to the village. He had a notion walking might be beyond you."

Maggie couldn't answer that, not having had occasion to attempt it. Still, her legs did feel quite weak, but that might have been due to MacGuigan's long frame taking up most of the cart. Their lower limbs were touching in places she was sure were not at all proper.

At one point he started to say something, then reached out and traced his fingers swiftly across the neckline of her gown. "Ach, you've lost your brooch."

Her hand flew to her throat in a panic—until she remembered her benevolent gesture in the barn. "I took it off," she said, not wanting to lie. Hoping to distract him from any more questions, she prodded at his knee. "And could you please stop crowding me, Master Longshanks?"

"You might be more comfortable in my lap," he responded with the mocking leer she was coming to detest. Who'd ever have thought she'd one day long for a man to leer at her in complete earnest?

Farmer MacNeill tsked at him over his shoulder. "Ye've developed a bit of a mean streak, MacGuigan, and it shames me tae see it."

Maggie shot her companion a smug grin; at last she'd found a champion on the island.

When they reached the waterfront, the farmer handed her down from the cart like the lady of the manor and took her arm as they went along the wharf.

"Pay him no mind, lass," he said, close to her ear. "He's grown sour as a spinster in the past two years. It's from all the weight he's had to bear after his father's death. But make no mistake, the MacGuigan's twice the man his father was."

Maggie was just about to ask him to elaborate when MacGuigan grabbed her elbow and practically dragged her off to the skiff.

During the trip back, his face remained shuttered, and he responded to all her overtures with bare monosyllables.

It occurred to her that he might be starting to doubt himself.

Lord knew she'd done everything in her power to chip away at his certainty that she was Alice Fescue, and it was possible he'd finally seen the truth. Not that such a thing made her feel particularly elated. Once her true identity was established—*and* MacGuigan had dissuaded the fishermen from poaching in the earl's waters—he'd likely waste no time sending her to Quintay. She'd be right back where she was three days ago, having to face his lordship and admit the loss of the necklace. Except that she'd be leaving some vital part of herself on this island. It seemed the Barkin emeralds were not the only thing she'd forfeited in her encounter with MacGuigan.

She stole a glance at him, relieved that he was not attending her but rather keeping his eyes on the billowing sail behind her. The cut on his chin was now barely perceptible, thanks, she was convinced, to the healing properties of the spring water.

She let her gaze roam freely over the rest of his face, committing each plane to memory so that years from now she would be able to recall the exact curve of his tanned cheek, the arched set of his nose, the heart-stopping contours of his mouth. She'd have only to close her eyes to see again the waving strands of his hair, the heavy black lashes forming a lacework of intriguing shadows around those pale, haunting eyes. She'd harken to him in every sea breeze, every field of heather, every crackling peat fire. His laughter would come to her from out of the darkness and the flash of his smile would light up her dreams.

Maggie turned her head sharply away. What on earth was she doing? She would not let herself become any more beguiled by this man. Her time with him was simply a stimulating interlude in an otherwise humdrum life. MacGuigan could be nothing more to her than a foolish fancy. Especially if he was the laird of St. Columba—and Barry MacNeill's parting comment had certainly fed into her suspicions on that front. Such men did not seek the favor of lady's companions. Not in the real world.

To distract herself from this deflating line of thought, she leaned back, splaying her arms on the seat, and began to sing. It was a sad, oddly soothing soldier's song, mourning the lost comforts of home and hearth. She was into the second verse, when MacGuigan grumbled loudly, "Have done, will you."

Maggie's mouth snapped closed for an instant. "I'm sorry. I know my voice is indifferent, but—"

"Your voice is quite pleasant," he said. "But for God's sake, you don't have to grind into my brain that you're homesick and missing your family."

Her eyes widened, "Homesick? I believe a person would need a home in order to feel homesick. Furthermore, I chose that song because I like the melody. I promise I wasn't trying to make you feel guilty—"

"I don't feel guilty."

"Then what do you feel?" she asked waspishly, wondering if this brangling was preferable to strained silence.

He looked across at her, dead on, his eyes never wavering. What she read there nearly sent her tumbling backwards off her seat. Blatant desire and open longing burned in that intense silvery stare, and she instantly felt a reciprocal heat flare up from deep inside her. The fierce flame danced between them for an endless moment, sparking like splinters of lightning striking a gutted oak, and Maggie wondered that the skiff didn't just ignite beneath them and burn to a cinder, sails and lines and all.

It was almost better than being kissed. Almost.

When he lowered his eyes, distracting himself with the tiller, she could still feel the scorching heat on her cheeks.

After that brief unguarded moment, he lapsed back into silence. She was frantic for him to say something, to explain himself—though it really wasn't necessary, she concluded after a time. When a man looked at a woman in such a way, words were superfluous.

He wanted her. Beyond that nothing much mattered.

MacGuigan did not invite her to share his supper that night, and she did not wander out to the fire. There was a new edginess, a simmering tension between them that only increased after they'd come ashore. The few times they'd brushed past each other in the cottage, the contact had set her pulse racing. Once, he'd come up behind her while she was refilling the water jug, and she'd nearly melted back against him, aching to feel his arms close around her. She'd heard the sharp intake of his breath and knew he'd been thinking the same thing.

Even now, as she picked at her dinner, she was sorely tempted to go out to him. But she wisely decided that each person's heart took its own time to discover its best, truest path, the way a stream needed eons to find its natural course along a riverbed. She only hoped it wouldn't take him quite that long.

No, she reflected, she trusted him not to make her wait. He was nothing if not rash. And as for herself, all her previous misgivings about him had been swept away by that one startling look they'd shared in the skiff. She could almost believe it was within her power to win him, and the mere notion of that made her giddy with expectation.

Her sack of mulch, which MacGuigan had troubled to carry from the MacNeills' barn in the dogcart, now sat on the porch, a pungent reminder of his thoughtfulness. The tiny acorn basket lay on the nightstand beside the bed. These were small, nearly insignificant tokens, but they might as well have been priceless treasures for all they meant to her. The man had taken away her liberty and given her quite another sort of freedom in return. The freedom to speak her mind, to test her body to its limits, to laugh and sing and dance in the sea. The more time she spent with him, the more the old Marguerite Bonheur rose up in her. It seemed inconceivable now that she would soon return to the stultifying life of a hired companion, forced to keep every feeling and opinion bottled up inside her.

Yet perhaps that was not to be her lot after all. There was a man out there on the shingle who might offer her a very different future. She had an inkling that tonight he was no longer standing guard but rather was keeping watch over her. The thought comforted and thrilled her.

Chapter Seven

*T*he next morning Maggie was lazing in bed, still a bit dazzled by what she'd read in MacGuigan's eyes yesterday, when a loud barking erupted outside the cottage. By the sound of things, Fabian had tracked down his master.

Two minutes later, there was a knock at the bedroom door.

"Miss Fescue?" It was a woman's voice.

Maggie was pushing back the covers when the door opened. A young woman peeked into the room. "I know it's a bit early for morning calls," she said with a hesitant smile. "I just wanted to meet you."

Maggie sat up, brushing back her plait of hair, and then stopped, one hand suspended, as she took in her visitor's appearance. It wasn't exactly like looking in the mirror, but close enough.

It's incredible, she thought.

Her visitor came into the room and approached the bed with some wonder, obviously experiencing a similar reaction. "Gulliver was right. We might be sisters—"

"Gulliver?"

The woman tsked merrily. "He still hasn't told you his name? It's not his real name, actually, it's what we called him as a boy. Because he towered over the other children on the island. Made us all feel like Lilliputians."

Maggie rubbed at her head, still confused. "I thought his name was Collum."

"That was his father. Black Collum they called him, because of his hair."

Maggie was beginning to think Captain Og had not told her one word of truth during the entire trip from Kilchoan.

"Then what *is* your cousin's name? And who are—"

"Dorcas!" MacGuigan's shout echoed from the front room, and the next instant he was inside the bedroom.

Her visitor cried, "No, Gull!" as he hustled her out and slammed the door, barricading it with his body.

"My cousin's the nosiest creature on this island," he said to Maggie. "She rode over from the village on her pony"—he raised his voice—"and she can ride right back, if she knows what's good for her."

There was a determined pounding on the door, and then what sounded like someone kicking it once.

Maggie was about to ask why he didn't want her talking to his cousin when she realized she was sitting there in her muslin night rail. She immediately drew the covers up to her chest.

He raised one brow. "This from the woman who cavorts half naked in the surf?"

"You know, you can be truly insufferable at times."

"I do work at it," he said with a grin.

"And are you just going to stand there leering at me while your cousin tries to beat the door down? I've never seen such a family for outrageous behavior."

"Dorcas is the wild one. I am tame as a pet lamb. And I am not leering. I was reforming my opinion of your nightwear. What appeared shabby in your carpetbag is quite charming on your person."

Maggie tugged the blanket up even higher.

A dark head appeared at the open bedroom window. "Gulliver," said Dorcas with apparent restraint. "You really are behaving like a cad. It's a good thing I came over this morning. . . . Miss Fescue clearly needs a proper chaperone. Now, get out of her bedroom."

"Or what? You'll climb through the window and box my ears?"

"It won't be the first time."

He walked over and shut the window in her face, latching it before he drew the curtains closed.

Then he returned and settled on the edge of her bed. Maggie watched him warily. He seemed all wry levity this morning, and she wondered if she had imagined that simmering energy between them yesterday.

"Now, listen to me," he said. "There are things afoot here, as you know, that have the potential for getting sticky. I don't want my cousin involved in any of this in case it should come to the law being called in."

"You should have considered that before you imprisoned me," she pointed out tartly.

He leaned back, wide-eyed, and made a sweeping gesture with each hand. "Imprisoned? Where are the bars? Where are the shackles?"

Maggie sniffed. "Very amusing. I do have a great oaf of a gaoler, however, who has now taken to stomping around in my bedroom."

He reached forward to trace his knuckles lightly over her chin. "Such a sweet maid. Still," he purred, "there's nothing a man enjoys more than a good tongue-lashing first thing in the morning."

His eyes danced with wicked humor.

Maggie glared back at him. "I believe your cousin has the right of it. You *are* being a cad."

His expression grew serious as his hand drifted up to stroke a wisp of hair behind her ear. "Ah, no, Maggie," he said, his voice barely more than a whisper. "A true cad would not have slept out on the shingle last night. I think we both know that."

She had no idea how to respond to such plain speaking. Though at least he was acknowledging that something had been set in motion between them. She took his hand and rested her cheek on it for a moment, looking up at him with open entreaty. "I do know. But please don't mock me . . . or this . . . situation you've placed me in. I never know from one minute to the next how to react to you."

He inclined his head until their noses were nearly touching. "I'd say you were doing fine." His fingers tightened on hers as he nudged her head back and kissed her softly.

Maggie forgot all about holding up the blanket; it settled at her waist as his free arm slid around her and pulled her close. Her breasts, with only their thin covering of muslin, pressed against the muscled wall of his chest, and she heard him sigh low in his throat at that first sweet contact. She answered with a ragged moan as he deepened the kiss, coaxing her mouth open.

There was a sort of safety in knowing his cousin was right outside the cottage; he wasn't likely to overwhelm her, and so she let herself be carried away by the moment, tasting him boldly, twining her arms around his neck, raking her fingers through the thick, sleek strands of his hair.

He was strong, much stronger than she realized, but he held his power in check. That mastery impressed her, gave her the courage to explore with her mouth and with her trembling hands. When she traced her lips along the side of his throat, his body arched into hers. When she stroked her hands down his back, she felt the tension of coiled muscles beneath his shirt. His eyes were closed now, his face taut with desire, and still he did not try to coerce her. Rather he seemed to be savoring her fledgling efforts to reciprocate. Further emboldened, she pulled aside his collar and set her mouth against his upper chest, biting softly.

"Sweet Jesus," he cried against her hair.

He fisted one hand around her plait and tugged her head back, kissing her openmouthed, roughly, with little finesse. Maggie knew his control was slipping, but it didn't matter. Her own was long gone. She'd forgotten all about her erstwhile chaperone—until a sharp tapping started up on the outside of the window.

"Gulliver!" came the muffled call. "What's going on? It's gotten very quiet in there."

He let her go so quickly she nearly fell backward onto her pillow.

"I *knew* you were going to be trouble," he said with a halting grin. There was not a trace of recrimination in his tone.

Maggie looked up at him, hoping her eyes were conveying the words her lips could not form. That she wanted more, that she would always want more from him.

He rose just as she was screwing up her courage to tell him how she felt.

"I'd best go out there and soothe my headstrong cousin. Meanwhile, you get yourself dressed."

Maggie drew her clothing on quickly; she wanted to get outside before . . . Gulliver . . . sent his cousin packing. She now had a source for information on her mysterious host, and she was not going to miss this opportunity to get some answers.

Gulliver found Dorcas behind the cottage, tossing feed to the chickens.

"I warned you not to come here," he said, tugging the tin plate from her hand and dumping the feed onto the ground, where the chickens descended on it *en masse.* "What happened to not wanting to risk your pretty neck?"

"Good thing you're not a farmer," Dorcas observed dryly as she watched the hens frantically attack their breakfast. "As for my neck, Guy would never do anything to harm me. You know that. Besides, I have a message for you from Fingal. He said you might like to know that the fishing fleet went out this morning on the first tide."

He handed the plate back, turned from her without another word, and went off down the beach. His spyglass was under the seat in the skiff, and it took only one glance to assure himself that the boats normally moored off the wharf were gone.

Thank God he hadn't sent the ransom note and gotten his lordship's bile up. But he still didn't like it that the fishermen were risking the waters off Quintay. Shandy Taybeck's promise to wait a few days had likely been overridden by the other captains, men too long without some gainful occupation. So off they'd sailed, after pilchard or whatever made its way into their nets. Something to eat, something to sell at market, something to give a man back his pride. Gulliver knew full well how that felt.

He also knew that pride could be as much of a burden as a badge of merit. It might be time he swallowed his own completely and made his plea to the earl in person. Miss Fescue or Maggie Bonner or whoever the hell she might be could leave St. Columba then, and he'd get his peace of mind back. He'd nearly lost his wits in that bedroom, nearly declared himself like the poor besotted fool he was.

She came out of the cottage at that moment, came hurrying through the garden with her dark hair in a wild tangle behind her, and he cursed those wayward fishermen. He'd much rather have bided here with her than go sailing after them. Especially since he'd just now decided on a course that would soon end this farce they'd been acting out. He and Maggie would have little time left.

Her eyes narrowed as soon as she drew near enough to read his clouded expression. "What's wrong, MacGuigan?"

He closed the spyglass with a snap. "The fishing fleet's gone out, bound for Quintay is my bet. I've got to go after them."

"Not in that little boat," she said, casting a dubious look at his skiff.

"I'll take the *Kestrel* out." He grinned. "You remember, the fine sloop that ran down the *Charles Stuart*."

She rolled her eyes. "As if I could forget that momentous encounter. But are the fishermen really in danger?"

"I'm not taking any chances," he said as Dorcas came up to them.

She wet her index finger and held it aloft. "Wind's from the west, Gull. Riding my pony around the bay would be quicker than taking the skiff across to the village."

"And that same wind should slow down the fleet somewhat." He turned to Maggie. "I'm going to leave Dorcas here with you. Um . . . try not to stab her or anything."

She nodded solemnly, then surprised him by gripping his arm and whispering, "Godspeed, MacGuigan."

Lord save him, the wench was worried about his sorry hide. He touched the side of her face. "I'm too wicked to die young, mignonne."

That got a smile out of her. He tweaked her hair once, then motioned his cousin to follow as he headed back to where her dun pony was tethered.

"I didn't want to make you an accomplice," he said in a low voice, "but it appears I have no choice. Will you stay here and see that she doesn't wander off?"

"She's not exactly a gibbering idiot, Gull. I think I can handle things." She averted her eyes and said half under her breath, "Though whoever thought I'd be looking after Guy's intended."

He knew he ought to tell Dorcas that his prisoner was no such thing and about the earl's bride running off. Especially that part. But he needed to be away from here before his resolve failed. Time enough later for explanations.

Dorcas was looking over her shoulder at Maggie. "You

know, if things had been different, I might actually have come to like her." She added with an impish grin, "She gives you a hard time, which places her high in my estimation already."

He muttered something under his breath, then untied the pony's bridle from the tree beside the henhouse. Fabian crawled out from under the structure and began capering around the pony's legs, set for a good run.

Gulliver got him by the collar and handed him off to her. "Keep him here with you." He paused. "And there's one other thing, Dorcas. I don't want you discussing me with that woman."

She tipped her head up. "But whyever not? What can she tell the earl about you that he already doesn't know?"

He couldn't admit to Dorcas that it wasn't the earl's censure he was worried about, it was Maggie Bonner's. He didn't want his cousin revealing anything about his past.

"I simply want my private business kept . . . *private*," he said at last.

"Very well, I swear not to say a word. Though it was a very promising topic—now I haven't any idea what we will talk about."

"Two women? Alone all morning? Trust me, you'll find something."

He climbed onto the pony's back and set off at a brisk trot toward the bog.

Maggie was standing beside the garden wall intently following MacGuigan's progress along the shingle when Dorcas rejoined her.

"I fear for your pony's back," Maggie remarked.

"Not a bit of it. Western Isle ponies are unusually sturdy. The Vikings rode them, you know."

"I can imagine that," Maggie said. "Your cousin has the look of a Viking chieftain."

She finally tore her gaze away from MacGuigan and met Dorcas's gimlet stare. Maggie felt totally caught out—she might just as well have been drooling over the man.

"Do you think he'll be able to turn the fishermen back?" she asked.

"He'll do his best. I doubt there's any real danger. Though

as you've probably gathered, Miss Fescue, my cousin feels responsible for everyone on this island."

"Yes, I had got that impression. And, please, my name is Maggie Bonner."

Dorcas tipped her head. "Still sticking to your story, eh? Gulliver told me about all about it. I'd just as soon you weren't Alice Fescue, as a matter of fact. So I'll play along if it makes you happy."

"That's a relief. Your cousin is not good at playing along. And I am sorry you have to stay here and be my watchdog."

Dorcas smoothed her hands over the stone wall. "None of this abduction business was my idea. But family loyalty runs deep on these islands . . . deeper than you can imagine. So I'll do what he asks, even if I disagree with the whole scheme."

She boosted herself up onto the wall and sat gazing across the bay. Maggie couldn't help noticing that her muslin gown was sadly out of date and that the brim of her straw bonnet was distinctly tattered. The first lady of the island appeared little better off than the villagers, in spite of her fine house.

"And here's another irritation," Dorcas said. "He made me promise not to tell you anything about him. It's ridiculous, really, but Gull's gotten rather secretive lately. Makes me wonder what he's up to."

"You mean besides robbery and kidnapping?" Maggie couldn't keep from pointing out.

Dorcas shifted around with a crooked grin that was much like her cousin's. "His mother always said he did things in a grand way. No petty crimes for the MacGuigan." She gasped and flung one hand over her mouth.

Maggie laughed. "Don't look so panicked. I've known his name for days now. I . . . um . . . looked through his desk and found a pile of invoices with C. MacGuigan on them. After what Og told me, I assumed it stood for Collum."

Dorcas shook her head. "I might as well tell you the whole of it, though he's bound to have my skin. His parents named him *Cadmus*. Isn't that boringly prosy?"

Maggie wrinkled her nose. No wonder he preferred Gulliver.

"Another of Og's little fibs," she muttered. "I wonder if anyone on this island would know the truth if it leapt up and bit him."

"Oh, don't take Og MacNeill as our exemplar," Dorcas said quickly. "Most of us only tell fibs out of the usual social necessity. Og's turned lying into a lifelong vocation."

Maggie let her gaze wander to the castle. "I also found an old etching of Whitesands in your cousin's desk. It must have been quite something back then."

Dorcas sighed. "It was grand."

"I don't suppose you know of a way inside? I walked the perimeter two days ago—until your cousin caught up with me."

"So you got away from him, did you?" There was that crooked grin again.

"For a time." Maggie explained about putting her disguise together and how she'd crossed the bog. She purposely omitted the kissing part.

"That took some pluck," Dorcas said, her eyes gleaming. "And it explains why he stayed here the past two nights. You're fairly slippery, Miss . . . Bonner. I wager he was spitting nails when he finally caught you."

"To put it mildly."

"Then it will be a fine payback for you if we can get into the castle. I don't suppose you found a large key while you were rifling through his desk? You see, Gulliver is the caretaker and he's the only one who ever goes inside."

Maggie was about to ask her if that had anything to do with her cousin actually being the laird, but Dorcas had pushed off the wall and was heading for the gate.

"Come on," she called over her shoulder. "I think we both deserve to have an adventure. If only we can find that key."

Maggie hoisted the sail and lashed the line to a cleat, following Dorcas's instructions. Her companion was seated at the tiller, while Fabian stood in the bow, tongue lolling, the breeze ruffling his ragged coat.

They'd found the key without too much searching—it had been at the bottom of a stoneware crock on the desk. After a quick breakfast, they'd set out, Dorcas stating her intention of teaching Maggie to sail. Together they'd got the skiff into the water, barefoot, with their skirts hiked up. Dorcas had leapt nimbly into the boat and tugged Maggie aboard in her wake.

Now that the sail had bellied out nicely, Dorcas showed her how to steer with the tiller. Then she lounged back on the opposite seat, bonnet off, bare feet jutting over the side.

"This is the freest thing I know," she said. "The wind carrying you, the water cradling you."

"It *is* very liberating," Maggie agreed. She was enjoying herself immensely. Somehow having a task took her mind off her uneasy stomach.

"We're lucky the wind's from the north now. Otherwise we'd have to tack." Dorcas made a zigzagging motion with her hand, and Maggie recalled Captain Og sailing that way on the journey from Kilchoan.

Dorcas took the tiller from her when they left the enclosed bay to come around the headland beneath the castle. Maggie was impressed by her skill on the open water.

Fabian bolted from the boat even before it was beached and went racing up a narrow path on the cliff face. The two women sat on the sand to replace their shoes.

"This is already an adventure," Maggie said as she laced up her half boots. "Lady Fescue and her daughter were not much for outings. I feel as though I've been cooped up in a musty old house for three years."

"Where was that?" Dorcas asked, knocking the sand out of one slipper.

"They lived in a rented manor house in Surrey. It was near where my father worked, at Lady Ashcroft's home, Summit House. Lady Fescue is a dedicated toadeater, so she was delighted to do Lady Ashcroft a favor by employing the daughter of her librarian."

Dorcas cocked her head. "You really *are* Maggie Bonner. No one could have made up a story with so many minute details."

"Your cousin thinks I ought to take up writing novels."

"Let's not talk about Gulliver," Dorcas said with a tiny frown. "Whenever I'm doing something I oughtn't, I always imagine he's right around the corner, about to pounce."

Maggie knew exactly how that felt.

They climbed the low cliff together, and then Dorcas led her to a small door on the north face of the castle that was nearly obscured by thick bushes. Maggie realized she'd walked right past it two days ago.

They ducked through the door, which led to a small chamber with a flagstone floor. "This is the scullery," Dorcas whispered as she took a candle from her pocket and lit it with Maggie's tinderbox. "Beyond it are the kitchens and the laundry. Everything here is self-contained, no outbuildings. There's even a stable and carriage house inside the portcullis gate."

"I gather you've been here before."

"Of course. It was quite a showplace years ago. Parties, masquerades, musicales . . . all before I was of age, alas."

"I understand the old laird had a son. Were you and he friends?"

Dorcas hesitated, then shook her head. "He was older than I was and quite full of himself. No, I'm not sure friends would describe our relationship."

They moved through the kitchen, barren of furnishings save for an enormous table in the center of the room. Dorcas led her up a narrow staircase to the ground floor, where they emerged into a large hall. The chandelier overhead had been wrapped in muslin, and the few pieces of furniture were obscured by holland covers.

"You don't really get the true effect," Dorcas said, still whispering. "This was where the laird's family held their public gatherings. When the chandelier and the wall sconces were lit, you would have sworn you were back in another century. That's a minstrel's gallery up there." She pointed to a stonework balcony. "Though the orchestra normally played on a dais set up beside the staircase."

Maggie followed her guide through room after room, all the while gauging how well the castle was suited to be a hotel. The dining room could easily have accommodated a dozen round tables, and the spacious drawing room would be the perfect place to entertain guests with music or charades. Or even, she thought wistfully, dramatic productions.

When Dorcas suggested the portrait gallery next, Maggie realized that there had been no paintings or works of art in the rooms they had passed through—and very little furniture. It seemed odd that the family had put their other valuables in storage and left the portraits up.

Dorcas led her to a long corridor that faced the enclosed courtyard and so did not have the windows shuttered. Light flowed in through the leaded panes and played over the rich colors of an oriental runner.

They began at the far end of the gallery, giggling over the cavaliers with their spaniel curls and plumed hats and the Restoration ladies with their powdered bosoms and lavish gowns.

"That's the old laird as a boy," Dorcas said as they came to the more recent portraits. "And there he is as an adult with his wife."

The old laird had a craggy face with a stern mouth and raven-dark hair. Maggie had hoped to see some resemblance to Gulliver, but there was none she could detect. Then she turned her gaze upon the female figure in the painting—and smiled. The laird's wife was a slender, delicate-boned brunette with dark-lashed, silvery eyes. Gulliver's eyes to the life.

A small brass plate at the base of the portrait read "Sir Collum MacGuigan, 9th Laird of St. Columba and his wife, Lady Katherine."

Maggie couldn't contain her question any longer. She pulled Dorcas closer to the row of windows. "Remember what you said earlier, that Gulliver feels as though everything is his responsibility? It got me thinking. Is your cousin the laird of St. Columba, by any chance?"

Her companion's eyebrows shot up. "Now, that would be a fitting and proper thing, wouldn't it? But, no, Gulliver is most definitely not the laird."

"But the laird's name was Collum MacGuigan, the same as Gulliver's father." She pointed to the plaque.

Dorcas chuckled. "It's clear you've been in the Hebrides only a short time. Otherwise you'd know that each of these islands boasts a very limited number of family names. Here, we are all MacNeills, MacGuigans or Taybecks. And there must be a dozen Collums."

Maggie must have looked noticeably crestfallen, because Dorcas snatched up her hand and said briskly, "Now, come along . . . I've a treat for you. I'm going to show you where the castle ghost is said to walk."

They pelted side by side down the corridor, like two school-girls off on a lark, and were breathless when they reached the master bedroom. The large chamber was also nearly empty of furniture but richly appointed, with hand-colored silk on the walls and exquisite rococo frescoes and carved figures adorning the domed ceiling.

Maggie stood there, head tipped back and candle held high, admiring the putti and cherubim, when Dorcas began speaking from behind her in a low, eerie voice. "'Tis said a lady walks here by night, crying for her lost love."

Maggie turned to her with a bemused smile.

"A crofter's daughter, she was, from the mainland. The third laird met her while raiding the coast and carried her off to Whitesands to be his bride. They say he wooed her as no man has ever wooed a woman before. But her kinsmen stormed the castle. There was a great battle, and they trapped the laird in this room and killed him. Then they tossed his battered body into the sea."

Maggie gave a shivery grimace.

"Her kinsmen took the lady away then, back to the main-land, where she died bearing the laird's son. But her specter dwells here where her lover was murdered, gazing out to sea, waiting for him to return to her."

"That's very romantic," Maggie whispered. "But sad."

"All ghost stories are sad," Dorcas said. "Happy ghosts don't haunt . . . that's what Fingal always told us."

"Have you ever heard her?"

Dorcas shook her head slowly. "They say only the descendants of the third laird can hear her mournful cries."

Just then a keening howl rose up from outside the castle walls. It came right through the closed shutters, resonating in the shadowy room. Both women shivered.

"Something's amiss with Fabian," Dorcas muttered. "Come, it's time we left anyway. We need to beat Gulliver back to the cottage."

They hurried down the two staircases and through the kitchen. Maggie, now in the lead, pushed the scullery door open for Dorcas, and they were both met by a fierce gust of wind.

Maggie flung her head back, gaping up at the sky, which had gone an ominous, unnatural shade of gray-green.

Fabian stood foursquare on the grass apron above them, facing into the west wind, howling like a soul in torment.

The sound went right through Maggie.

"Something is wrong," she hissed as they started up the incline. Once they were free of the moat, the wind whipped at their skirts and tugged at their hair, while the sea beyond them churned, the waves dancing up like flames in a bonfire.

"What is it, boy?" Maggie whispered, crouching down beside the dog and, after a second's hesitation, wrapping her arms around his neck. He was trembling all over, never taking his eyes from the western horizon.

Maggie looked up. "Something is very wrong—he's shaking like a leaf. Oh, Dorcas, what does he know?"

Dorcas scanned the sky to the west. "I'm not sure. . . ."

"It's MacGuigan!" Maggie cried. "Something's happened to MacGuigan. Dogs know . . . they know these things."

Dorcas made no response. She took Maggie's wrist and hauled her to her feet. "Come on, we've got to get back." There was an odd urgency in her voice.

Maggie's throat tightened. "What is it? You have to tell me."

"A squall," she said tersely. "They sometimes blow out of nowhere. You can see the edge of it there in the distance." She thrust her arm out, the wind licking at the sleeve of her gown.

"It's over Quintay, isn't it? Right where Gulliver and the fleet are."

Dorcas nodded as she headed for the cliff. "But those boats were built for heavy seas and high winds."

"What about the *Kestrel*? It's not as large as the fishing boats."

"Gulliver's been sailing since he was a boy. He'll know enough to outrun it and find safe harbor on the island."

Maggie stopped her and spun her around almost roughly. "Then why do you look so worried?"

Dorcas bit at her lower lip. "Maybe it's that silly ghost story. It still makes me shivery."

"Dorcas," Maggie said sternly.

Her companion took a deep breath. "Squalls can be much worse than storms. They come upon you suddenly, out of nowhere, and the wind keeps shifting. It's almost impossible to sail, all you can do is ride them out."

Fabian was whimpering beside Maggie now, and she lowered her hand to comfort him. It was more than she could do for herself.

"Gull's been out in squalls before this," Dorcas added as they skittered down the cliff path. "And for all we know, he might nearly be home. He could be moored in the bay by the time the squall hits St. Columba."

"You mean it's headed here?" Maggie asked breathlessly as they hurried across the beach.

"The wind is from the west again . . . It should be here in less than an hour."

They didn't bother to remove their shoes this time, just pushed the boat into the rising surf and climbed in, wet to the knees. Dorcas kept her post at the tiller all the way across the bay, and Maggie had a time of it controlling the sail with the wind so strong at their backs.

Even the protected waters of the bay were choppy, mimicking the great swells that rose out in the open sea. There was a glory to it that Maggie might have appreciated—the skiff virtually flying across the water, heeled over and straining at her lines—if Fabian's behavior hadn't upset her so much. She'd never owned a dog, but she'd heard plenty of stories about faithful hounds who knew with an uncanny animal prescience when their owners were in trouble.

It had started to rain by the time they reached the shallows, fat drops splatting on them as they dragged the boat far up on the shingle. Maggie snatched up the spyglass from under the seat before she raced after Dorcas into the cottage. She needed to keep an eye on the harbor, needed to know the instant MacGuigan returned.

Dorcas was already at the fireplace, stoking up the embers, when Maggie came through the door, dragging Fabian with her. He had made it clear that he wanted to remain outside, but she couldn't stand to think of him fretting out there in the wet wind. They'd hold their vigil together.

Dorcas made tea, and then they pulled the settle before the fire and sat sipping from their mugs, watching the peat burn, while Fabian paced behind them, every so often scratching at the door and whining.

The wind soon rose to a screaming fury outside the cottage, while rain lashed the roof. It was dark as night outside now, and dark inside, except for where the fire threw its glow.

"Squalls don't last long," Dorcas said. "There is that."

"Won't your people be worrying over you?"

"Gulliver had to leave my pony at the house. I'm hoping he told someone that I stayed behind here."

Dorcas found an old pack of cards in the desk, and they occupied themselves playing piquet, but Maggie couldn't settle down. Once or twice Fabian came over and laid his chin on her thigh, sighing as he gazed up at her. It amazed her that she had once been frightened of this dog who was as good natured as any beast she'd met.

Once the rain let up, she finally gave in to Fabian's unspoken entreaty and went to the window with the spyglass. The late afternoon light was watery, but the worst of the storm clouds seemed to have departed. She raised the spyglass, focused it on the harbor—and gave a little cry.

Dorcas was at her side the next instant.

"It's the fishing boats," Maggie said. "They've come back."

Dorcas took the glass from her. "Mmm. But I can't quite see if the *Kestrel* is among them."

They both went outside to find a better vantage point.

"No," said Dorcas as she lowered the glass. "He's not back. But that doesn't mean anything, truly. He could have put into a cove on this island and decided to overnight there. The *Kestrel* has a small cabin."

"But he knows we'll be worrying about him."

Dorcas gave her a long look. "He's a man, Maggie. I wager it never occurred to him."

Maggie humphed in annoyance. "Then I won't waste another minute worrying. And look, Fabian's completely calmed down."

The dog was now sniffing along the edge of the water as if he hadn't a care in the world.

"It was likely the squall that put him in such a quake," Dorcas said. "I had a terrier once who hid in the privy whenever a storm blew up. Brassiest dog on the island, but he'd sit there shivering and whining like a pup until the thunder stopped."

Since they'd missed lunch, they decided to have an early supper. The two of them sat companionably at the table while they prepared the fixings for a shepherd's pie.

"Gulliver should see you now," Dorcas said. "You'd make your case with him, sure enough. I bet the real Alice Fescue never set foot in a kitchen in her life."

"Maybe I should bake him a cake," Maggie suggested.

"Or a pudding."

"Ah," said Maggie with a broad chuckle, "because . . . the proof is always . . . in the pudding."

For a few seconds she was lost in laughter. But when Dorcas commented lightly, "Besides, cooking is still the best way to a man's heart," Maggie's face went instantly blank.

"I think some other woman will have to follow that course."

"Oh, no," said Dorcas with an impish frown. "It won't fade. I caught that look in your eyes when he rode off, that . . . beguiled yearning. I saw how agitated you got when you thought he was in danger. You *have* formed a *tendre* for him, haven't you?" She added softly, "As though things weren't tangled enough."

Maggie nearly groaned. *Was it that obvious?*

"You are quite mistaken," she managed to get out—and in a nice frosty tone. "Your cousin and I find each other mutually and hopelessly irritating."

Dorcas gave her a sly smile. "You've never been in love, have you?"

Maggie shook her head. She'd nearly answered, "Not until now."

"I didn't think so," Dorcas continued with a certain smugness. "Otherwise, you'd know that irritation, especially the mutual sort, is one of the earliest symptoms of attraction."

"And I suppose you have been in love?" Maggie asked a bit snappishly, not at all pleased with how the conversation was evolving.

"Since I was fifteen." Before Maggie could ask her to elaborate, she said quickly, "I didn't mean to bring it up. It's not something I ever dwell on."

They worked without speaking for a time, then Maggie said

tentatively, "It wouldn't make any sense, would it? I mean, my forming an attachment to your cousin. Our lives are literally worlds apart, not to mention the fact that he's holding me captive."

Dorcas crossed her arms and leaned them on the table. "When does love ever make any sense?" she asked sagely. "And you wouldn't be the first woman to have a care for her captor. Just think of our castle ghost. No, I wouldn't blame you. . . . He's a bonny man and a good man in spite of this nonsensical abduction business. But I should warn you, he is not likely to come courting. The young women here keep casting out lures, but Gulliver remains impervious."

Maggie felt like a complete paperwit. What did it matter that he'd kissed her repeatedly? Or that he'd looked at her yesterday as though she was his last hope of paradise? Surely Dorcas knew the state of his mind—and heart—better than she ever could on only four days' acquaintance.

"No, even if he does care for you," Dorcas went on, "there's no guarantee he will pursue you. Believe me, I've had some experience with a man who cares but will not come forward." She hesitated, then said, "There's something else you ought to know. Gulliver and Guy, since they were boys, have made a great game of stealing each other's possessions. If my cousin still believes you are plighted to the earl, I'm not sure that hasn't increased your currency in his eyes."

Maggie felt her own last hope fade.

Dorcas must have seen the pain in her face. She reached over and rubbed her shoulder. "I hope I'm wrong. Maybe Gull's finally outgrown that silly game."

"It doesn't matter," Maggie said, as she busied herself slicing the four remaining sausages. "It was only a foolish fancy. After what you've told me, I'll consider myself forewarned."

The rain began again while they ate their supper, not in such torrents as when the squall had hit, though sharp gusts of wind frequently rattled the shutters. The conversation had strayed onto the neutral topic of books and Maggie tried to regain her animation. It reassured her to know that Dorcas had herself suffered heartache and yet somehow moved on with her life and even managed to present a cheerful exterior to the world.

"I wish there was some way to get word to your people," Maggie remarked during a lull in the conversation. "I can't help thinking they'll be frantic with worry. I promise not to run off if you want to sail back to the village."

Dorcas shook her head. "Fingal knows Gulliver took the *Kestrel* out, and when he sees the light in the cottage window, he'll assume I'm here."

"Who is this Fingal? You and your cousin often mention him."

"Fingal works for my family . . . ah, but he's much more than a servant. I'd call him the heart of St. Columba—our harbormaster, head of the fishermen's guild and deacon of our little kirk. He raised us all, to some extent. Me, Gulliver . . . even Guy."

"And the laird's son, did he bother with him?"

"We were all the same to Fingal. Nuisances who needed to be educated and made into proper folk. Not that he was so very proper. In his youth he'd been a smuggler and a cattle thief, though not on this island. But woe to any child who did not mind his manners with Fingal MacNeill. It's odd, because he didn't do a very good job of it with his own son, Og."

"Oh, Og," Maggie said darkly. "Mr. Treachery himself."

"May I tell you something? I'm glad he put you ashore on St. Columba. I'm still not sure he intended Gull to take you captive, but whatever his reasons were for marooning you, I'm delighted you're here. I think we are well on the way to becoming friends."

Maggie felt her face grow warm. "Thank you. I've never had a real friend before now, and I can see that I've been missing a great deal."

Dorcas seemed surprised by this revelation, so Maggie explained about growing up on the road. "Of course, the actors were my friends, as much as any adult can be to a child. And my parents were very entertaining to be around. Still, I was rarely with children my own age."

"Wasn't Miss Fescue your friend?"

"No, I was her French tutor at first. And then her mother hired me to be a sort of governess-companion. Alice and I got along fairly well, but she never confided in me or expressed any interest in my life. Although I do recall telling her about the

Players to distract her when she had the toothache. I made her swear never to tell her mother. Though I suppose it doesn't matter any longer. Lady Fescue and I will part company once we return to London."

"And you'll have to find another situation?"

Maggie nodded. "I know this will sound odd, but being here has been akin to having a holiday. Maybe it won't be so bad now, finding another employer. I expect I'll be quite refreshed and rejuvenated after my visit to St. Columba."

There, Maggie thought proudly, *that was putting a good face on things.*

Dorcas took her hand. "Why don't you stay here?"

Maggie drew back.

"No, I'm serious. You can be *my* companion. I can't afford to pay you, unfortunately, but you'd eat what we eat, and you'd have a nice room in my house. Bridie would fuss over you, and Fingal could tell you all the old, familiar stories we've long ago grown tired of."

There were tears in Maggie's eyes now. No one had ever extended such kindness to her.

"I can't," she said sadly. "The money I earn goes to my father, who is ill and needs a caretaker."

"Bring him here," Dorcas said, undaunted. "The sea air and fresh spring water will do him good. Just look at Fingal. Ninety, if he's a day. And one of our captains, Shandy Taybeck, claims to be older still."

Maggie took a moment to wonder if it was St. Columba's spring that gave the inhabitants such a long span of years. She'd give ten years of her own life to see her father recover his mobility. Perhaps if she found a generous employer, she could put aside a small sum and bring her father here for his own holiday.

"That is a truly gracious offer," she said. "But my life is elsewhere. Who knows, maybe I can return in a few years."

"None of us might be here then," Dorcas said flatly. "If Gulliver can't turn things around, everyone will have to leave." Then her eyes clouded. "I just thought of something. Gulliver's the reason you won't stay, isn't he? Here I am blundering about, insisting you come here to live . . . but it wouldn't do, would it?"

Maggie shook her head. She could just imagine herself tagging along after MacGuigan like a lovesick mooncalf. It would be beyond humiliating.

"Especially living in your house, Dorcas, where I would be bound to see him."

"Well, isn't that just like a man," Dorcas muttered, "to complicate a perfectly promising friendship."

Chapter Eight

*T*he rising wind whipped at the skirts of Gulliver's greatcoat as he went along the cobbled lane toward the castle. Like Whitesands, Luray Castle had been erected on a hill so that it loomed, bold and majestic, over the more humble dwellings. But unlike St. Columba, this island boasted a proper town with a bustling market square and an impressive Gothic church, its bell tower soaring like a needled tor above the slate-roofed shops.

The people here were prosperous, well fed and of an entrepreneurial disposition. The resident earl might have been an Englishman, but he had fostered wide-ranging commerce and modern methods of agriculture on Quintay. Acres of nursery stock spread out behind the castle, this being a pet project of his lordship, who was intent on restoring the dense woodlands that had thrived on the island centuries earlier. Among his holdings there also numbered cattle and sheep farms, while a large portion of the island's protected interior was given over to the cultivation of timothy, wheat and maize.

Gulliver felt like a pauper going to supplicate a prince as he passed through the castle gate and headed up the front drive. It didn't help to remind himself that his own bloodlines were fully as ancient as the English earl's. After all, he mused, if the prosing ministers were to be believed, every soul on the planet could claim lineage directly from Adam and Eve. No, bloodlines were not proof of worth these days. It was now the jingle of coins in his pocket and the quality of his cloak and boots that gave a man stature.

That thought amused Gulliver almost as much as it discouraged him. He had been reared by a father who'd taught him that a man's true value lay in two things—his treatment of others and his sense of fair play. So far, though, generosity and honor had not been offering Gulliver much return on his investment. Maybe that was why he'd finally succumbed to temptation and stolen back the necklace. And why he'd played along with Og's game of abduction. And look where that little stunt had gotten him—embroiled with a lively termagant whom he couldn't court and dared not seduce and who, furthermore, likely thought he was a filthy beast.

Well, he *had* been fairly beastly toward her. Always pushing her about, making her work to exhaustion, forcing his kisses on her. While his rough-hewn Highland ancestors might have winked approvingly at such treatment of a lady, his own father, a courtly gentleman to his boot tips, would have been appalled. He didn't even try to imagine how his mother would have reacted.

He knew now, without a doubt, that he'd imprisoned the wrong woman. He knew, further, why he'd remained deaf to all her protests and stayed blind to the signs that she was no pampered society miss. It did no good telling himself that his refusal to see the truth had not arisen out of stupidity but out of fledgling desire, the result of the startling attraction he'd felt for her aboard the *Charles Stuart*. He wanted her to be Alice Fescue, if only because that gave him a reason to keep her close by.

Lust was definitely the stupidest reason on earth for a man to do anything, he reflected sourly. It was time he started engaging the clever brain that nature had blessed him with and stopped following his—

"You there! Halt at once!"

Gulliver snapped out of his musings. A tall footman in wine-colored livery was rapidly approaching across the great hall.

Gulliver realized with a start that he'd walked right through the castle's front door—out of longstanding habit.

"How dare you enter without leave?" the man snarled softly. He was not one of the servants from the old days, more's the pity, and his eyes flicked over Gulliver and dismissed him in practically the same instant.

Gulliver wished his coat wasn't so shabby and that his boots weren't so scuffed and worn. He hadn't shaved that morning, and there was already a dark stubble sprouting on his cheeks. The footman had probably taken him for a sneaking tinker.

"I'm here to see the earl," he said, putting his chin up and brazening it out.

"And what business could you possibly have with his lordship?" the footman sneered.

Gulliver stepped closer to the man, met his glare dead on and said evenly, "I am not in the habit of confiding my private matters to . . . *hirelings*."

The footman was unfazed. "That hardly signifies. His lordship is not at home." He stalked to the oak door and held it open meaningfully. "Now, good day."

Gulliver ignored him, moving a bit farther into the hall. It was much grander now than he remembered it, the result, no doubt, of that bottomless Faulkner purse.

"I say!" the footman cried. "You are not to wander at will in his lordship's home. If you do not leave at once, I shall summon the head watchman and his dogs."

"You do that," Gulliver muttered, unconcerned. He assumed old Wat Darwin was still looking after the grounds. It wouldn't hurt to see a friendly face right about now.

From the open doorway, the footman give three sharp blasts on a whistle, and Gulliver smiled to himself. To possess such power must be very gratifying.

It was not Wat, however, who appeared with a brace of mastiffs tugging at their leashes, but a large, chesty, red-haired young fellow with an ugly smile. Gulliver turned away from the open drawer of a delicate French table—he'd been searching for a scrap of notepaper—and put his hands behind him. He was itching for a fight now but had no intention of brawling in the earl's front hall.

"Where's Wat Darwin?" he inquired of the footman, who had taken up a bold position—behind the watchman.

"Mr. Matchem had him dismissed for stealing."

"Oh, I see," Gulliver purred. As though Wat would have pilfered so much as a sou. "So it's Neddie Matchem who's running things here at Luray. That explains a great deal."

"Mr. Matchem is his lordship's right hand," the footman said staunchly. So staunchly that Gulliver knew his old enemy had been responsible for hiring this self-inflated insect.

"Do ye want me to set the dogs on 'im?" the watchman inquired of the footman.

"Not inside his lordship's hall," the footman hissed. "It's impossible to get blood out of marble tiles. Just . . . take him out of here."

The burly man came toward Gulliver, his small, bright eyes watching eagerly for any sign of resistance. Gulliver leaned back on his heel and shoved one hand negligently into his coat pocket.

"You don't know who I am, do you?" he said softly. "Ah, but I recall you. Your father was head stableman in the old days, Donald Rennie. He had two red-haired sons . . . you must be Brian, the elder. And if I'm not mistaken, those two ferocious beasts you are barely restraining are the get of Little Peach, the old earl's favorite mastiff. Gad, what a great lump of amiability she was."

With that, he knelt down, drawing from his pocket the dried bits of chicken liver he always carried for Fabian. He reached out and offered them to both dogs. They came forward, sniffing, then gobbling the treats, licking his fingers and tugging forward to lick his face. He ran a hand over each massive, rounded skull and looked up smugly at their handler. "It appears your dogs approve of me, which is more than I can say for the people around here."

"Master Gulliver?" the watchman said haltingly as recognition dawned. "Ye always did have a way with the beasts. Lord, but it's been an age since I set eyes on ye."

Gulliver rose. "Nine years, Brian, to be exact. So they've made you chief bully boy around here. Must be hard work keeping up your status, considering all the other bullies that have overrun the castle."

Brian Rennie grinned, to his credit taking Gulliver's meaning at once. "I am the outside bully. His lordship has a great fear of intruders."

"Ah. And how does your family go on, Brian?"

"Here, now," the footman protested, stepping between them. "This will not do." He took Rennie by one shoulder. "You are to throw this scoundrel out, not pass the time of day with him."

"Oh, stow it," Rennie shot back, shaking him off the way a horse flicks away a deerfly. "If you didn't have more hair than brains, you'd know that this gentleman is Gulliver MacGuigan, master of St. Columba, not some housebreaking gypsy."

The footman snarled, "I don't care if he's the reincarnation of St. John the Baptist. He has no business loitering here with the earl away from home."

"He lordship's gone off to dine with the squire," Rennie confided to Gulliver. "Had the carriage sent around less than an hour ago. Ye might do better to come back after dark."

"I'd like to leave a note," he said. "If yon footman would be so kind as to bring me some paper."

"I will do no such thing!"

Rennie turned to the man and with a toothy grin made as if to set his dogs on the fellow. The footman danced back from the two gaping maws, his own mouth stretched in a rictus of fear.

"Ye heard Mr. MacGuigan, Woodbine. Paper and pen, if ye please."

The footman collected himself, tugging at the hem of his velvet jacket, and then sailed blithely off toward one of the rooms that opened onto the hall.

"Simpering toadeater," Rennie muttered. "He's Matchem's eyes and ears in this place, Master Gulliver. Not someone ye want to cross."

"You just did," Gulliver pointed out.

Brian Rennie shook his head. "My position here is secure. I know a few things about Neddie Matchem he doesn't want the earl to get wind of."

"Anything you'd like to share?" Gulliver inquired silkily.

Brian let out a low rumble of laughter. "You always were a cagey sort, Master Gulliver. Come down into the town and have a pint wi' me once ye've written your note to the earl. We can catch up on old times, and I can tell ye how things are faring here at the castle."

Gulliver smiled broadly. "Yes, I think I'll do just that."

Chapter Nine

*D*orcas retired early, but Maggie was too restless to sleep, still fretful over Gulliver's prolonged absence. When she let the dog out during a lull in the rain storm, he ran off. She went outside and called and called, but he had disappeared.

"Gulliver's back in the village," she told herself. "That's where Fabian's gone, to find his master."

She settled down in the armchair, listening to the sound of rain on the slate roof tiles and imagining herself a permanent resident of this cottage. A fresh coat of paint, a few braided rugs, some charming botanical prints on the walls and crisp white curtains at the windows would improve the place all out of recognition.

She could find a room for her father in the village, perhaps hire someone pleasant-natured—the basket seller came to mind—to look after him. The island was flourishing again in this scenario; Gulliver had found work with his sleek ship, carrying supplies from the mainland to all the Western Isles. Dorcas would be a regular visitor, and Maggie and Gulliver would return the favor, dining in her fine home, perhaps with a child or two in tow.

So rich was this image, so replete with everything she'd never admitted to herself that she craved—home, husband, a family of her own, security, a sense of belonging—that she nearly wept when she saw that it could never be. It was just a pretty dream.

As usual, everything came down to money. Without that commodity, she and Gulliver could have no life. Maggie was not so imprudent as to believe that anyone could live on love.

Right now he was more bound to the islanders than to her, and rightly so. She was sure he could go to the mainland and find suitable work as a steward or a bailiff that would support them both. But his heart's blood ran all through St. Columba as surely as the water from the saint's spring. It was not a solution.

Of course, she reminded herself for what must be the hundredth time, MacGuigan had never given her reason to hope for anything between them, especially marriage. Dorcas's comments had quickly set her to rights about that. But this was a daydream, after all, and great leaps of logic were allowed.

It would help her cause, she decided, if she could prove to him how much this island had come to mean to her, to show him they had a common concern. She had to do something more than giving away a brooch or helping to seed a field—it must be something enduring.

That's when the plan really began to come together in her head. What was more enduring on this island than poverty? Only one thing—the curative powers of St. Columba's spring. She was not surprised the locals took it for granted; that was always the way, people not seeing or appreciating what was right under their noses. But she'd seen . . . and been stunned. Her pounding headache gone in an instant. Gulliver's blistered hand healed overnight. Fingal MacNeill spry at ninety. Captain Og, blast his leathery hide, still hale and sharp-witted—and strong enough to carry her—at nearly seventy.

She also grappled with the outstanding flaw in her theory— Gulliver and Dorcas had both lost parents whom she assumed were relatively young, which did not bode well for the spring's powers. Then again, she reasoned, the gentry were more likely to drink wine than water. The villagers, on the other hand, would drink ale—she'd have to ask Gulliver if they brewed their own here using water from the spring.

The more she thought about it, the more convinced she became that she'd finally stumbled across the one thing that could bring prosperity back to the island. Lady Ashcroft, her father's former employer, had dozens of aged friends who were always journeying to Bath—for all the good that odiferous water did them.

St. Columba could offer visitors clear, refreshing spring water, as crisp on the palate as a fine white wine. She'd entreat

Lady Ashcroft to come, and once she'd seen the benefits of the spring, it wouldn't be long before all in her acquaintance would come flocking. The castle would need to be leased from the laird, of course, and they'd need to make it presentable for guests. But Maggie was certain he wouldn't stand in their way. He clearly had no use for it himself, and, furthermore, if her scheme worked, he'd end up lining his empty pockets with gold. She only hoped Gulliver knew where to reach him.

She was still musing over her glorious plans for St. Columba when she dozed off, her head canted sideways on the back of the chair. The candles they'd lit for supper guttered eventually; the hearth fire, left unfed, cooled down to ember and ash. The room lay in darkness, unrelieved by even a trace of moonlight, since the rain continued unabated outside.

A fragment of peat exploding in the hearth roused Maggie, the sharp pop intruding on her disordered dreams. She opened her eyes but sat without moving, wondering if Dorcas had come into the room and restored the waning fire. That made no sense; if Dorcas had been in here she'd have ordered Maggie to come to bed.

She was just stretching her chilled feet toward the fire, when the tiny hairs on the back of her neck stood straight up.

A man was standing in the shadowy corner beside the fireplace.

Maggie's whole body tensed. It was not MacGuigan; the man was neither toweringly tall nor broad in the shoulders. She slowly raised her eyes to his face—and nearly cried out. He was staring directly at her.

A low voice came out of the darkness. "What have you done with her?"

Maggie leapt up with a wavering cry, heading straight for the door. But what about Dorcas, her brain screamed, Dorcas asleep—and unaware—in the bedroom?

She turned back abruptly and collided with the intruder. With a stifled cry she tried to push away from him, her fingers splayed on his rain-wet coat. He got one arm around her waist, but she managed to thrust back from him, banging up against the desk. The ironstone crock practically fell into her hands.

She turned quickly, raised it up high, and smashed it down over the stranger's head.

He stood there goggling at her for a long moment, uttered something that sounded suspiciously like "Dorcas" and then collapsed onto the floor.

Maggie reeled back against the desk, gasping for breath.

"What on earth's going on out here?" Dorcas stood in the bedroom doorway, a lit candle in one hand.

"An intruder," Maggie panted. "I . . . I hit him on the head with a crock."

Dorcas took a few steps toward the fallen man, but Maggie quickly pushed away from the desk and ran to head her off. "Stay back! Please! I don't know if he's knocked out or only dazed."

But Dorcas skirted her, moving forward so swiftly she seemed to float over the ground. She gave a little cry as she fell to her knees beside the prostrate form. Maggie watched in disbelief as Dorcas put her ear to the man's chest and murmured, "Thank God," just before she began to trace her fingers gently through his hair.

Maggie came closer. "Do you know him?"

Dorcas looked up, her eyes glassy. "Your intruder, the man you coshed on the head, is none other than William Broderick Faulkner, Baron Tewksberry, Viscount Guisewaithe—"

"No!" Maggie keened. She knew where this was going.

"—the most honorable Earl of Barkin."

Maggie sank to her knees. "I didn't kill him, did I?"

"No, but there's a rather deep cut above his right ear."

Maggie couldn't believe it. She'd never in her life struck another person. Now in a mere four days she'd knifed a possible laird and coshed a genuine peer on the head. Good thing the Regent was off in London and safely out of range.

"I am so sorry," she cried.

Dorcas sighed. "He was daft to come here in the middle of the night. You only hit him. Gulliver would have been more likely to put a bullet through him."

"I . . . I think he mistook me for you. First he said, 'What have you done with her?' and then just before he passed out he said, 'Dorcas.'"

"He normally wears spectacles, but I suppose he took them

off in the rain." She brushed a lock of hair back from his brow with great tenderness. "Ach, he's bleeding here, as well." She reached down and tore the ruffle off Maggie's best nightgown, which she'd borrowed earlier, and wadded it into a pad to press against his wounds.

"What is he doing here?" Maggie whispered sharply. "Your cousin never sent a ransom note. So how could the earl have learned that I—I mean Miss Fescue—was being held on St. Columba?"

Dorcas blew out a breath. "I have no idea. Maybe Gull did send the note. The main thing is, he's here now, and we have to deal with him."

"Shouldn't we call in a doctor? There must be one on the island."

Dorcas's mouth twitched. "You're looking at her. Doctor, schoolteacher and postmistress. Though I think I can handle this. First thing, we need to get him into the bedroom. But we can't muck about, Maggie. If he's got a concussion, he'll need delicate handling."

Maggie knew this to be true. One time the Players' pert Columbine, Belle Ferrars, had been struck on the crown by a piece of falling scenery. The foolish girl had laughed it off— and ended up bedridden for nearly two weeks.

Maggie rose and snatched Og's oilskin from the peg by the door. "Look, we can spread this on the floor and ease him onto it. Make a sort of sling."

Together they managed to drag the earl into the bedroom but were unable to lift him onto the high mattress, not without jostling him. Dorcas shook out the featherbed and laid it before the hearth. Once they got the earl settled on the pallet, Dorcas went off in search of her cousin's medical kit.

Maggie knelt beside the earl, patting his hand reassuringly, while she watched anxiously for any signs of returning consciousness. She was surprised at how young he appeared, quite close to her own age, she imagined. His complexion was pale, the skin nearly translucent, like the faces of saints she'd seen in a cathedral painting. And though his features were not as boldly drawn as MacGuigan's, there was a measure of beauty to them. High, prominent cheekbones rose above a chisel-cut jaw, while his generous nose was finely etched and properly noble. He might have been a scholar or a cleric, she thought, with that intelligent brow and narrow, serious mouth.

Maggie drew back when Dorcas returned and settled beside him, watching as she snipped bits of hair away from the two wounds.

"You don't happen to have a sewing kit?" Dorcas asked without looking up.

"I always carry one," Maggie said, "but surely you're not going to—"

"Stitch him up?" Dorcas grinned. "Won't be the first time. When he was twelve he came running to me with a gash in his calf. He'd been jumping off the portcullis bridge. Strictly forbidden, but I'm sure Gulliver teased him into it."

Maggie quickly found the kit in her bag. "I'm not sure I can stand to see this. I feel guilty enough as it is."

"Then go make tea. Isn't that what you English do during a crisis, drink tea?"

"If there's no brandy to be had."

"I wish we did have some brandy. These cuts need to be cleaned out. But Gulliver does not keep strong spirits about."

"We've got something even better than brandy," Maggie said. She went to the parlor and fetched the bucket of spring water and a cloth napkin. She wet the napkin and handed it to Dorcas. "It probably wouldn't hurt any if you could get him to drink a bit of it."

Dorcas looked up. "So Gulliver's been telling you about our spring."

"I've seen with my own eyes. Your cousin burned his fingers in the fire and I poured some water over them. The next day the blisters had completely disappeared."

Dorcas shrugged. "We MacGuigans are speedy healers."

Maggie again wondered, as she went to put the kettle on, how these islanders could remain so casual about something so miraculous.

Dorcas was just finishing her handiwork, fixing a length of gauze around the earl's head, when this eyelids fluttered and then opened. He stared up at her with apparent incomprehension until she mustered a strained smile and said, "Hello, Guy."

"Dorcas?" he rasped. *"A-a-a-h—"* He raised one hand toward his brow, but she quickly caught it and set it again at his side. "What the devil happened to me?"

"Someone smashed you over the head with a crock," she replied matter-of-factly. She knew she shouldn't have been so glib, but Maggie Bonner had only done what she'd longed to do for nine years. Maybe the other woman had finally knocked some sense into him.

"Who hit me?" he said under his breath. "That hulk of a MacGuigan?"

"No. It was . . . a young lady he has staying here." She wasn't sure how much she should reveal to him. Wiser to wait until she got an idea of how much *he* knew.

"You're not going to tell me it was Miss Fescue who hit me. The girl's as timid as a rabbit."

So he *did* know about the abduction. She wouldn't have to dance around the subject. Then his words sank in, and she began to tremble—in anger and in resentment. Was that truly what he'd wanted all along, someone timid and . . . and *rabbity*?

She kept her voice firmly under control as she replied, "I'm afraid I've never had the pleasure of meeting your Miss Fescue."

His mouth tightened. "Then Gulliver must have her hidden away somewhere else. At least he's kept you out of this infernal business."

"There is no 'infernal business,' Guy. Og MacNeill stranded a young woman on the beach in Withy Cove. Gulliver's been looking after her."

"And this woman denies being my intended bride?"

"Vehemently. I believe you saw her earlier, sitting in the chair by the fire."

He shook his head, then groaned softly. "It . . . it was you I saw." His voice softened. "I was watching you sleep."

"Without your spectacles," she pointed out, trying to stay brisk and businesslike. It was difficult; his wide-set blue eyes seemed to peer right inside her. "She and I look very much alike from a distance. But she had no idea who you were, and I believe you frightened her."

He boosted himself up onto one elbow and then snarled when she tried to force him to lie down again. "Stop fussing, Dorcas. A little bump on the head isn't going to keep me from finding Miss Fescue—or from having things out with Gulliver."

Dorcas kept silent as he attempted to stand, at last pulling himself completely upright by gripping the edge of the mantel. It was one of the things she loved most about him—he never stopped fighting back. Sickly and frail as a child and then finally struck down as a young man, he had refused to give in to his infirmities. But his face had gone quite gray now as he leaned heavily upon the mantelshelf. She rose and moved closer to him, in case he fell.

"Where is your wretched cousin?" he asked between clenched teeth.

"I honestly have no idea. He sailed off yesterday morning. There was . . . a problem with the fishing fleet. I imagine he got caught in that squall earlier and took shelter in a cove."

"He was in Luray yesterday. I assumed he'd be back here by now."

Dorcas cocked her head. "What do you mean he was in Luray? You mean in the town?"

"No, in my home. The scoundrel had the gall to deliver his ransom note in person. Unfortunately I was away at the time."

Dorcas was mentally scrambling to keep up. Gulliver had said nothing about going ashore on Quintay, let alone visiting the castle.

"Do you have this note?"

He fumbled awkwardly at the pocket of his waistcoat, and Dorcas finally reached over and drew out the folded paper.

As she scanned it, her eyes widened.

I need urgently to speak with you. Time is running out and things are growing desperate. You alone can remedy the situation. If you do not heed this, if you continue to ignore me, I cannot answer for the repercussions to those you care about.

He took it back from her and drawled, "You're not saying anything, Dorcas."

"It's not a ransom note," she answered in a dazed voice. She was reeling over how utterly Gulliver had abased himself to write those words. Things must be even worse than she thought.

"It's hardly an invitation to tea," he said in an odiously smug voice.

"And where, pray," she returned just as archly, "does he mention holding your fiancée?"

"He didn't need to. Og already brought me news of the abduction." He added in an undertone, "Four days ago, that was."

Dorcas nodded thoughtfully. "Ah. And I see how quickly you rushed to rescue your lady." She was gratified when he winced. "What kept you, Guy? Was there a delivery of crumbling statues you needed to examine? A crate of broken pottery, perhaps, that you simply had to sort through?"

His cheeks narrowed. "We both know how it is with Og and the truth. They are typically miles apart. So, naturally, I did not believe a word of his story. At least not until I received that note."

"Gulliver was asking you for help," she said flatly. "Not ransom money."

"What sort of help?"

"For the islanders. Things have been very grim here over the past three years."

He sighed deeply, almost regretfully. "I'm not surprised. Ned Matchem says Gulliver's drained the place of all its resources, most likely to repay gaming debts left over from his days in London."

Her eyes flashed. "And you believed that oily snake?"

"Why shouldn't I? He's served me well for years as my steward."

"And I suppose you've conveniently forgotten how much he hates Gulliver?"

"Hates?" he scoffed. "That's a bit extreme. And over what—losing a bout of fisticuffs to him when they were lads? What were they scrapping over anyway? A fishing rod? A bag of peppermints?"

Me! Dorcas wanted to shout. *They were scrapping over me. And they weren't lads. . . .*

Ned Matchem had been fully sixteen and she fourteen when he'd cornered her in a barn behind Luray Castle and tried to force himself on her. Thank God Gulliver had heard her whimpering cries and come for her, dragging Neddie out of the barn by his hair. Gull had nearly battered him to a pulp, he'd been that frenzied. Guy had only heard about the fight secondhand, and never the truth of what caused it. Dorcas had sworn her cousin to secrecy, knowing that Neddie wouldn't dare breathe a word of it. Not if he didn't want another thrashing.

"Trust me, Guy, there is no love lost there on either side."

"Be that as it may, there's no way I am giving Gulliver MacGuigan tuppence."

"But these islanders—"

"Hang these islanders!" he cried, wheeling away from the mantel. "I wish them at the devil. For years now you have placed them before your own welfare. If you asked me for money, I would open my coffers to you. But only if you promised to go away from here, to leave this sorry place."

"Where would I go?" she asked forlornly. "The only place away from here I could bear to live is closed off to me now."

He took her meaning at once. "Ah, Dorcas," he said, reaching out a hand to her. "It wasn't meant to be like this. But you had refused me—"

"I rejected your terms," she interrupted in a quaking voice. "I don't recall you giving me the chance to refuse you anything."

"Have it your way, then. Still, you can't deny you turned your back on me. So I determined to get on with my life without you."

"It appears you've found someone to compensate you for that loss."

"No . . . you don't understand."

"Then edify me," she said curtly, hoping she wasn't opening herself to more pain.

He turned from her, lowering his gaze to the fire. "It happened while I was in London last month. I went there to see yet another physician." He gave a dry laugh. "This one was worse than all the others. . . . The wretch took away what little hope I had. Mere months left to live was his diagnosis."

Dorcas took a step back and sat on the bed like one in a stupor. "No, Guy."

"Yes," he said with a measure of acceptance that cut her to the quick. "And so there I was, wandering through St. James's

Park in a daze, trying to face the inevitable, when I came upon a young lady and her mother feeding the swans. The girl was pretty and charming—"

"I don't think I want to hear this."

He spun to her. "I told you, you need to understand how it was. I felt only a mild interest in her at first. But then we started discussing the swans—it turns out she is quite fond of birds." He grinned wanly. "She said I reminded her of a chimney stork. So I told her about Quintay, about all the seabirds and songbirds and the great migrating flocks that pass over in the spring on their way to the arctic. She was quite enthralled. And that's when it occurred to me that here was someone who might brighten my life a little, someone I could stand to be around."

Dorcas blinked several times. "Someone you could *stand* to be around?"

His blue eyes darkened to indigo. "You can't have any notion of how frightening it is to face your last months alone."

She shook her head as if to clear it. Then spoke directly from her heart. "And you would prefer the company of a pretty stranger to a woman who has loved you for most of her life?"

His eyes burned into hers. "Those feelings didn't sway you two years ago."

Dorcas stood up. She'd rubbed her face in things quite long enough. "I think you'd better leave now, my lord, or we are bound to come to blows. I trust you have a boat of some sort."

"Og brought me over. But I'm not going anywhere until I find Miss Fescue."

"She's not here!" Dorcas nearly shouted. "She's never been here. The woman Og set ashore is her companion, Miss Bonner."

"Well, what the devil was she doing sailing from Kilchoan without her mistress? *And* carrying the Barkin emeralds, if Og's to be believed."

"Oh, she had the emeralds, right enough. And now Gulliver's got them."

"So she's in league with your cousin."

Dorcas was glad there were no stoneware crocks in the bedroom—only the Sevres vase that had belonged to Gulliver's mother—or she'd have been tempted to cosh him herself.

"Why I am even talking to you?" she groaned. "How could

I have forgotten that once you get something into your thick head, you hold onto it like a rat terrier?"

He took a step closer, his mouth now white at the edge. "And I don't know why I'm bothering with you. I've warned you enough times in the past about what Gulliver has become. And that was before he'd turned thief and kidnapper."

"You told me nothing," she shot back. "Except to make veiled insinuations that Gulliver's behavior had 'gone beyond the mark.' As though I would give him up forever based on such vagaries."

He stalked right up to her. "So you want plain speaking, do you? Very well. I've told myself to keep out of things, but he's brought the fight to me now, and in no uncertain terms. Fact is, I have it on the authority of several reliable men—not Og, by the way—that Gulliver's been wrecking ships off Craigleigh Point."

Dorcas gave a shout of disbelief. "That's preposterous!"

"Not as preposterous as the odds of four ships foundering there in three years."

"But wrecking? That knock on the head's obviously given you fits. It's true a number of ships ran aground since Gulliver returned here, but I promise you they weren't lured onto land. You've sailed off Craigleigh Point. . . . You know how treacherous those currents can be."

"Two of the ships were bringing supplies to Quintay. Both captains spoke to Ned Matchem afterward and swore they'd seen a beacon light on the cliffs, drawing them in to land. As for their cargo, well, the islanders swarmed onto the beach and made off with everything they could carry."

She put her chin up. "That's always been the custom here, when there's a wreck."

"How convenient."

"Besides, no one was injured. Gulliver went into the water any number of times to pull sailors from the surf. It's my understanding that wreckers kill anyone who manages to come ashore." She shuddered at the brutal image.

"Your cousin is lucky no one did die, else he'd be rotting in irons, or worse. Even if you don't believe me about the wrecking, you must see that he's crossed well beyond the mark now . . . and I fear you will be implicated with him."

"What do you mean, implicated? The necklace is his by right. And he didn't abduct Miss Bonner—Og stranded her here and Gulliver's been watching over her."

The earl gave a hiss of disbelief. "See, he's got you lying for him now."

Red-hot anger flared up in Dorcas, stoked by the fact that what he'd said was partially true.

"What right do you have to come here and make accusations about *our* behavior? Your family nearly beggared this island nine years ago and you don't see me pointing my finger at you. Gulliver's crimes are likely all in your head, while the crimes of the Faulkners against St. Columba—the withholding of fishing rights off Quintay, the calling in of mortgages, the embargoes on trade—are still an open, festering wound to these people."

He squared his shoulders. "You hold me responsible for the deeds of my father?"

"No, but you have done nothing to rectify even one of them." Her voice lowered. "And there I was all those years, sneaking off to meet you in secret, hoping that when you took the title things would change for the better." She prodded him sharply in the chest. "Do you know how much of a traitor I feel? Still feel? Consorting with the enemy is what they call it. That is my only crime, my lord, wasting my time with an ineffectual, impotent coward."

Guy's eyes blazed. There was an instant she feared for her safety—when his hand snaked out toward her. But instead he leaned around her to where the oilskin lay in a jumble on the bed, a silver flask jutting from one pocket. He snatched it up, yanked off the top and sniffed at the contents. "Whisky, thank God," he murmured reverently before he took a long, deep swallow.

"I really don't think—"

"What?" he snarled, looking at her over the raised flask. "Not good for my health? I'll tell you what's not good for my health: standing by and watching you throw your life away on a parcel of ungrateful islanders and a worthless cousin who is surely bound for the gibbet."

He offered her a mocking toast, then finished off the whisky, tossing the empty container back onto the bed.

"I want you to leave," she said in a low, shaking voice. "This instant. You can wander around the island in the dark for all I care, looking for your pretty, precious Miss Fescue. But I won't have you defaming Gulliver in his own house. Which, you might have noticed, does not bear any resemblance to the home of a man grown fat off wrecking ships and the pillaging of his own people."

She stood there, hands fisted, fury snapping in her eyes. She could hardly bear to look at him. On the surface he appeared much as she remembered him, but his character had altered beyond recognition. Where he had once been good-hearted and trusting, he was now sullen and suspicious. In spite of possessing great wealth and an illustrious title, he was a petty, vindictive man. And he was dying.

No, she wouldn't, couldn't, think about that or all her resolve to put him from her would wither. She'd convince herself that these changes in him were brought on by solitude and illness, that his true nature needed merely to be reawakened.

Only a fool could believe in such miraculous turnabouts.

He'd finished fastening up his greatcoat and now stood watching her cautiously. "Thank you for tending me," he said in a carefully modulated voice, and then added with a small shrug, "I suppose this is our last good-bye."

She tried to remain strong and upright, but those words pierced her like a dagger.

"Just go," she managed to rasp out, keeping her eyes averted.

It took her by surprise, the speed with which he crossed the room and caught her up in his arms, the strength with which he held her tight against him, the heat and force of his mouth as it swooped down over hers, crushing her lips, searing her with its intensity. He'd never kissed her as a lover before, and especially not like this, without any restraint, stamping her with his imprint, bruising and tearing her tender mouth, until she was nearly crying out for him to take her—propriety and Miss Fescue be damned.

"Ah, Dorcas," he crooned against her throat. "Don't . . . please . . ."

She pulled back and looked up into his blue eyes, so fiercely tender, and felt herself begin to slip.

"It's over, Guy," she whispered raggedly, while she still had the strength of mind to say the words. "Let it go."

As abruptly as he'd come at her, he spun away. She stumbled backward, swallowing her desperate entreaties for him to stay as he moved toward the door. Three steps from the threshold, he began to weave unsteadily, one hand reaching out blindly for something to grasp. He gave a low, wavering cry of disbelief, and as she watched in horrified shock, his legs gave way beneath him and he crumpled to the floor.

Maggie had been waiting by the bedroom door, which was conveniently ajar, wondering if she should go inside with the tea tray or stand there blatantly eavesdropping. Her suspicion that Dorcas was in love with the Earl of Barkin was apparently well founded. Not that their conversation was at all loverlike, but Maggie remembered what Dorcas had said about mutual irritation. It certainly seemed to be a strong link between those two. Although the earl was not coming across as a particularly pleasant person. He'd made several ridiculous accusations against MacGuigan and seemed determined not to listen to any of Dorcas's words in his defense.

Maggie was so engrossed in the melodrama that it wasn't until she heard Dorcas order the earl to leave that something significant dawned on her—Dorcas still believed Alice was going to marry the earl. Gulliver, in typical male fashion, had never shared that part of Maggie's tale with his cousin.

She was about to burst in on them and announce theatrically that every impediment had been removed, when Dorcas herself came flinging through the door.

"Oh, come quickly!" she cried, clutching Maggie by both shoulders. "He's passed out again and I cannot rouse him. His head wound must be far worse than we thought."

Maggie set down the tray and hurried after her. His lordship lay on his back in a relaxed sprawl halfway between the bed and the door.

Dorcas was nearly weeping. "We were fighting—oh, God, it seems all we ever do is fight—and I am so afraid I gave him an apoplexy. The doctors warned him that he hasn't long to live and—"

"Nonsense," said Maggie. "You can take everything doctors

know and put it in a thimble—and still have plenty of room for your thumb."

Dorcas grinned through her tears. "My mother used to say that about men."

Maggie hugged her. "I know. Mine did, too. Now, calm down and help me figure this out. I heard him moving around in here. Maybe he just overtaxed himself." She crouched down beside him. "His breathing appears regular." Maggie sniffed and then leaned closer to his lordship's mouth. "Is he foxed, Dorcas? I smell spirits on his breath."

Dorcas pointed to the flask lying on the bed. "He found it in the pocket of that oilcloth cape."

Maggie shook her head, laughing softly. "Not foxed or concussed," she said, looking up. "Drugged. That whisky was drugged."

"How on earth . . . ?"

"Og used it on me. I believe it was originally intended for Mr. Matchem, in case he was traveling with the Fescues to Quintay."

"Og made *you* drink it? That's horrid. I wonder you can stand the sight of any of us, after what we've put you through."

"It's been an adventure," she said truthfully. "But I have to tell you, two swallows from that flask put me out for at least an hour, maybe more."

"Guy drank it all."

Maggie grimaced. "Then I hope you don't have any plans to move him for some time."

The anxiety returned to Dorcas's eyes. "We need to get him away from here before my cousin comes back. I might not have given the earl an apoplexy, but Gulliver's the next likely candidate for the job."

Maggie thought for a minute. "Didn't he say that Og brought him here?"

"Yes. The old rascal's probably lurking close off shore."

Maggie ran out to the garden and scanned the bay on all three sides. It was growing light off to the east, and the rain was no more than a fine drizzle. There was nothing visible out on the water, least of all a tall-masted ship like the *Charles Stuart*.

It appeared his lordship was yet another victim of Og's whimsical treachery.

She returned to the bedroom. "Og's gone. Maybe we can carry the earl to the skiff and take him to your house."

"No, I still haven't ruled out a concussion. I'd prefer to keep him bundled by the fire for another few hours at least. But I don't know what we will do when Gulliver returns. Guy's been through enough already tonight."

Maggie thought for a moment and then said with a sly smile, "I think you can leave the handling of your cousin to me."

After they'd settled the earl on his pallet, Maggie made a fresh pot of tea and they retired to the table in the parlor.

"I'm sorry I was eavesdropping," Maggie said a little sheepishly. "But there seems to be so much going on around here . . . and no one tells me anything."

Dorcas shook off her apology. "You're embroiled in this now . . . so there's no point in keeping the story from you. Just how much did you overhear?"

"Enough," Maggie said. "Though it sounds like a complete comedy of errors. I can't believe Og told Lord Barkin your cousin kidnapped *Alice*—I really think someone needs to horsewhip the good captain."

Dorcas gave a mirthless laugh. "I'd almost think the old scoundrel was playing matchmaker, trying to lure Guy here on false pretenses, except that the earl is no longer a free man."

Maggie saw it was time to play her trump card. "I . . . um, gather it was his lordship you spoke of earlier, the man you've been in love with since you were fifteen."

"You might have also gathered that there are no longer any gentle feelings between us."

Maggie blithely tossed Dorcas's own words back at her. "Nothing but a great deal of mutual irritation."

"There is that," she agreed. "But it's the mean-spirited sort that comes at the end of things, not the exciting, stimulating kind that marks a new beginning."

Maggie pondered this. Perhaps it was true that Dorcas and the earl had only the bitter dregs of love between them. But she also had a fair notion that the long silence in the bedroom, just before the earl collapsed, had involved a heated bout of kissing. Hardly bitter dregs.

Maggie leaned forward. "So you wouldn't be interested to learn that Alice Fescue is no longer promised to his lordship?"

Dorcas's head shot up. "What are you saying?"

"Didn't it ever occur to you to ask me why I was traveling alone to Quintay with the necklace?"

"I assumed Miss Fescue had sent you on ahead to arrange things at Luray. And as for the necklace, I believe ladies' retainers often carry their mistress's jewels."

"True. Except in this case, I wasn't carrying them . . . I was returning them."

There was an audible hitch in Dorcas's breathing, as though she knew something momentous hovered just out of sight.

Maggie reached across the table and took her by the wrists. "You see, Alice Fescue no longer had a claim to that necklace. Seven days ago she ran off with a captain of the militia."

Dorcas stood up so swiftly, she overset her chair. "Miss Fescue's n-not going to m-marry Guy?"

Maggie's brows meshed into a parody of deep concentration. "That might be difficult. I expect she's already wed to her officer."

Dorcas righted her chair, then stood there clutching the spindled back, her eyes wide with disbelief. "I . . . I can't seem to focus."

"Sit down," Maggie said gently. "And let it sink in."

Instead, her companion turned toward the bedroom, one hand reaching out toward the closed door. "But he doesn't know . . . he *can't* know." Tears welled up in her eyes. "And he won't be awake for hours."

With a purposeful sigh, Maggie rose and got her settled again.

"You must think me a total ninny," Dorcas said. "But it's such a shock. I thought I'd got used to the idea of him marrying someone else. I see that I only pushed the pain away. . . . It's flooding over me now, as though I'd just this minute learned of his betrothal. Isn't that strange?"

"Not necessarily," Maggie reflected. "Perhaps it's only after the pain's been truly averted that we dare to prod at the wound."

"I don't think I could have borne it," Dorcas said intently. "I've been living a great lie since Gulliver told me. Perfectly fine on the outside, dying a little every day on the inside."

"And does his lordship know how you feel?"

Dorcas rested her cheek on her hand and groaned. "I think everyone on both islands knows. But Guy has always held me away. Perhaps because of his health being so indifferent." Her eyes met Maggie's. "Though by the time we were both fifteen, he'd got over most of his childhood ailments. . . . He seemed to get fitter every week. His parents had never sent him away to school, so he spent a great deal of time here, staying with the laird's family at the castle. I remember one blazing hot day in July—I was walking along the wharf and Guy came sailing up. I looked at him, grinning up at me from the deck of his sailboat, and knew that I loved him beyond anything. It was odd, because the two of us spent most of our time arguing. Yet in spite of that, I couldn't bear being apart from him. I . . . ached when he wasn't here."

Maggie had a fair notion of how that felt. MacGuigan's absence of less than a day had left a hole inside her a mile wide.

"I was sure it was only a matter of time before Guy told me he loved me." She looked down at her clenched hands. "But within the year something dreadful happened. I . . . I don't believe I can speak of it without going back on my promise to Gulliver. Suffice to say our future together did not look rosy."

"I do know there was a rift between your two families," Maggie interjected softly.

"Yes, there was. But I would not let family politics keep me from him. Every few months I managed to sail over to Quintay on the sly—Gulliver was off in London by then, so I'd take the *Kestrel* out myself. Guy would meet me in a deserted cove or in a small wood beyond the town. For years we managed to preserve our friendship in small snatches of time—though Guy never gave any sign that he wanted things to progress beyond that. Then two years ago, a year after Gulliver returned here, Guy told me he wanted me to come to Quintay to live."

Dorcas's voice shook. "I was ecstatic. I thought we would be married, and it would mean the end of the feud. But all he wanted was to get me away from here, nothing more. He told me I had to promise him that I would never again set foot on St. Columba."

Maggie frowned over this high-handed bungling. "So you

were to leave everything that was familiar and forsake your kin? And not even for an offer of marriage."

"Exactly. Gulliver's mother was ailing, his father had just died. . . . They were all the family I had left after my own parents passed on. I told him it was a heartless, senseless request. That's when he started up with those vague accusations against Gulliver. And so I taunted him, told him he was jealous because Gull had been living a rather colorful life in London, while Guy was moldering away in his castle, collecting bits of old statues."

Maggie winced. "Rather a low blow."

"It was a measure of my anger. Guy turned very white—it's his heart that is weak, you see—and I knew then that we could never be together, that we would always be fighting over my loyalty to my family and to this island."

"And you sailed away and have not seen him since?"

"Yes . . . and so even if he is free, I don't honestly know that I could walk into that bedroom and throw myself at his feet. Because, basically, nothing's changed."

"I'd say a great deal has changed," Maggie observed emphatically. "You've both had a good dose of what it feels like to face permanent separation. So how could you wake up tomorrow—and every day after for the rest of your life—knowing you had your heart's desire within your grasp and lost it for lack of holding on?"

"You make me feel like a paltry, fainthearted creature," Dorcas murmured. "And perhaps I was. I should have given Guy a few weeks to cool down and then presented myself to him on a platter. Instead, it's been two years wasted."

"And if that doctor *was* correct, you might not have much time left," Maggie reminded her gently.

"I would take him if all we had was a month or a week."

"That sounds like a recipe for heartbreak, if you'll pardon me pointing it out."

"That's because you've never been in love, Maggie. Sometimes all you get is one day. And yet, it's enough."

Maggie stood up and collected the teacups. "Then you'd best not delay. I'll see that your cousin is distracted when he returns, and you and the earl can have some time to yourselves."

"*If* he ever wakes up," she said fretfully.

"And if MacGuigan ever returns," Maggie added under her breath.

While she tended to the dishes, she thought about what Dorcas had said, that sometimes one day was enough. She wondered if she'd look back at these few days with MacGuigan and count herself lucky to have shared even so brief a time with him. This was likely to be her only venture into romance, she knew. The life that lay ahead of her, working as a governess or a companion, would not offer her any opportunities for courtship. Such women were barely acknowledged by their employers and nearly invisible in society.

It was a lonely, loveless road that loomed before her, and she renewed her determination to wring as much joy from this island sojourn as she could.

Chapter Ten

*I*t was well past sunrise when Dorcas came hurrying out of the bedroom. Maggie stirred in the armchair, where she'd been trying to make up for a night of little sleep.

"I was sitting by the window," Dorcas said. "The *Kestrel's* just come into the harbor."

Maggie breathed a prayer of thanks. Dorcas, however, appeared more agitated than relieved.

"If Gulliver fetches my pony from the house, he could be here in less than fifteen minutes."

"Are you sure that would be such a tragedy? Gulliver's anger at Lord Barkin can't be that great . . . not if he tried to see him yesterday. And since the chief impediment between you and the earl is his cork-brained notion that your cousin is a blackguard, why not let the two men meet and iron things out? MacGuigan certainly isn't going to attack the earl outright"—not the way she had, she mused—"and his lordship's in no condition to start a fight."

Dorcas mulled this over. "It might just serve. Maybe it is time my cousin had the chance to answer one of his accusers face to face. But not until I'm sure Guy is recovered." She gave Maggie a grim smile. "You've seen full well how my cousin can be when he's riled—high-handed and overbearing. He'll come barging in here, full of recriminations and accusations, and Guy and I will never get to sort things out."

Maggie had to admit that Dorcas knew the two men far better than she did. And she'd certainly got the right of things about her cousin's pigheadedness. "Think first, act later" was clearly not the MacGuigan family motto. Maybe all the common sense in the clan had gone to Dorcas.

"At least I've thought of a way to keep your cousin from coming into the cottage. But you've got to stay quiet and make sure the bedroom curtains are closed."

"I wish Fingal was here," Dorcas moaned. "He's the only one Gulliver or Guy ever listened to in the old days."

Maggie thought a moment. "Write him a note and I'll see that it's delivered. Between the two of you, you should be able to get the earl away from the cottage."

"Where can we take him? My house is rather public— someone's bound to notice us dragging an unconscious man along the High Street."

Maggie looked out the window to the promontory across the bay. "Take him to the castle."

Dorcas made a little moue. "It will be difficult, being there with him again after so long."

"You never know, it might help . . . familiar ground and all that. And I promise to keep MacGuigan distracted until the two of you can patch things up."

Dorcas gave a low chuckle. "I hope you've got enough stamina for that. From my experience with his lordship, it could take weeks."

Maggie patted her hand, then nodded to the bedroom. "He kissed you in there, didn't he? Ah, I was right . . . and spent rather a long time at it, too. You might want to think about returning the favor, once he wakes up."

Dorcas gave a weary sigh. "He's still out cold. Though I did manage to trickle a little water down his throat."

"Don't stop," Maggie said firmly. "You may think it's only an old wives' tale, but I'm convinced there are great healing properties in that water."

Great enough, she prayed, to cure a dying man—and save a dying island.

Gulliver berthed the *Kestrel*'s dinghy at the wharf and was met at the top of the steps by Fabian, who greeted him with a wild lashing of his whip tail and a deal of foolish groveling.

"Bad dog," he muttered fondly, scrubbing at his briary head. "I left you behind to guard the ladies and here you are sauntering about the village like a town beau. What's the matter, things get too tame for you over there?"

The dog yipped once and gnawed at his cuff, then together they set out for Dorcas's house. Gulliver was anxious to get back to the cottage, but first he needed to have a talk with Fingal.

Things on Quintay had not gone at all as he'd hoped. After being turned away during his initial visit to the castle, he'd spent four very edifying hours with Brian Rennie, snugged away from the lashing rainstorm in one of Luray's waterfront taverns. On his second visit later that night, however, he'd discovered that the earl had disappeared. Not even the officious footman seemed to know where his master had gone. He'd decided to try again that morning, hoping Guy had resurfaced. A flustered housemaid had answered his knock and told him artlessly that most of the staff was off searching for the earl. He'd had a fleeting urge to offer his help but then thought better of it when the maid informed him that Mr. Matchem, returned late last night from the mainland, had everything well in hand.

Gulliver didn't have time to waste dealing with Neddie Matchem—even if the man could have shed some light on the whereabouts of the real Alice Fescue. Anyway, if he knew Guy, his lordship had doubtless gone off yesterday afternoon to inspect his nursery seedlings, got caught up in discussing horticulture with one of his overseers and, rather than ride back in the teeming rain, had likely spent the night in the man's lodge. They'd done it often enough as boys, without a word to anyone.

Still, if Matchem was back, then his lordship would soon learn of Alice's defection. The earl would be bound to wonder where Alice's companion had got herself off to with his necklace. Gulliver knew he had to make a decision—and quickly.

Twenty minutes, seated across from Fingal MacNeill in Dorcas's kitchen, was all it took.

His old friend heard him out without comment and then made one of those uncomplicated pronouncements that came readily to a man of nearly ninety years. "Appears to me, lad, ye're letting your heart get in the way of yer brain. And doin' justice to neither organ. Ye made one mistake—now, don't compound it by wafflin' about. Ye know the proper thing to do . . . ye always did know, even as a lad."

When he didn't respond immediately, Fingal added, "Sometimes the way it plays out, ye give up one treasure only to find there's another right behind it."

Gulliver wasn't so sure about that. It occurred to him, as he rode out of the village on Dorcas's pony, that he was being asked to give up *all* his treasures. Still, there was no other way he could truly square things with Maggie Bonner—even if it would put a severe hitch in his plans for reviving the island. His only alternative now was to dispose of his last major asset, a course he'd been avoiding for months, since it meant relinquishing a cherished link with his father.

He looked back to where the *Kestrel* was moored, his expression wistful but resigned. A man without a boat in these islands was akin to a knight without a steed, a sorry soul with no means of transportation or livelihood. Nevertheless, he had no choice, not if he wanted to regain a crumb of his honor.

He was whistling softly as he crossed the bog, Fabian sticking close behind the pony. Whistling in the dark his mother called it, when you needed to muster your courage and face your worst fears.

Not that he feared Maggie Bonner, precisely. Rather it was wondering how her absence would affect him that left him unsettled. Still, he knew she couldn't stay on here, especially after his talk with Brian yesterday.

He'd been shocked and nearly appalled to discover that somehow—though it wasn't a stretch to imagine Neddie Matchem's poisonous whispers behind the rumor—the earl believed he had been wrecking ships off St. Columba. Not only that, his lordship also had the crackbrained notion that Gulliver was plotting with his islanders to raid Quintay.

It explained the presence of the armed cutter—and further explained why all Gulliver's requests for aid had gone unanswered. The earl had not, as he'd assumed, merely been sitting in his fine castle stewing with resentment against him for a sin he'd unwittingly committed years earlier. No, his lordship had apparently been nourishing a great hatred for the people of St. Columba in general—and Gulliver MacGuigan in particular.

This was all inconceivable to him. Nine years ago, the two islands had existed in harmony, sharing trade and fishing rights, not to mention the close blood tie the two chief families had shared. And even though it was because of Gulliver that their longtime amity had been disrupted, it never occurred to him that the rift might one day lead to armed conflict. Nevertheless, he'd seen the earl's gunboat himself that morning, cruising off the south coast of Quintay; he'd drawn close enough in the *Kestrel* to spy the stern chasers and cannon ports.

How it had come to this pass remained beyond his understanding. He'd never have taken the damned necklace or played along with Og's abduction scheme if he'd known the earl now regarded him as a ruthless scoundrel. The bond that had been between them since childhood, the latent affection he'd taken for granted all these years in spite of the gulf between their families, had clearly ceased to exist. Guy would not be thinking of Gulliver's actions as just another version of their boyhood competition, something done to tweak him. No, he'd have seen them as an overt declaration of hostile intent. And if Neddie was behind the slander, then Gulliver, in seeking to aid St. Columba, had played right into Matchem's hands *and* placed the islanders at great risk.

He wondered if the only reason Guy hadn't yet made a pre-emptive strike was Dorcas's presence on St. Columba. Not that that would prevent Gulliver from sending her away to safety. And Maggie Bonner, as well.

Even if Brian was wrong—and Gulliver still had a faint hope that he'd overstated the danger—he had no choice but to treat this threat as though it was genuine. Perhaps the best thing, once he'd made his peace with Miss Bonner, would be to go to Luray Castle and give himself up to the earl—after a short detour to thrash Neddie Matchem into next Christmas. Then he'd force Guy to listen. If there was a shred of his boyhood friend left in the man, Gulliver would make him see the truth. It was a rash plan, he might very well end up in prison, but it was the only thing he could think of to defuse the situation.

Maybe Maggie Bonner will visit me in the Tollbooth, he thought wryly. Better yet, he wouldn't put it past her to over-power his guards and set him free. They could run off to the Highlands and live in happy obscurity.

No, that was not likely to be the way things played out. She'd return to England, return to supporting her father—he'd make sure she got a stellar reference—and if the earl believed him, he'd end up back here, still trying to keep the island afloat.

As he neared the cottage, Fabian raced past the pony and began his usual yapping among the chickens, who squawked and fluttered about without having the sense to run away. Not unlike himself, Gulliver reflected sourly, choosing to stay here and fight in the face of impossible odds.

Someone inside the cottage must have heard the commotion in the yard. There was the thud of the front door slamming, and in seconds Maggie Bonner came pelting around the garden wall. Gulliver slid off the pony and held out both hands to greet her. She never slowed her pace but careered right into his chest.

"MacGuigan," she panted. "We were so worried . . ."

Her hands were stroking over him, over his chest and down his arms, as though she needed to reassure herself that he was whole.

"I'm not exactly returned from the wars," he said.

She looked a delight this morning, in a summer-weight gown of pale amber muslin with her dark hair in a loose plait down her back.

Her eyes narrowed. "You got caught in that squall, though, didn't you? Your wretched dog scared the life out of Dorcas and me. . . . He started up howling and baying. We knew you were in some kind of danger."

He rubbed his hand over her bare wrist, liking the feel of her skin under his palm. "The worst danger I was in was from the very bad ale at the Balefire Tavern on Quintay."

"So you overnighted there?"

"Mmm . . . I never did meet up with the fishing fleet. Turns out they hadn't gone to Quintay after all. Fingal told me they decided to try again south of the island. Apparently they got a decent haul."

"Good for them. Maybe the seals brought the fishing back after all. But then how did you end up on Quintay?"

He gnawed at his lip. "I . . . I need to speak with you about that. But let me get cleaned up first."

He started to move past her, but she put both hands on his arm, gripping tight.

"No! You mustn't!" Her hold on him eased and she said more calmly, "Last night your cousin came down with a wretched head cold. *We* did get caught in that squall, you see, we were . . . um, walking out along the shingle. Then she was up all night coughing and sneezing, and now she's finally fallen asleep. I'd rather you didn't disturb her."

"That's odd. It's not like Dorcas to get caught in a storm. Besides that, she's rarely ever sick."

"I don't think she's in any danger, just cranky and out of sorts."

"There's a neat irony. I leave her here to look after you and you end up looking after her."

"I'm not much of a nurse, but I do know she needs to rest. I'm thinking you can wash up there"—she pointed to the cistern—"and I'll fetch you some clean clothes."

Before Gulliver could object, she was heading back toward the garden gate. She looked just as appealing from the aft end as from the fore, but he made himself turn away. He had a new mandate now, and it did not include ogling her backside.

He was still washing up at the cistern, his shirt off, hanging tucked into the waistband of his breeches, when she came around the side of the cottage, a pile of clothing in one arm, a basket over the other. He turned to her, mindless of the water running in rivulets down his bare chest, and his breathing nearly ceased. She had stopped ten paces away and was regarding him with an expression of raw hunger he'd never before seen on a woman's face. Hunger for him.

His whole body reacted to that look, quickening fiercely. His blood surged through him, primal and equally hungry. The few kisses he'd stolen had been but a fleeting taste; he needed to consume her entirely to be sated.

A swift, potent image rose in his head . . . of thrusting her up against the side of the cottage . . . of kissing her until she cried aloud . . . of sinking down deep into her warm body . . . until he was lost to everything but the mindless bliss of completion.

Lost . . . Aye, he'd be lost indeed if he ever did such a thing.

Without hesitation he dunked himself, head and shoulders, into the rain barrel. The cold water shocked him back to his senses, cooling his body, if not the heated images in his brain. He came up with a gasp, pushing away from the barrel, flinging his head back and sending water droplets spraying from his hair in every direction.

When Maggie finally approached him and laid his things on a wooden bench, he was drying himself with his shirt, his equilibrium nearly restored. Until she took a towel from the top of her pile and said, "Here, best let me do your back. You're still soaking wet."

He nearly growled as she turned him about and began rubbing the cloth briskly over his shoulders and down along his spine. He steeled himself to her touch, all the while aching to catch her in his arms and tug her against his naked chest.

Fortunately, she did not linger over her task. She handed him a clean shirt, and he was relieved when she looked away as he drew it on and tucked it into his breeches.

"I really should shave," he said, rubbing his hand over two days' worth of bristles. "I'm starting to look like a hedgehog."

"I think I can bear it," she said. "It adds to your roguish appeal."

She was gazing at him again with that open hunger, and he nearly blanched.

Why now, he wondered irritably, when he'd finally made up his mind to let her go? For four days she'd given him nothing but sauce, and all of a sudden she was practically throwing herself at him. It ought to have dulled the edge of his desire, but it only made the wanting more acute. He'd take her full of battle and sharp words or melting and compliant.

Except that he couldn't take her . . . not in any way. He dared not even think about it.

He reached for a clean neckcloth, knotting it carelessly, then drew on the waistcoat she held out. As he buttoned it, his stomach rumbled audibly.

"I don't suppose you'd let me into my own kitchen for some breakfast?"

She shook her head and opened the lid of the basket; it appeared laden with food. "I thought we might have an al fresco picnic."

He scowled. "I see you've planned this all very neatly."

She shifted on her feet, and he began to get the notion that she was holding something back. Her normally open countenance was shuttered, her eyes uncharacteristically avoiding his.

"What's really going on?" he asked in a carrying voice. "Why are you so determined to get me away from here?"

"Why, nothing's going on . . ."

He motioned toward the cottage. "Dorcas isn't sick, is she? The two of you have cooked up some intrigue between you."

Before she could respond, a loud hacking cough emanated from the bedroom window behind her. Followed by an audible bout of wheezing.

Maggie's eyes widened. "I'd best see to her."

She disappeared again, around the garden wall. He looked down at Fabian and rolled his eyes.

"She's gone back to sleep," Maggie announced when she returned. "I fear your shouting disturbed her."

Gulliver refused to look abashed, not for speaking in a perfectly normal tone of voice outside his own cottage. Jesus preserve him from females and all their odd starts.

"And since we can't stay here," Maggie was saying, "I thought we might have our picnic up in the hills. Though I have a note for Fingal from your cousin—something to do with her missing a meeting of the ladies' church guild—if you don't mind stopping first at the village."

"The village is exactly where I plan to take you," he said. "To the *Kestrel*."

Her head tipped to one side and she said assessingly, "I suppose we could picnic off the seal rocks. It would be a treat to see them up close."

He felt a tic start up below one eye. "We're not going on a blasted picnic," he said, then added bluntly, "I'm taking you to Quintay."

Her mouth fell open, but no words came out. If he'd expected her to be pleased by his declaration, he was far off the mark. If anything, she looked incensed.

"Now?" she said at last. "Just like that?" She glowered at him for a long moment, then shook her head. "No, I don't think so."

She spun away from him and started walking in the direction of the bog. He went striding after her. "Do I have to remind you that you hardly have any say in the matter?"

She slowed a bit and turned. "Hasn't anyone ever explained to you that the exact method for *not* getting your way is to put the other person's back up? Honestly, MacGuigan . . . it's no wonder you need to go about ravishing women. You haven't a shred of charm."

And then she started walking again, with even greater determination, the hem of her gown scudding around her ankles.

Maggie wasn't sure how things had progressed from him looking at her as though he wanted to devour her to this display of sheer male arrogance.

As she passed the pony idling beside the henhouse, she tugged his reins off the rickety fence and began hauling him after her. Once she got safely past the bog, she'd need a swift mount to beat MacGuigan to his cousin's house. It was time she had a few words with Fingal MacNeill—alone.

MacGuigan was following her some twenty paces back, muttering threats, while Fabian loped at his heels. The man clearly had no idea she was about to bolt.

Something significant must have happened on Quintay to bring him to this sudden—and most unwelcome—decision. She couldn't imagine what, since the earl was here on St. Columba. She told herself to focus on the tasks at hand—delivering the note and getting MacGuigan away from the village—rather than dwelling on how callously he'd announced his intention of sending her away.

But the more she walked, the more her pain and anger mounted. So much for the romantic reunion she'd been anticipating. And how dare he just blithely order her from his life? As though he'd never confided in her and laughed with her, as if he hadn't kissed her and beguiled her and made her love him.

MacGuigan almost managed to catch up with her at the beginning of the bog, but she paid him no mind—he wasn't likely to tackle her on the narrow, precarious path.

"Maggie Bonner," he called to her. "See? I'm finally acknowledging that that's your real name."

"No, it's not," she shot back.

"Damn it!" he sputtered. "What in blazes is that supposed to mean?"

"My name is Marguerite Bonheur," she said over her shoulder—without slowing her pace. "That is whom you are dealing with now. Maggie Bonner was a tame, spineless creature who allowed you to push her around and order her about. But you can't intimidate Marguerite. . . . She is more likely to snap her fingers right in your face." Maggie turned and did just that. "And then tell you to go to the devil."

"Maggie!" he cried. "Stop!"

"No, I absolutely will n—"

She was a few feet in front of him, but he made up the distance with a great bound and lifted her right off the path. And then held her tight in his arms to keep her from struggling.

"Quagmire," he breathed up against her ear. "You were just about to march yourself into the worst quagmire on the island."

Maggie craned her head around. They were standing on the edge of a semicircular patch of damp, innocent-looking peat.

"Are you daft?" she muttered.

He kicked at a loose rock with one boot. It landed six feet away—and set the whole sodden mass to trembling. Then with a sickening plop, the peat burped open, and the rock was swallowed up.

"Sweet Jesus," Maggie breathed and buried her face in his shoulder.

"I should have let you go in," he whispered raggedly, his mouth brushing her hair. "Just to put the fear of God into you . . . just so you'd listen to me for a change."

She tipped her head back. "But then you'd have pulled me out, wouldn't you?"

He looked down at her, his jaw set. "I'd probably have needed some time to think it over."

"Wretch," she said.

"Is that above or below the status of rogue?"

"Below," she said darkly. "Definitely below."

His arms tightened. "Ah, Maggie," he said with a sigh. "However will I manage without you here keeping me in my place?"

She feared he was being sarcastic, until she saw the rueful, almost dismal expression in his eyes.

"Then why are you sending me away?" she pleaded.

"Because I must." His mouth twisted. "The farce has played out; now the melodrama is about to begin. And I don't want you here if things turn ugly."

Her fingers dug into the fabric of his greatcoat. "Tell me what you mean! You can't just send me off like this, not knowing what's going to happen."

"Trust me, this is for the best. Now, get on back to the cottage and fetch your things. I'll bring the *Kestrel* over—"

"No!" she cried. "At least let me deliver your cousin's note."

He held out one hand. "Give it to me."

Maggie couldn't risk that. If he read it, Dorcas and the earl would be discovered—well before they had time to straighten out their tangled affairs. She'd failed in her mission to take the Barkin emeralds to Quintay, but she vowed she wasn't going to fail in this.

He was now glaring at her. "You don't seem to understand that time is of the essence here."

"Well, how could I?" she huffed, "when you won't tell me what's really going on. I am heartily sick of all your secrets, MacGuigan. And let me remind you, this farce, as you call it, was all your doing. If you'd listened to me that first day, if you'd *paid attention,* I'd have left the island on the next boat out. But, no, you had to keep me here, until I started to care . . . more than I ever thought possible. So don't you dare be angry at me for not wanting to leave."

"What do you mean, started to care? Care for what?"

She had such a desire to dump her basket over his head. How could a man be so obtuse?

He took her by the shoulders and shook her once. "Maggie, what are you saying?"

She thrust back from him. "I'm not talking to you anymore. I'd do better conversing with Fabian—I'm likely to get more openness and honesty from that dog than I'll ever get from you."

She was retracing her steps when she realized MacGuigan was not behind her. She turned. He was still beside the quagmire, staring off into space. This was the chance she'd been waiting for. The pony had wandered a was down the path; she ran up to him, snatched at the trailing reins and scrambled onto his back, thankful she'd often ridden astride as a girl.

MacGuigan gave an angry shout as she trotted off, but she was beyond heeding him. She let Fabian lead her through the bog, while MacGuigan stormed after them, audibly cursing the dog for a turncoat.

Once she was clear of the swamp, she dug her heels into the pony's side. He took off so quickly she was nearly unseated and hung half out of the saddle for a good ten strides until she was able to right herself.

When she reached Dorcas's house, she tethered the pony to a bush in the drive and ran up the front steps. She knocked several times, waiting fretfully until a reedy old man in corduroy knee breeches opened the door.

"Mr. MacNeill?" she panted. "My name is Maggie Bonner. I've brought you a message from Dorcas."

His eyes brightened. "Ah, the MacGuigan's captive. 'Tis a pleasure to meet ye, lass."

He looked beyond her, to where his master was striding purposefully along the shingle, and he grinned. "It appears you've not yet shaken your gaoler."

"I haven't much time," she said. "Dorcas needs you at the cottage."

His eyebrows rose.

She took the note from her basket and thrust it into his gnarled hand. "It's all in there. But please, don't say a word to MacGuigan. He believes she's laid low with a head cold."

His bemused expression at once grew wary, but he duly scanned the note, then tucked it into his moleskin vest. His keen gaze darted to her face. "I ken my master isn't the only one with a taste for intrigue."

"He wants to take me to Quintay . . . and the timing couldn't be worse."

"Sorry, lass. 'Twas me advised him to set ye free."

"Three days ago I would have thanked you. But now I've promised Dorcas to get her cousin away from the village — not that sailing to Quintay wouldn't answer, except then I won't be here to see how it all turns out."

She paused for a breath, looking up at him intently — and realized with a shock that she'd seen him before. He was hard to mistake, tall, almost regal, with a thatch of pure white hair and teak-colored skin that was stretched so tautly over his skull, his face appeared almost ageless. In spite of that, he bore a distinct resemblance to the craggy Captain Og, something in his wide-legged sailor's stance and his keen blue eyes. Was he the old man she'd seen MacGuigan speaking with at the street market? Yes, but where else? Then it came back to her.

"It was you!" she cried sharply. "You were piloting the boat when MacGuigan held up the *Charles Stuart*."

He'd been weathering her scrutiny with a grin, but now his smile faded. "I've crewed the *Kestrel* now and again."

She couldn't believe it; Dorcas had made him sound so wise and saintly. "And you approved of your master risking his neck to steal those emeralds?"

"No one values the MacGuigan's neck more than me, lass."

Maggie's brow furrowed. "Then why did you aid him? Did he order you to do it?" She leapt ahead before he could answer. "Your master's the laird of St. Columba, isn't he?"

Fingal stroked one forefinger along his jaw and she could have sworn there was regret in his eyes when he said, "Not that I know of, lass."

Maggie nearly screamed. There were a thousand things she wanted to ask him, but MacGuigan was approaching the porch steps, a thundercloud on his brow.

Maggie shot Fingal an imploring look. "Please, you must tell me—"

MacGuigan had got her by the wrist, in a nearly painful grip. Fingal glowered down at him from the doorway, his blue eyes flicking from MacGuigan's face to the tanned hand that encircled Maggie's arm. MacGuigan released her at once.

"She's a menace," he pronounced hotly in his own defense. "To herself and God knows who else. She barely missed walking into a quagmire and then nearly tumbled off that pony right onto her—"

"None of those things would have happened if you hadn't been . . . bullying me," Maggie interjected.

"She's got you there, lad," Fingal observed.

"You haven't even begun to see bullying," he said between his teeth. "Now, you are going to march yourself to the wharf so we can sail over to the cottage and fetch your things."

He had taken her by the hand, less roughly this time, and was trying to tug her down the porch steps, but she was holding tight to the railing. Fingal was watching this byplay with an expression of great relish—again putting Maggie in mind of his scapegrace son.

"Leave off now, MacGuigan," he said at last. "The puir lass

has suffered enough at yer hands. 'Tis amends ye should be makin', not threats."

"Amends?" MacGuigan echoed incredulously. "This . . . shrew has been haranguing me for days to set her free. First she attacks me with a knife, then she runs off to the castle and hides. And now, when I tell her I'm finally taking her to Quintay, she runs off . . . again." He thumped his palm against the side of his head. "I'm dashed if I know what she wants."

"One day," Maggie said quickly. "Just one day more. Please."

"And what difference will one day make?"

All the difference in the world, she longed to tell him.

"Just give me a little time to get used to the idea," she said. "If you still want me gone tomorrow, I promise I will not make a peep."

"I'd pay to see that," he said under his breath.

Fingal sniffed. "Sounds like a fair request to me."

MacGuigan turned to him. "Have you forgotten what I told you not an hour ago—that unless I get Miss Bonner to the earl, the whole island may be at risk?"

Fingal touched his vest, over the spot where he'd stashed the note. Maggie had seen him read it; he knew Lord Barkin was right here.

"Things are not so desperate as ye think. As ye said, Master Guy's gone from Luray Castle; he's doubtless off somewhere seein' to his . . . nursery. It doesna sound to me like his lordship is about to launch an attack."

"Attack?" Maggie echoed. "Surely he'd never attack St. Columba."

MacGuigan's narrowed gaze slid to her. "And what, pray, do you know about him?"

Maggie swallowed hard. "I . . . only what you told me. That the earl cared for this island once."

"That's clearly in the past," he muttered darkly. "He now views us as a lot of . . . cutthroats and scoundrels."

"Steady, lad," Fingal said as he came down the steps and took him by the arm, drawing him away from Maggie. "Don't be so hasty to fear the worst."

She saw what Fingal was doing, giving her a chance to get away.

She sidled noiselessly down the steps, then sprang across the grass to the pony. MacGuigan gave a shout when she clambered onto the saddle, but she was already urging the pony along the drive. She'd dropped the basket in her flight—Fabian was nosing around in it on the lawn—but she had other things on her mind besides breakfast. She was going to lead MacGuigan to the one place on St. Columba she still needed to see, the logical spot to tell him of her wonderful plan: the saint's spring, the heart—and possible last hope—of this island she had unaccountably come to love.

Chapter Eleven

*M*aggie had made it as far as the alpine valley when he caught up with her. He was mounted on a graying bay hunter and had her basket lashed to the back of his saddle.

"I have strict orders not to bully you," he said grudgingly as he rode up.

Her eyes twinkled. "I think I could grow to like Fingal enormously."

"He said I should listen to you for a change. As if I haven't been doing that for the past four days."

Maggie raised one brow. "You listen, MacGuigan, but how much do you actually *hear*?"

"Not enough, obviously."

"Perhaps you'll hear better with food on your stomach. I was thinking we could ride up to the spring. Is it far?"

"Not on horseback. It lies above the meadow where I found you."

She waited for him to move off, but he just sat there gazing into the distance, his face washed of any expression. She nudged the pony up closer, and he finally turned to her.

"I'm sorry, Maggie, I've no heart for this right now."

She'd never heard him so forlorn. "MacGuigan, what happened on Quintay?"

"Let's just say I lost a foolish illusion."

She leaned over and gripped his hand. "Come to the spring . . . I've something to tell you that might raise your spirits."

He gave her a wan smile and then set his horse in motion. What had seemed like an endless trek that first day was now

accomplished in barely a quarter of an hour. It wasn't long before they were traversing the final hill before the meadow.
Halfway across the slope, MacGuigan veered off the trail, setting his horse directly up the side of the gorse-covered hill.
Even when the bracken gave way to rocky scree, he continued
doggedly upward until they came to a flinty track that ran
below two towering crags. They were high enough now to see
the bay and the castle but happily too far away to make out any
small craft on the water.

They rode single file down into a hidden glen, a gradually
widening ravine carved between the two peaks that ended in a
shallow bowl. At its east end, an outcropping of rock thrust
away from the side of the mountain, forming a shelf perhaps
twenty feet across, narrowed at the end like an adze. It jutted far
out over a clear, colorless pool.

Maggie slipped from her pony and went at once to kneel at
the water's edge. The pool was half in shadow, half in sunlight,
the lighted portion revealing the slightly distorted geometry of
the granite bottom. The grotto possessed a serene, almost oth-
erworldly aspect; not a weed or wildflower sprouted from the
hard rock to distract the eye from the limpid surface of the crys-
talline water.

"It is rather magical," she said, looking up at MacGuigan.
"Does the spring rise from the middle of the pool?"

"No, the source lies deep under that ledge." He dismounted
and then led her along the length of the pool, to where the
ground fell away. Across a ten-foot gap the solid wall of the ad-
joining peak rose opposite them.

"And here," he said, standing at the very rim of the chasm,
"is where our water comes from. Ah, carefully . . ." He slid one
arm around Maggie's waist as she peered out over the edge.

The water from the pool drained through a narrow opening
in its bank, sluicing out as from a rainspout, to cascade down
the jagged cliff face below them.

"But how does the water get beyond this chasm to the rest
of the island?"

"Don't you know that water runs down, Maggie? It always
runs down. Down to our village, down to Cranlochie." He
pointed off to the north. "Fingal says the spring has carved a
great river beneath those hills. The streams from that river find

their way through limestone and granite and silt, always seeking sea level."

"And they all emanate from this one spot?"

"Precisely. If the spring were to dry up, the island would have only rain water to sustain it. But that's not likely to happen. It's apparently been flowing since the days of the Vikings."

"It just appeared here one day?"

He rubbed at his chin. "Well . . . the local legend is that St. Columba was marooned here by some Celts who didn't fancy being browbeaten into Christianity. It was intended to be a death sentence, since the place was an uninhabitable rock. As the story goes, he came up here to pray for succor and took shelter beneath that ledge. During the night he had a dream that compelled him to awake and strike his staff hard on the ground. When he did so, the spring rose up, right through the granite, and brought the island to life."

"And has it been healing people since that time, do you think?"

He shrugged. "Those old wives' tales had to start some time."

He moved away from the edge. "And now if the history lesson is over, I'd like some breakfast."

He went to his horse and untied the basket from his saddle. Maggie lingered beside the drop-off, impressed by the rugged beauty of water plummeting over the mossy rocks. How could MacGuigan be thinking of food when surrounded by such wonders? The man didn't have a sensitive or fanciful bone in his body.

She craned around. "And you don't believe any of those tales?"

He'd seated himself on a flat rock beside the pool and was exploring the contents of the basket. "I'm delighted that you've taken the island and all its fairy stories to your bosom, but don't expect me to be so awed."

She suddenly grew fearful of revealing her plan. In his present mood he'd likely scoff and accuse her of cooking up ridiculous schemes to stay on the island.

He held out a scone to her as she stalked past him.

"No, thank you. I've lost my appetite."

He threw it down and rose to his feet. "Now what have I done?"

"Nothing," she said in a rasping voice. "Just . . . *nothing*." She flung one arm out toward the pool. "You don't value it or esteem it . . . or honor it. To you it's just water running downhill. But if you weren't so obsessively focused on getting money from Quintay, you'd see that all the help you need is here. Right here!" She took a breath. "This water has miraculous healing powers, MacGuigan. And once word of that got out, people would flock to St. Columba."

He came toward her warily, as a man approaches a child in a tantrum—or a dangerous lunatic—with his arms held before him, hands open. "It's just a spring, Maggie. There's no magic . . . only the magic of sustaining life on this island."

"You're wrong!" she cried. She needed to believe it, needed to know that rare and special things existed in the world, things that could balance out the pain and the disappointments and the humiliations.

"I suppose I should thank you for even trying to come up with a solution," he said, "however impractical."

"It's not impractical. How can you be deaf and blind and so infuriatingly stubborn, all at the same time?"

His voice rose. "And how dare you come here and tell me how to save my island?"

She took a step toward him and snarled, "I didn't *come* here."

His mouth twitched, his anger giving way to wry amusement. "No. No you didn't. Some waggish sea god cast you up on my shores to torment me." He set a hand tentatively on her shoulder. "Please, have some breakfast. It's quite a novelty to meet a woman who's actually testier than I am on an empty stomach."

Maggie grumbled all the way back to the rock where he'd laid out the contents of the basket. He tugged off his greatcoat and spread it over the hard surface for her to sit on. She plumped down, facing the water.

"I don't blame you for being taken in by all the tales," he said in an attempt to be conciliating. "I suppose Dorcas told you the most recent one . . . Fingal's amazing recovery."

"No," she said sullenly.

"Now, don't add this to our list of miracles; it was strictly circumstantial. The thing is, Fingal was taken hard with the influenza last autumn. He lay close to death for days . . . to the point where some of the village men came up to the meadow and dug his grave."

She was growing interested now. "I'd always meant to ask you why there was an empty grave sitting there."

"He was born in that meadow—his mother, Adelaide, was gathering herbs there when her time came upon her. And so it was there he wished to be buried. But Og and Bridie were convinced they could save him. They carried him up here in a litter and laid him in the pool. I'm not exactly sure what transpired, but I saw him walk into the village the next day . . . a veritable Lazarus."

"And you still refuse to credit the spring?"

"He had a raging fever. The cool water simply brought his temperature down."

Maggie jabbed her open hand under his nose. "What about the blisters on your fingers? What about the nick on your chin. Both healed in a matter of hours. What of the great span of years these islanders boast and all the old men still capable of working like young men . . . Barry MacNeill, Og MacNeill, Captain Taybeck?" She grasped his wrist. "This may not be the fountain of youth, MacGuigan, but to someone who does not take the spring for granted as you do, it surely appears to be a fountain of good health."

"I probably shouldn't tell you this," he said with a rueful smile, "but I may be the greatest argument for your case."

"Then you must tell me."

"Very well . . . I suppose it's light enough penance for all my sins against you." His gaze drifted to the still water. "Since I turned twenty, I'd made my home in London, supporting myself by gambling." She saw the side of his mouth twist up. "Dice, drink and doxies were my sole pursuits . . . and not necessarily in that order. I was burning the candle at both ends. Hell, I'd have burned it in the middle if given the chance."

"Not uncommon behavior for green young men," she said.

He shook his head. "I was neither green nor so young. I was merely hell-bent. Then three years ago, it all caught up with me. I fell ill." He had begun to fret his fingers against his palm. "I had banished St. Columba from my thoughts for so long, but all I could think of then was that I needed to be home. Some friends put me on a ship bound for Barra—I don't remember much of the passage—and the captain set me ashore here."

"So you came home to recuperate?"

His eyes flashed. "No, Maggie, I came home to die."

Her mouth fell open.

"The scarlet fever I'd survived as a youth had only been biding its time to strike me down. The doctors told me there was no hope, that my heart was failing. But once I was back here, within weeks, my strength returned. Fingal and Bridie claim it was the spring water they'd forced on me by the gallon." He paused. "I don't know . . . maybe I never credited the water because I didn't want to admit I'd really been that ill."

Maggie herself had a hard time believing it; she'd never met a man so fit. She suddenly recalled what Dorcas had told her, that the earl's heart was also afflicted.

"Did Guy have scarlet fever as a youth?"

He turned an incredulous frown upon her. "How the devil did you know that?"

"Just a guess . . . you do keep harping on his frail state. And is there more to this story—of why you left the island and put it so firmly from your mind?"

He turned away. "None of this is your concern any longer."

She stretched her hand out to cup his chin. "Look at me, MacGuigan. It's no wonder you can't deal with the present if you keep the past locked up tight. What happened here nine years ago that you are so afraid to tell me?"

"Damn, you are worse than Dorcas for prodding at a fellow." He met her eyes, his expression full of anger and remorse. "I nearly killed Guy is what. Out of my own caprice and foolishness."

"You? Father Christmas and Robin Hood all rolled into one? It's unthinkable."

"It happened just the same. I'd been sent down from university for some boyish infraction, and I set off for home, thinking it was all a lark. The diligence out of Edinburgh was crowded. I shared the compartment with an entire farm family, from a babe in arms to a doddering old gaffer. I decided it was best if I took a boat to Quintay—if I'd come here, my father would have parted my scalp with his tongue when he discovered what had happened. Guy was more than happy to let me hide in his rooms at the castle. He was bored to flinders when I wasn't there. So I made an accomplice of him for a few days . . . until I began to sicken."

Maggie felt an icy chill steal up her spine.

"I imagine one of the farm children had scarlet fever— Lord, they were all red-faced and cranky. Guy was soon forced to tell his father that I was there and growing sicker by the hour. The physician on Quintay immediately had me quarantined in a remote part of the castle. But it was too late. By the time I was recovering, Guy had fallen ill."

"And he was already sickly."

"No, that's the irony. He'd been improving for a number of years. But the scarlet fever hit him hard and then worsened to rheumatic fever . . . and I was sent home in worse disgrace than you can possibly imagine. The earl was so distraught, he cut off all communication with my family, with this island. He held notes against my father and Dorcas's father—and he called them in. He banned all fishing, all commerce with St. Columba."

"Couldn't the laird have intervened on their behalf? You didn't intentionally carry sickness from the mainland." A thought occurred to her. "Or did the earl strike out at the laird as well?"

"The laird suffered with all the islanders." MacGuigan smiled grimly. "So you needn't wonder why I made myself scarce."

Maggie scuttled right up beside him and slid her arm around his shoulders. It was the comforting gesture of a friend, not of a lover. "And you feared I would have judged you as others have?"

"No one can judge me as harshly as I judge myself." He hissed in a sharp breath. "No, that's not true. I do care what you think . . ."

"I know that. I only wish you cared enough to . . . to . . ."

"What, Maggie, to let you stay here? How daft is that? I've no money, no prospects, not even a decent coat."

She nearly winced as she drew back; his words sounded so

final. "Once I told you about my scheme, I thought you might not be so eager to ship me off to Quintay."

"I never said I was eager. D'ye think I am so willing to give you up almost the instant I convinced myself you're not promised to the earl?"

Maggie was not heartened by this declaration; she saw now what Dorcas meant about a man who cared but would not come forward.

"But that doesn't mean I'm foolish—or selfish—enough to keep you here. I want you to get on with your life. And to do that, you'll need this—"

He'd taken the necklace from his coat pocket and set it in her hands before she knew what he was about. Maggie nearly dropped it. She'd never even touched it before, since Lady Fescue herself had placed it in Maggie's bag. It was heavy with the weight of the gold setting and the large stones—and with the weight of all the trouble it had so far caused.

"*No, MacGuigan*—" she cried softly, trying to thrust it back at him. "I don't want it."

He took her hand and folded her fingers tight around the gold links. "You need it to smooth things over with your employer. It's the only way I can guarantee you won't suffer for this misadventure."

She wasn't going to suffer, she promised herself. Chiefly because she had no intention of going to Quintay. Or back to Kilchoan, for that matter.

"And so what were you intending to do with me?" she baited him, barely keeping her anger in check. "Just put me ashore in Luray and blithely sail off? I . . . I swear you're no better than Og MacNeill."

He shook his head. "I intend to meet with the earl and tell him the truth. That I took the emeralds—which crime, incidentally, I have reason to believe he will overlook—but that I did not carry you off from the *Charles Stuart*."

"And what about holding me captive?" she drawled. "A bit tricky to put a nice veneer on that."

"As I said, I'll tell him the truth." His eyes traced over her face. "That I was instantly smitten with you—standing there covered with mud in Fingal's grave—and couldn't bear to let you go."

Maggie's heart soared. She might hear prettier compliments in her lifetime, but none so precious. "And *is* that the truth?" she managed to whisper.

He peered at her through his brows, his mouth curled into a wry smile. "What do you think?"

Maggie couldn't seem to form any words. To hide her confusion, she bundled the necklace and tucked it into the pocket of her gown. She'd deal with it later, once her brain was working again.

When she glanced up, he was still looking at her with that fierce, hungry light in his eyes.

She set her chin. "I observed once that you island men have trouble holding on to your women. It's no wonder, if you send them packing the instant things get sticky."

He hitched one shoulder. "We're a protective race."

"I don't wish to be protected. Especially when the danger is all in your head." She took up his hand, large and warm and rough, and said as calmly as she could, "Will you listen to me for two seconds? There's something I need to tell you. It's been burning a hole in my conscience . . ."

His eyes widened. "Don't tell me you really are Alice Fescue."

Maggie chuckled. "No, she is well out of our lives. This is something you've got to take on faith, because I can't explain it just yet. You do believe that I am not a liar or a fabricator of tales?"

He nodded.

"And so you must trust me when I say that there is no danger to you or the islanders from the earl. None today, none tomorrow, likely none ever. I know this for a fact."

"And I am not to ask how you know this?"

"No. I'm thinking you owe me this one gift . . . that for once you will suspend your disbelief."

He surprised her by saying, "Done. It is suspended. Partially because Fingal seems to be of a similar mind. He's rarely led me astray."

"Oh, and I have?"

"When haven't you?"

She pulled a face at him.

He leaned back on one elbow and drifted his hand down her

arm, stopping to let his fingers draw lazy circles on her wrist. "You know, I've never done this with you before . . ."

"What?"

One cheek narrowed. "Asked if I might kiss you."

Maggie's eyes flashed up to his face. "Not wise," she said quickly.

"To kiss you?"

"To ask. You know how balky I can get."

He slid his arm around her waist and tugged her closer. "Better to just do it?"

"Mmmm . . . don't give me any time to arg—"

He didn't.

He had her on her back, pinned down by the muscular weight of his upper body, and was kissing her senseless before she could come up with any argument against it. She was sandwiched between a slab of hard rock and a man's rock-hard body, and she'd never felt so delicious in her life. Even the Barkin emeralds gouging into her hip didn't trouble her. Nothing mattered beyond MacGuigan's hungry mouth, MacGuigan's urgent hands.

"Ah, Maggie," he sighed into her throat. "Bonny Maggie Bonner. What am I going to do with you?"

She thought what he was doing *to* her was rather fine. Especially when he drew the lace tucker away from her collarbone and proceeded to place tiny, nipping kisses along its entire length. His two days' worth of beard rasped against her skin in a such a stirring manner that she nearly rose up beneath him. He seemed to know exactly what to do to make her frantic for more.

He had reached the point of her shoulder, when she tipped his head back and asked playfully, "MacGuigan, just how many women *have* you ravished?"

"Plenty," he shot back, his eyes glittering.

"How many?"

He growled softly, trying to hold back a grin. "At least one or two."

"Hmmm . . ."

"What?" he coaxed, caressing the skin behind her ear until she shivered.

"I'm thinking it's more likely to have been the other way

round. My guess is that women hurl themselves at you and beg for your kisses."

He looked around the grotto and sighed. "And not a one of them here, alas. I suppose I'll have to make do with a sharp-tongued shrew."

She tugged his head down until their mouths were almost touching. "You will, indeed," she said, and then leaned up and smiled against his lips.

Chapter Twelve

*G*uy had a fair idea he'd returned to consciousness, but in spite of having his eyes open and most of his brain functioning, he knew he must still be asleep. He couldn't possibly be lying on a couch in the drawing room of Whitesands castle. The old relic had been closed up years ago. He looked around the large room and saw the holland covers on the few remaining pieces of furniture and the barren walls.

It's a dream, he told himself, one of those wretched dreams where you mistakenly think you're wide awake. If he *was* awake, then there had to be some explanation for the knife-sharp pounding inside his head.

Is this it? he mused bleakly.

Had his time come upon him and found him neither alert enough to fight back nor dazed enough to go under unresisting?

He closed his eyes and tried to turn his face into the cushion. The pounding grew worse, and a tiny groan rasped up from his chest. He instantly sensed a presence beside him; a cool hand drifted across his throbbing brow, a soft voice uttered his name.

"Guy?"

He felt his head being lifted gently and then tasted the acrid lip of a tin mug as it was pressed to his mouth. "Drink, Guy . . . just a sip . . . please."

He swallowed slowly, fearing that even that miniscule action would worsen his pain.

When he opened his eyes again, Dorcas MacGuigan's face, taut with concern, was the first thing he saw.

"*I'm dying . . .*" he managed to gasp.

She shook her head slowly. "No . . . you're going to be fine.

The whisky you drank was drugged. One of Og's infamous concoctions."

He stretched his mind back what seemed miles to Gulliver's bedroom. There was a silver flask . . . he was fighting with Dorcas . . . kissing Dorcas. Lord, it was such a jumble. He wished he could remember all the details of kissing her—it was the first time he'd ever overstepped his strict rules of conduct where she was concerned. Stupid rules, he thought now, ridiculous, idiotic rules. He did manage a fleeting recollection of how she'd tasted, of how her body had felt in his arms. It was enough to make a man weep, having experienced that bliss and knowing it could never be repeated.

She was watching him, her deep green eyes focused intently on his face. Worry had made her a little haggard, but she was still the most captivating woman he'd ever met, like a siren who'd left her sea palace behind.

She made him drink again, then asked him if he wanted to sit up. He was about to refuse, to explain about the crushing pain inside his head, when he realized it was gone. Completely gone.

He shifted his legs onto the floor and sat up quite on his own, sinking back into the corner of the couch. She rose and settled beside him, holding the mug clasped tight between her palms.

"Let me know when you feel fit enough to talk," she said a bit stiffly. "There's something you need to know—and I'm afraid it might come as a shock."

"Tell me," he said, canting his head back onto the cushion and looking at her over the rise of his long Faulkner nose. "I'm fairly shockproof at the moment."

"Two minutes ago you were dying," she reminded him with a touch of her usual spirit. She fiddled with the mug, then turned, and met his eyes. "It has to do with Miss Fescue."

"Has *she* finally turned up?" Then he grimaced, vexed over the disordered state of his brain. The chit wouldn't be here; she'd be in Luray.

"Wrong castle," he murmured. He cocked an eye at her. "We *are* in Whitesands, are we not?"

"Of course we are. Though I'm not surprised you don't recognize it . . . it was alive the last time you were here. Now there's nothing here but ghosts."

He reached for her hand, to stop her fretting with the mug and because he needed to touch her, to feel her warmth against his ice-cold skin. She grasped his fingers and he tightened his hold.

"About Miss Fescue—"

"Devil take Miss Fescue," he muttered. "I don't want to talk about her. Can't you just sit here with me like old times? That was all I needed for so many years . . . knowing you would be beside me, believing our friendship would go on forever."

"Those times are long past, Guy." Her voice sharpened as she slipped her hand from his. "Not to mention I was never that fond of being relegated to the role of friend."

He pushed away from the couch back and sat upright. "But you knew . . . you had to know . . . that it was all I could offer you."

"I did get that impression . . . eventually. What was it, Guy, my lack of rank or your perpetual illnesses?"

His brows meshed. "Your rank never entered into it. I'm hurt that you could even suspect such a thing."

"*You're* hurt?" she said. "I'm the one who spent nine years chasing after you, only to have you offer a virtual stranger the one thing you'd withheld from me."

"My name?"

"Your future," she whispered hoarsely.

His eyes widened. "I thought you understood. God, Dorcas, I was sure you knew why I never claimed you. I . . . I didn't want to hurt you, to make you suffer marriage to a man who was bound to leave you brokenhearted after so little time. My death probably won't faze Miss Fescue, any more than losing a chance-met acquaintance would. But I couldn't imagine putting you through such an ordeal."

She thrust up from the couch and spun to face him. "If you'd wed me when you came into the title, once you had some say over your own life, we'd already have had four years together. Just think on that. And here's another thing—did you believe I would mourn you any less for not being your wife? Bah!"—she wheeled away from him—"I don't know which is worse . . . callous men who boast they know nothing of a woman's heart or smug fellows who credit us with thoughts and emotions that are a million miles from how we really feel."

Guy stretched his hand out to her. "It was a mistake, Dorcas. There, are you satisfied? I made a mistake in London. Oh, it seemed reasonable enough at the time, finding myself a pleasant companion for my final days. For two years, I had subsisted on memories of you, everything we ever did together, every conversation—and argument—was my daily fare. But once I discovered I was living under a death sentence, I decided to put those memories behind me. I would make a new start, I told myself, for however brief a time I had left."

"I do understand that," she said a bit more gently. "I was the one who sailed away from you in anger and never tried to make things up. I had no right to blame you for moving on."

"But you *did* have the right," he said, "because I never did move on. Not truly. I was barely one day out of London when I realized I'd made a terrible blunder. Marrying the wrong woman was rapidly starting to seem as hellish as living without the right one." He rubbed his fisted hand against his forehead. "Not that any explanation can make up for my error. I've set this comedy in motion and I can't very well cry off now." He glanced up at her and said with a bitter laugh, "Do you know that when Og showed up in Luray and said there was some problem with my fiancée, I actually hoped he was going to tell me the chit had drowned?"

Dorcas appeared to bite back a smile. "I don't think she ever got that close to the water. I believe she was last seen heading inland."

Guy rose slowly to his feet. "Is that some sort of jest?"

Dorcas took a step closer, her eyes bright. "She ran off, Guy. Seven . . . eight days ago. Your little bird fancier apparently also fancied a militia captain in Kilchoan."

He stood there weaving, disconcerted that the pounding had started up again in his head. Only it wasn't his head; it was his heart that was thumping so loudly, almost jubilantly, inside him. That frail, damaged heart that had betrayed him all those years ago was now beating strong and steady, brimming with the force of life.

He reached for her, holding her by the shoulders, while he

studied her face. There was a scattering of tears on her lashes now, and nothing but joy in her eyes.

"Dorcas," he whispered. "Can you ever forgive me for being such a cloth-headed dolt?"

She sniffled. "If you can forgive me for being too proud to give you a second chance."

He enveloped her in his arms and heard her sigh as he settled with her on the couch. "I'd forgotten how strong I always feel around you. As though your own great energy and zest for life were somehow transferred to me. I only wish . . ."

"What? What is it?"

"I wish there were some way I could be strong for you. Gad, I am such a paltry fellow—"

"No," she cried, grasping him by the arms. "You are . . . you have always been my truest example of someone who soldiers on, no matter how bad things seem, no matter how frightening the circumstances. It goes beyond strength, Guy. It's courage and determination, ferocity—"

"Stubbornness," he added with a grin. "Remember, I'm the rat terrier."

"Well, there is that," she agreed, her eyes dancing. "But all those things I mentioned, they've not only been an example to me, but to Gulliver as well. If he hadn't seen and admired those traits in you when you were boys, I doubt he'd have been able to muster the strength and tenacity these past three years to keep St. Columba afloat." Her fingers tightened. "And he *has*, Guy. I don't care what you've heard, it's been positively awe-inspiring the way he's thrown himself into helping everyone."

"Including the drastic measure of selling most of the furnishings in this castle?"

She nodded. "Oh, I know . . . the laird wouldn't have approved, but Gulliver had no choice. Not if we were to eat and feed our livestock."

"You should have said something. We were still meeting on Quintay for almost a year after Gull came back from London. Why didn't you tell me how badly off you were?"

"You know Gulliver—he's got more than his share of pride. He was sure he could turn things around. And then you and I . . . parted. I wouldn't have dreamed of asking you after that.

And maybe Gulliver still felt too guilty over what had happened all those years ago to ask you for help."

"I wonder if Gulliver did write to me," he mused. "The note he left in Luray seemed to imply there had been other letters. Gad, is it possible Matchem destroyed them?"

"Not only possible. I would say quite likely."

Guy hated to acknowledge that such a thing could be true. Still, he had to admit his steward never missed an opportunity to point out Gulliver's misdeeds—first with stories of his infamies in London and then, once he was back on St. Columba, with dark tales of wrecking and sordid gossip about the parade of doxies coming over from the mainland. More recently, there had been dire warnings of his plans to revive the old custom of cattle raids. Matchem certainly seemed bent on painting MacGuigan in the worst possible light.

He frowned. "I still don't understand. Why should there be such longstanding enmity between the two of them?"

Dorcas took a deep breath and then said in a constricted voice, "Ned Matchem tried to rape me when I was fourteen. *That* was what he and Gulliver fought over."

Guy half rose from the couch, rage surging up from his gut and suffusing his face.

She clasped his arm and drew him down again. "I said he *tried*. I was none the worse for it, truly."

He touched one hand to her cheek. "Sweet Jesus, lass . . . why did you never tell me?"

"I wanted to forget it ever happened. Bad enough that Gulliver had made a bitter enemy of him."

"And yet you let me put my trust in Matchem for the past four years?"

"You always swore he served you honestly. I'm just not sure he treated anyone else to that virtue in the same measure."

He slipped one arm about her waist. "I'll make it up to you, see if I don't. You, Gulliver and the islanders. My investments keep doubling, though I rarely bother with them"—he chuckled softly—"maybe that's the secret. Anyway, there's plenty of gold for St. Columba. And you'll be relieved to know I'm done with my . . . crumbling statues and bits of old pots."

"I don't mind, truly. I know you enjoy collecting old things." She looked up into his face and smiled ruefully. "In fact, I've often wondered how old I'd have to be before you'd want to collect *me*."

"Not one day older, Dorcas. Not one second older."

He nuzzled her throat, then kissed her mouth softly, carefully.

It was very nice, Dorcas reflected, but she couldn't help recalling wistfully how he'd taken her at the cottage, all heat and haste and hot temper. She was wondering how to tell him that this gentle salute was fine for a friend, but that she preferred something a bit more impetuous, when he cursed under his breath.

The next instant he had bent her back and was kissing her deeply, his arms nearly crushing her. Dorcas responded with all the passion and hunger she'd held pent up for nine endless years.

"I will give you my future," he gasped against her throat. "And the protection of my name. No one will ever hurt you again."

He laid her back against the corner of the couch and rested his head upon her breast. When he spoke at last, his voice came out like a sigh. "I'll hold you and keep you for however long I have . . . and bless every day we can be together."

Dorcas brushed her lips over his hair. "I'm not worried. Those things I listed, your courage and tenacity, yes, and your stubbornness—they are what will keep you alive, Guy."

"And your love," he said.

"*And the water*," she added under her breath, certain beyond any normal logic that Maggie Bonner was right.

Chapter Thirteen

$\mathcal{M}$acGuigan had finally left off kissing Maggie. It had soon become obvious to both of them that a slab of granite was not conducive to a comfortable ravishment, not if one valued elbows and knees and hipbones. Still, they had managed to engage in some skillful maneuvering that had left Maggie breathless, if a bit bruised. MacGuigan was again canted back on one elbow, watching her with bright eyes, while a tiny smile played along the edges of his mouth.

"Not bad for a woman who's never been kissed," he said, toying with the lace on her cuff.

She chuckled softly. "I think I've made up for lost time this past week." She added with a sly look, "I should thank you for schooling me."

He winced theatrically. "Lord, I was beastly to you that first day."

"That was Maggie the drudge," she said. "You've been rather splendid with Marguerite."

"Ah, Marguerite," he echoed. *"La bonne Marguerite Bonheur."* He reached out to trail his fingers along her collarbone, which still bore the faint marks of his amorous assault. "So tell me about Mademoiselle Bonheur," he purred. "She sounds like a woman with a very mysterious past."

Maggie's mouth twisted. "She was just a girl who traveled across England with Harry Topping's Top-Rate Players. Her mother was the daughter of a solicitor who ran off with a dashing French actor."

"The world well lost for love, eh?"

"Love and a lot of greasepaint and shabby boarding houses, I'm afraid."

"And you hated it?"

"I adored it. Dorcas told me that sailing was the freest thing she knew. I used to think while I was with the Fescues, that my childhood was the freest thing I'd ever know. And then I came here."

His smile faded slightly. "Freedom often has a high price, Maggie."

"I know that. My parents paid dearly for the life they chose. They gave up family and comforts. My father especially. His own father had some remote connection to the Comte de la Toureville Fantin and acted as his steward. Papa was raised with the comte's own sons. When he was eighteen, he went to Paris and became an actor in the *Comédie-Française*. But when the Terror started, and his connection to the comte put him at risk, he fled to England and joined a band of traveling players."

"And did you ever think of going on the stage yourself?"

Her brows rose. "Mama would never have allowed it. As a child I was sometimes called on to perform. I played Puck in a very indifferent version of *Midsummer Night's Dream*. But once I put my hair up, she made sure my behavior was beyond reproach."

"She had aspirations for you, then."

"Doesn't every parent? Frankly, I think she was a bit naive . . . what gentleman would want a wife who'd been traipsing around England for sixteen years? Anyway, after she died, my father gave up acting to become Lady Ashcroft's librarian. That led to Lady Fescue hiring me as her daughter's companion."

"I take it Lady Fescue knew nothing of your past."

Maggie shuddered. "Good heavens, no. I was plain old Maggie Bonner by then."

He said slyly, "Ah, but you did happen to mention your father's connection to the comte."

Her smile was impish. "Of course. Mama always said you need to use every little scrap to make a decent quilt."

"You do indeed. Though I often think it would be nice to have a blanket made of whole cloth . . . not something piecemeal. At times I grow so weary of this piecemeal life, Maggie."

He looked down at his shabby clothing, clean and pressed, but equally darned and patched. Her own dress was not much better, faded and let out a half dozen times.

She took his hand. "We may be in motley, Gulliver, but our hearts are of whole cloth. That has to be worth something."

His fingers gripped hers tightly as he drew her closer. "It's everything, Maggie. Everything in the world." His voice softened. "I think that's the first time you've ever called me by name."

"Gulliver," she said again, just to see him smile.

"And you would throw in your lot with this great oafish fellow and not mind toiling and starving and living on this barren rock?"

"I would." She leaned forward and kissed him gently, on one cheek and then the other. "But it's not barren. And maybe it could even be prosperous if you would only consider my plans for your spring."

He fetched a heavy sigh. "Very well, let's suppose you are right about its healing properties. Then what? How does the island benefit?"

Lord help her, he was such a dear dunderhead.

"You lived in London; you saw how the excesses of the gentry played havoc with their health. Gout, dropsy . . . a whole slew of ailments. And what do these wealthy sufferers do when their pleasures are finally curtailed? They go to a spa, like Bath or Harrogate." She paused dramatically. "Or St. Columba."

A slow, canny smile dawned on his face. "And I assume they pay well for their time in such places, whether they are cured or not."

"Plenty of people return from Bath without a trace of bodily improvement. But their spirits are lifted." She tweaked his hair. "Everyone benefits from a rest cure, you know."

"Even you?"

Maggie laughed softly. "Especially me."

He stretched back on the rock and crossed his arms behind his head. "Let me think on this a while."

She sprawled over his chest, her fingers toying with the folds of his neck cloth. "You think . . . I'm going to kiss your throat."

His hands stole to her waist. "I doubt there's a man born

who can think clearly while a green-eyed woman is kissing
his—"

A thunderous *ka-boom!* shattered the air above them, rever-
berating through the hills.

They both stilled for a heartbeat, then MacGuigan leapt to
his feet, dragging Maggie with him. Up out of the glen they ran
without a word, up into the open where they could see the bay.

A three-masted ship was cruising just off the castle promontory. Another *ka-boom* split the air, and a puff of smoke rose up
from one of the cannon ports.

Maggie let out a long, shivery cry. "They're firing on the
castle . . . and Dorcas and Guy are inside!"

MacGuigan whirled around and grabbed her by the shoulders. "What did you say?"

"The earl's here on the island," she explained rapidly. "He
came to rescue Alice—he sneaked into your cottage late last
night and I . . . I hit him on the head. Dorcas has been tending
him." She clutched at his waistcoat. "But we didn't want you to
thrust your great bullish head into things, MacGuigan. They
needed time to sort it out themselves."

He stood there blank-faced for several moments, processing
what she'd just told him.

She was trembling so badly she could barely stand. "I'm
sorry," she cried weakly. "I told you no harm could come to St.
Columba."

His hold on her eased. "It's all right. The ship's not firing on
Whitesands; she's sending out warning shots."

Maggie had no clue how he could be so sure of that. And
who on earth had ordered the earl's ship to frighten the village?

"Still," he said under his breath. "I don't much care for gunships sailing into my harbor."

"This is madness. . . . Who would do such a thing?"

"I have a pretty fair idea."

He went striding back to where they'd left the horses. Maggie stumbled after him, still in shock. He was shrugging on his
greatcoat as he said, "Look, Maggie, you've got to promise me
that you'll stay here."

"No!"

He mounted his hunter and caught up her pony's reins. "I

don't want you down there if it comes to any sort of fighting. Promise me—"

She must have nodded, because he was riding away, dragging her pony behind him.

Finally her wits cleared, and she went racing after him up the incline. "MacGuigan!" she shouted. *"Gulliver!"*

When he didn't stop, she bellowed out, *"Ca-a-d-mus!"*

He reined in and waited stony-faced as she came panting up to him.

"Who told you that?"

She grimaced. "Your cousin."

"I'm going to kill her, see if I don't. Cannonballs will be too good for the minx. Now, what is it? I am a bit pressed for time."

She latched onto his boot with both hands. "Suppose something terrible happens to you down there."

He reached out to cup her chin. "If the worst happens, then you'll just have to cart me back up here and toss me into that blasted spring."

She smiled swiftly, but then her panic returned. "You can't leave me. It's inhuman. Just think how you'd feel if the tables were turned?"

He paused a moment, his mouth pursed, and then handed over the pony's reins. "You've made your point. I would hate it like the devil."

Maggie didn't spare a moment to savor this rare victory. She mounted and set off behind MacGuigan, determined—yet again—to keep up.

A longboat from the gunship had drawn up at the wharf by the time they rode into the village, and a dozen armed sailors were now streaming up onto the High Street. A throng of villagers, alarm written clear on their faces, had already gathered there.

When she and MacGuigan reached the front of Dorcas's house, he pulled up and flung himself off his horse.

"Stay here," he ordered, before moving swiftly forward to confront the tall, russet-haired man who was forming the sailors into ranks.

"Matchem!" he called out. "You'd better have a first-rate explanation for this outrage."

Maggie's head reared up in surprise. There was no mistaking his lordship's steward—strapping and fleshily handsome, his looks somewhat marred by a jutting, oversized jaw, which reminded her of a wooden marionette. She hadn't liked the man when she'd met him in Kilchoan and was even less disposed to like him now.

Matchem didn't bother to answer MacGuigan; instead, he swung his arm up, mustering the sailors behind him. "Take him!" he cried.

The instant the men swarmed toward MacGuigan, the villagers rushed forward—and a melee quickly ensued. Bodies clashed on the cobbled street in a tangle of flailing limbs punctuated by the sound of thumping blows and sharp, guttural grunts.

Maggie watched anxiously from atop the pony, gnawing at her knuckles. Though by the look of things, twelve sailors and one oily overseer were no match for MacGuigan and the islanders.

Gulliver had been itching for a fight for days now, and he'd finally got his wish. He laid about him with his fists, knocking aside a man swinging a rifle and clouting another on the side of his head. Thank God the sailors were not firing their weapons, especially since his villagers—both men and women—had leapt into the fray with great gusto. Gulliver had lost Neddie Matchem in the confusion and continued to push his way through the tangle of heaving bodies in search of him.

He'd no sooner caught up with Matchem and got him by the throat, when a booming gunshot reverberated above their heads.

"Give over!" a voice commanded. "I order you to give over this instant!"

Gulliver looked up.

Guy Faulkner was standing on the stone seawall, the butt of a shotgun resting on his hip. At his feet stood a white-faced Dorcas and beside her, looking as though he wanted to knock a few heads together himself, was Fingal MacNeill.

At the earl's words, the sailors eased back from the villagers.

Guy leapt down from the wall and handed the gun to Fingal.

With a curt nod, he ordered the sailors back to the longboat, then strode toward Matchem with blue fire in his eyes.

"What in God's name are you doing here?"

The man squared his shoulders and smoothed down the front of his waistcoat. "I came here to rescue you, my lord."

"Rescue me from what?"

Matchem jerked his prodigious chin toward Gulliver. "From him. When I arrived in Luray last night, I was told you had disappeared. Then this morning, the head footman informed me that this . . . knave had been skulking around the castle yesterday. Not only that, Og MacNeill's ship was seen leaving the harbor last night. I feared they had carried you off."

Guy rolled his eyes. "I sailed over with Og quite voluntarily. There was no abduction."

"You can't blame me, sir, for thinking the worst of this ruffian." He glared at Gulliver.

But Gulliver wasn't attending him; he was looking at Guy. In spite of the bandage on his head and his unnatural pallor, there was a gleam of combativeness in his eyes that enlivened his whole face. Gulliver brushed past Matchem and went up to him.

"Well met, my lord," he said, holding out one hand.

Guy looked at it warily but did not take it. Gulliver feared a rebuff, but instead the earl set his hands on Gulliver's shoulders and smiled. "It's just like the old days—you in the thick of a fight and me trying to save your bacon. I . . . I've missed those times, Gull."

Matchem thrust forward. "But, sir! You cannot seriously be encouraging this scoundrel."

The earl turned, raking him with his glance. "We need to have a few words, you and I. For one thing, I'd like to know who's been filling your head with slanders against this man? I'd guess it was Og, if I didn't know that what little loyalty he possesses is given to the MacGuigans."

"Hardly slanders," Matchem hissed. "Do you doubt the word of the captains whose ships were destroyed and looted on this island? And as for Og, his loyalty may be to MacGuigan, yet I've heard him in his cups at the Balefire . . . complaining about his master's cruelty and vice."

Gulliver nearly laughed. Og never could resist putting on a willing subject.

"Everyone knows Og MacNeill's dicked in the nob," the earl pronounced. There was a deal of head nodding from the villagers and a muttered oath from Fingal. "For one thing, he told me Miss Fescue had been abducted from his ship."

Ned Matchem smiled slowly, and Gulliver felt a jolt when he said, "Then he truly is demented, because Miss Fescue is in Kilchoan awaiting passage to Quintay."

"No!" Guy and Dorcas cried at the same instant.

Matchem shrugged. "I saw her myself yesterday, nearly re-covered from a bout of influenza."

"And before that?" the earl queried sharply. "What about earlier in the week?"

"I never actually met her when I arrived in Kilchoan. Lady Fescue sent me off directly to recover a piece of missing luggage."

The earl took a step closer to his steward and gripped his arm. "We were told the young lady ran off with a militia man a week ago."

Matchem's head reared back. "According to whom?"

Dorcas spoke up. "Miss Fescue's companion was, er, way-laid here. She told us."

"Ah, Lady Fescue warned me that Miss Bonner might have tried to stir up some trouble. The girl was about to be dismissed from her post and must have got the wind up."

"Then why did Lady Fescue entrust her with the necklace?" Gulliver asked.

"Yes, why was Miss Bonner even carrying the necklace," Dorcas put in, "if there was no reason to return it to his lord-ship?"

Matchem did not appear discommoded by these rapid-fire questions. "Lady Fescue sent the girl ahead to inform the earl that his intended was ailing and would be delayed. Her ladyship decided it would be prudent to let her transport the necklace. No one would ever suspect that such a . . . dowdy creature might be carrying a fortune in gems."

He's been coached, Gulliver thought, seething. Coached and schooled by Maggie's scheming employer. He almost had to give Lady Fescue some credit; her daughter had clearly been caught and brought to heel, and now the woman was doing her best to turn a flat-out defeat into a stunning victory.

He urgently scanned the crowd, trying to find Maggie in their midst. She'd soon set this all to rights.

Matchem cocked his head. "I gather, my lord, that Miss Bonner never reached Quintay."

The earl's eyes flicked to Gulliver. "She met with a mishap and, as Miss MacGuigan said, was waylaid here."

"I abducted her," Gulliver said bluntly. "And took the emeralds from her." He grinned wickedly at Matchem. "Just more capital crimes you can add to my list, Neddie."

Dorcas caught Gulliver's hand and pulled him aside. "Where *is* Maggie, Gull?"

"She rode into the village with me, but I've not seen her since." He glanced again to the spot where he'd left her. His uncle's aged hunter was drowsing in the sun, now that all the fireworks had calmed down, but Maggie and the pony were gone.

"Yes, where is the chit?" Matchem said silkily. "Let's see what she has to say for herself."

"She's around somewhere," Gulliver said. She *had* to be.

"And where are the emeralds?" Matchem raised one brow. "Not with Miss Bonner by any chance?"

"They're in a safe place," Gulliver shot back.

Dorcas wilted against the earl, who drew an arm around her. "It's going to be all right, sweetheart," he said softly. "Miss Bonner had no reason to lie."

"Lie?" Matchem sneered. "She's been lying to Lady Fescue for years, never once told her about her sordid past as an actress in a troupe of traveling players. But Alice Fescue recently got the truth out of her . . . and told her mama like a dutiful daughter. They were only waiting until this journey was over to send the girl packing."

Damn. Gulliver had to admit the fellow was good. Calm, convincing—wise enough to have left the Fescue women behind, since it was always less risky for one person to commit perjury than a whole group.

Gulliver was determined to shake Matchem out of his sangfroid. He'd seen the look that passed between Dorcas and Guy, one of forlorn hope. He knew it was up to him to protect

the frail new bond between these two people he cared for. And
to further preserve the good name of the woman he was coming to love.

"I gather Miss Fescue's been returned to her mother's keeping," he said, moving to stand directly before Matchem. "What
I'm wondering is how much gold Lady Fescue offered you to
cover up her daughter's flight so that the marriage could go forward as planned?"

Matchem drew himself up. "I don't need gold. The earl sees
to me very well."

Gulliver smiled tightly. "And when he doesn't see to you,
you put your own hand in the pot."

The steward's face darkened. But before he could speak,
Dorcas interjected urgently, "There will be witnesses at the inn
in Kilchoan. People who knew Miss Fescue slipped away.
Chambermaids . . . ostlers . . . Lady Fescue's servants. Someone had to know."

Ned Matchem shook his head. "Ah, but the young lady was
sick in bed with only her mother tending her. Though now she's
fit and ready to come to her bridegroom."

"Then why didn't you bring her back with you last night?"
Gulliver said. "I'll tell you why—because you needed to come
here first and pave the way with your own lies. Ah, but the earl
was gone and you had no audience for your trumped-up tale.
You had a bride, but no bridegroom. How fortunate for you that
your pet snoop, Woodbine, saw me at the castle and so sent you
here. I wasn't skulking, however; I went there bold as daylight
to see the earl. Oh, I also happened to run into an old acquaintance, Brian Rennie." He watched Matchem's cheeks narrow.
"We had a rather interesting talk, he and I. It's not surprising
you say you don't need bribe money from Lady Fescue, Neddie . . . not when you've been helping yourself to the earl's gold
these past four years."

Matchem flung himself at Gulliver, wrapped his hands
around his throat. The earl and Fingal quickly pulled him back.

"That's a filthy lie!" he raged, struggling to get free. "Rennie is a drunken lout."

"He was sober enough the night he saw you selling pilfered
silver plate at the wharf in Luray."

The earl tightened his hold. "You told me it was Wat Dickens stole the silver."

"It was," Matchem gasped. He was starting to sweat now.

"And," Gulliver continued inexorably, "Rennie also happens to know you've been reselling the earl's grain—for a tidy profit."

"Now who's speaking slander?" Matchem cried. "I won't stand here and be accused by a filthy, lying freebooter."

Guy caught him by the shoulder. "Will you stand and be accused by your own master, Ned Matchem?" He leaned in close and whispered something into his ear.

Matchem blanched, and then sputtered, "It was a silly misunderstanding . . . I meant nothing by it. Good God, I was a only a lad."

"Tell that to Miss MacGuigan," came the earl's clipped whisper.

Matchem's gaze darted to the faces surrounding him. "Don't you be judging me, ye pack of sorry sheep." He spun to the earl. "And that goes for you, too, ye pitiful worm. A man who doesn't tend to his property deserves to lose it. Taking money from you was child's play."

The earl's mouth grew taut. "I believe it would be best if you went back to Quintay and collected your things," he said softly. "If you leave quietly, I won't press charges against you."

"Go ahead and dismiss me," Matchem muttered. "It won't change anything. I'll still have the better of you all. Miss Fescue will be here in a matter of days for her wedding"—he looked right at Dorcas and sneered, then swung his overbright gaze to the earl—"And you, my fine lord, will be dead before the first harvest."

Gulliver leapt forward to strike him, but the earl got there first, sending him reeling backward with a neatly placed jab.

Matchem's gaze speared Guy as he swiped at his bloodied mouth. "You don't have a prayer. And as for you, MacGuigan," he snarled softly. "It's still not finished between us. Not yet."

"Just go," Gulliver said, battling to hold his temper in check. "Get off my island."

The crowd parted as Matchem stalked off toward the wharf. Once he was gone, Guy gripped Gulliver's arm. "I . . . I don't quite know what to say. 'I'm sorry' doesn't begin to do justice to my feelings. I was a fool to believe him."

Gulliver shook his head. "Dorcas and I were both fools for not telling you what we knew of the man's character."

The earl leaned in closer. "And are you certain that this Maggie Bonner was telling the truth about Miss Fescue running away? I find I suddenly have no wish to marry her, but a gentleman can't very well cry off."

Gulliver clapped him on the shoulder. "Take a leaf from my book, Guy. Pretend you're not a gentleman for a day or two. Write to the girl and tell her you've had a change of heart."

"I haven't." His gaze slid to Dorcas—and softened noticeably. "My heart's never strayed from your cousin."

"Then I wish you joy of her. There's nothing like a head-strong woman to keep a man properly humble."

"Speaking of headstrong women," Dorcas muttered fret-fully, "where did Maggie go?"

Gulliver rubbed at the back of his neck. "I'm dashed if I know. It's like the earth swallowed her up."

"P'raps Miss Bonner was a selkie," said Fingal with a sly wink. "Gone back to her home in the sea now that she's worked her magic here."

"She'd hardly take the pony with her," Gulliver drawled.

Still, a sharp pang of worry was twisting his gut. What if she really had gone away? Sneaked onto the gunship somehow, or ridden off to Cranlochie to find passage to the mainland? He'd given her the emeralds—and the possibility of a worry-free existence for herself and her ailing father.

No, he reminded himself, she'd been battling him to stay right here. She'd even promised to throw in her lot with him. He trusted her . . . more, he realized, than he'd ever trusted anyone.

But where the devil had she gone?

Chapter Fourteen

*O*nce Maggie had seen MacGuigan and the earl make their peace—and further, seen the earl place his arm protectively around Dorcas's shoulder—she knew everything was going to work out. The feud was over, the lovers were reunited and the two islands would once again dwell in harmony. All that remained was for her to return the emerald necklace to Lord Barkin, and then she and MacGuigan could begin to plan St. Columba's future.

She felt in her pocket for the necklace . . . and pulled out a crumpled handkerchief. She reached in again, pushing aside the folds of her gown, digging her fingers deep into the bottom of the fabric pouch.

The necklace was gone.

Fighting off her panic, she tried to recall where she might have dropped it. During their frantic ride down from the hills? Or perhaps on the rock beside the pool, where she'd engaged in some strenuous acrobatics with MacGuigan? Wherever it had fallen, she absolutely had to find it. She'd already lost the wretched thing once.

Her gaze shifted to the crowd by the seawall. Mr. Matchem was speaking to the earl and every soul, including MacGuigan, was attending him. There was a chance she could find the necklace and return before anyone noticed she was gone. She turned her pony and walked him out of the village, keeping her eyes fastened on the ground. She was sure she would see it—the sun overhead would be striking sparks of light off the golden links.

She tried to retrace the exact route they'd taken earlier as she rode across the pasture and up the hill path. At the mouth of the alpine valley she turned to look at the village. The gunship was sailing out of the harbor, and most of the crowd on the High Street had dispersed. She thought she could make out Gulliver and his cousin walking with the earl toward Dorcas's house. She wondered if they'd even missed her in all the excitement.

She followed along the high trail, dismounting every so often to investigate the occasional bracken that edged the path, in case the necklace had fallen into a patch of weeds.

On and on she rode, until her eyes itched and her head ached from probing the ground so intently.

A pox on that necklace! He should never have given it to her—she was cursed. She lost gloves and genteel positions. She fell into holes and into love with overbearing, conscience-riddled men.

She was almost delirious with worry by the time the pony climbed up the scree on the last hill before the meadow. If it wasn't by the pool, she didn't know how she could face MacGuigan or the earl. She'd wanted to prove to Gulliver that she was capable and clever, a worthy partner. Losing the one thing he'd entrusted to her was not a stellar beginning.

The pony made its careful way down into the glen, and as they neared the bottom, her heart sank. There was nothing lying beside the pool except the basket and a few crumpled napkins. She slid to the ground beside the flat rock, then went down on her knees and crawled around it. All she found were some damp patches of moss.

She shifted onto the rock and sat gazing numbly at the water, praying to St. Columba for another miracle. She waited and prayed, half expecting the necklace to levitate before her eyes. Finally, she gave up. Even saints could only do so much.

All that remained now was to ride back to the village and admit defeat. She'd ask MacGuigan to form a search party; maybe one of the villagers would be able to find the blasted thing—unless it had fallen from her pocket while she'd been galloping on the trail above the bog. That hadn't occurred to her before, that the jewels might have tumbled down the cliff and into a quagmire.

She set her hands over her face. How this could have happened now, just when everything seemed to be working out so neatly? The tears started up, the first time she'd cried since she'd been left on the beach of Withy Cove in a drugged stupor. In spite of all she'd endured over the past five days, she had never once resorted to weeping. This wasn't a disaster of such monumental proportions, she reminded herself. No one had died, after all. So why was she stretched out, sobbing, on a rock?

Maybe it was the same phenomenon that Dorcas had experienced when she discovered the earl was free of Alice Fescue. Maggie could finally let all her tangled emotions—the fear and anger and frustration, the giddiness and wonder and joy of self-discovery—come pouring out. Because, in the end, everything was going to be just fine. Dorcas had her earl, Maggie had MacGuigan and the people of St. Columba had their miraculous spring. One lost family heirloom wasn't going to change that.

She gave a few final sniffles, blotting her face with one of the napkins, then leaned over the edge of the pool to scoop up a handful of water to ease her swollen throat.

The Barkin emeralds lay there under a foot of clear water—wavering before her eyes like a desert mirage.

Maggie gave a crow of victory as she pushed up her sleeve and thrust her hand into the pool. The necklace came up shimmering, as fine as any pirate's booty plucked from the briny deep. She quickly dried it off with the napkin—she almost kissed it, she was that relieved. Instead of returning it to her treacherous pocket, she fastened it around her neck, arranging it beneath her tucker. She vowed she would ride back to the village with one hand on the center stone the entire time.

When she heard the pony nicker, she didn't think anything of it. She finished gathering up the remains of their picnic and was just getting to her feet when she heard the sound of boot-steps approaching on the hard scree beyond the glen. Not MacGuigan; he'd have come up on horseback.

Some primal instinct made her hurry to the drop-off. She tossed the basket into the gulf, then climbed gingerly over the edge and wedged herself between two tumbled boulders, clinging to an ancient, weathered vine.

Of course, she'd forgotten about the pony.

She watched, wide-eyed, as Mr. Matchem came down the passage into the glen, carrying a large, bulky rucksack over one shoulder. He went right up to the pony, grabbed at the reins, and then called out, "Hallo! Who's here?"

Maggie shut her eyes—a reflex left over from childhood that insisted that if you couldn't see someone, they couldn't see you.

What was *he* doing up here? Was he possibly part of a search party sent to find her? That seemed unlikely; he was the last man MacGuigan would have enlisted.

He called out several more times, then scouted the area, but never came close enough to the drop-off to spot her. She heard him moving off, and when she finally steeled herself to peep over the edge, she saw him standing at the opposite side of the pool, gazing up at the outcropping that thrust out over the water. He began climbing, hand over hand, up the jagged rocks that led to the top of the ledge. Once he'd pulled himself up onto the shelf, he moved to the center of the space, then knelt down and took a small keg and several tools from his rucksack.

The loud *thwang* went right through her as he set a chisel and hammered it against the granite surface. Again and again he struck.

Sick fear rose up from her belly the instant she realized what he was doing. She heard the words MacGuigan had spoken that morning: *If the spring were to dry up, the island would have only rain water to sustain it.*

God in heaven, the man couldn't be that heartless, to take away the island's only source of water. But she also knew that if Ned Matchem wanted to strike at MacGuigan, there was no better way than through the people he cared for.

She was wracking her brain for some way to stop him or some way she could escape and warn Gulliver, when the vine she was clinging to gave way with a brittle crack. Barely stifling a cry of terror, she grabbed onto the hard, cutting surface of the rock and dug her toes into the nearest crevice.

Surely Matchem had heard her, but he continued on with his task, not even looking up. He'd finished gouging a hole in the ledge and was now doing something with the cask.

It was gunpowder, she knew, from the earl's gunship. How ironic that Lord Barkin would unwittingly be responsible for this calamity, one that would wipe out the island more surely than any trade embargo.

She inched her way up from the chasm; while he was distracted she intended to make a run for it. Once she got the pony out of the glen, he'd never be able to catch her. She crept along the pool and had just gotten hold of the pony's reins when Ned Matchem stood up.

"I was wondering when you'd come out of hiding," he called down to her. "Ah, Miss Bonner, is it? You've no idea the trouble you have caused me. Lady Fescue is not going to be happy."

Maggie hadn't a clue what he was talking about. Not that she cared. She had one foot in the stirrup, when he pulled a long-barreled pistol from his waistcoat.

"Not wise," he said, holding the pistol straight out and taking aim. "I suggest you move away from the beast."

Maggie stayed behind the pony, praying the fiend wouldn't shoot the poor animal.

He gave a muffled growl as he strode across the ledge and came clambering down to the level of the pool, somehow managing to keep the pistol trained on her.

She tried to run as he approached her, but he got her by the hair and dragged her roughly to the edge of the water.

She had a pretty fair comparison now of what it was like to tangle with a man who didn't care if he hurt her, as opposed to her run-ins with MacGuigan, who had manhandled her but never yanked at her hair hard enough to make her eyes tear. She was flailing at Matchem as he thrust her down onto the hard stone.

"Unlace your boots," he ordered.

"What?"

He rapped the side of his gun sharply against her head. "Just do it. I've a mind to make you suffer a little before I dispatch you."

With numb fingers she undid her laces and held them out to him.

He knelt down then and tied her hands together behind her, drawing the leather thong tight around her wrists before he knotted it. He did the same with her ankles.

"Now," he said as he rose. "If you can manage to wriggle over the edge of the drop-off, you might find it a less painful death than waiting for that ledge to fly apart."

She sneered. "Your paltry keg of gunpowder isn't going to budge that ledge."

He smiled, his great chin moving forward so that his face appeared almost grotesque. "It's all a matter of science, Miss Bonner. You find the spot where the stress cracks run through the stone, and it's as easy as breaking off the scored neck of a wine bottle. Besides, I've been blasting rock to make acreage for his lordship's nurseries these past four years. This is all in a day's work for me."

She watched helplessly as he climbed back to the ledge. The leather laces were cutting into her skin, leaving her with little feeling in her hands or feet. There was a slim chance she could throw herself over the pony's back like a sack of grain and pray that he'd carry her away from here. Before she could struggle to her feet and try it, however, Ned Matchem had come down from the outcropping.

"It won't be long now," he said with an encouraging smile as he caught the pony and mounted it. "And I should thank you for bringing me the means to a speedy exit."

He clapped his bootheels against the pony's side—and the beast leapt away with his customary dispatch.

Ned Matchem, caught unawares, flew backward over the pony's hindquarters and landed on his head, striking the hard granite ground with a sickening *thunk.* The pony kept on going, clattering up and out of the glen.

Maggie wriggled closer, watching with horror as blood began to seep out from under his hair. She had a very strong inkling he was dead. As she would soon be if she didn't get away before his charges ignited.

She was just steeling herself for rifling through his waistcoat with her teeth, hoping he had some sort of knife on him, when another set of footsteps sounded from above. She looked up.

MacGuigan was coming down the passage, dusting himself off.

"That damn pony," he was muttering, "ran right into my horse and scared him nearly off the trail. Blasted beast threw me. It's lucky I escaped with my—*Oh, Jesus!*" He came toward her at a run and dragged her away from Matchem.

"You must get away, Gulliver!" she cried. "He set a charge up on the ledge. . . . It's going to explode."

He looked up quickly, then down at Matchem. Kneeling, he thrust his hand against the man's throat. He shook his head. "What the devil did you hit him with?"

"I didn't hit him," she moaned. "He fell off Dorcas's pony. But that hardly matters. That whole ledge is going to be flying to bits any time now."

He fiddled at her wrists, trying to untie the boot laces, and then cursed. "They're knotted too tight, and hang me but I haven't got a knife. That's usually your department, Miss Bonner."

"Don't be making jokes," she wailed.

He scooped her up, but she started to wriggle. "No!" She was almost in tears now. "You can't run if you're carrying me. Just leave me here. . . . Oh, please, Gulliver, I couldn't bear it if you died."

"And you think I don't feel the same way about you?" He was carrying her, not toward the passage, but to the pool, where he set her down in the shallow water.

"Just a minute," he said, stroking the hair away from her face.

"We may not have a minute."

"So you don't think I should climb up there and try to defuse his charges?"

"There isn't time." She looked up at him and pleaded. "If you care for me, you will go. There's no point in both of us dying."

"No, there is not," he said as he lifted her from the pool. He easily slipped the laces from around her wrists and reached down to tug them off her ankles.

"It's a miracle," she breathed.

He leaned down and kissed her swiftly. "Leather stretches when it's wet, Maggie. Now, come on."

He raised her to her feet and coaxed her toward the passage.

"Go on ahead," she urged him. "I'll be right behind you."

The truth was, she could barely walk. She still had little sensation in her feet, and without the laces on her half boots, she feared to stumble and slide right back down into the glen.

When he turned and saw her wincing steps, he heaved her over his shoulder and then scrambled up the remainder of the incline.

They were out on the scree surface now, treacherous footing at the best of times. He was making his way toward the lower, gorse-covered slope, when the glen behind them exploded with a thunderous roar. A plume of dark gray smoke roiled up from the opening, peppered with chunks of flying granite.

MacGuigan threw her down and covered her with his body, and seconds later, as the ground beneath them continued to rumble ominously, he leapt up again.

"Can you run?" he cried.

She plucked off her half boots and scrambled to her feet. "I can now."

"Then run like hell, Maggie. That explosion's about to bring half the mountain down upon us."

He caught her arm and dragged her straight down the slope, turning only when they came to the trail. "Into the meadow," he panted.

Small rocks were clattering past them now, bits of scree and larger shards of shale. They were fifty feet from the spot where mountain gave way to meadow when she dared to look back.

Several tons of rock were tumbling down the side of the peak above them, the landslide gathering momentum as it picked up more and more granite debris. A great cloud of dust rose above it, like the spray above a surging waterfall.

"Not the meadow!" she cried. "There's no cover there."

"Trust me," he said, propelling her forward again. She knew he could easily have outstripped her, but he stayed at her side, setting an arm around her waist and practically carrying her whenever she flagged.

They were onto level grass when the first of the larger rocks came bounding down around them. Maggie felt a sudden surge of energy, as though she could fly if she needed to. She was even with MacGuigan now, no, she was pulling a little ahead, when he caught her in the crook of his arm, and the next instant they were airborne, locked together and falling.

They landed with a jarring thud at the bottom of Fingal Mac-Neill's grave. MacGuigan immediately thrust her up against the wall and sprawled over her, both hands capping her head.

"I love you, Maggie Bonner," he whispered hoarsely against her shoulder. "If those are the last words I ever say, I will have spoken my heart."

The roaring of the landslide reached them then, booming like a terrible storm, full of thundering and clashing and the awful, awesome sound of great, weighty bodies in rapid motion.

Whether it was luck or the surface dynamics of the meadow—or the sanctity of Fingal MacNeill's grave—the larger rocks bypassed them. A great shower of debris fell upon MacGuigan's shoulders and a few apple-sized stones battered the inner sides of the grave, but when the dust finally settled and the roaring ceased, they were both relatively unharmed.

He dug her out of the shale and, as he had done before, boosted her onto the grass. Only there was little grass to be seen in their immediate vicinity. The peak had deposited its detritus well into the opening of the meadow, in a sloping pile of slag and soil that rose to ten feet at the base of the hill. Maggie crouched amid the scattered rocks, coughing and trembling, trying not to cry. MacGuigan took her in his arms and rocked her.

"We're alive, sweetheart," he crooned.

She reached up and gently wiped a trickle of blood from his cheek. "I would have died if you hadn't found me."

His eyes held hers for an instant. "You're too wicked to die so young. We've got that in common."

"How did you find me?"

"Fabian tracked you down. I told you chasing runaways was his favorite sport."

"Oh, Fabian!" she cried. "In the explosion."

He shook her gently. "It's all right. He went bounding off after my horse, who was chasing your pony. All three of them are probably halfway to the village by now. Which means we'll have to walk out of here on foot."

He looked down at her stockinged feet, then slid back into the pit to find her buried boots. Once he'd unearthed them, he handed them up to her but stayed where he was, gazing about him. "Looks like we'll need to dig out Fingal's grave—again," he said.

"Not for some time yet," she said hopefully. "He'll have bairns to look forward to now."

MacGuigan cocked one eye at her. "How very indelicate of you, Miss Bonner. I haven't even proposed yet."

Maggie refused to blush. "I was referring to Dorcas and the earl."

He was grinning as he climbed up and settled beside her. He helped her put on her boots, his fingers warm and so very gentle on her bruised feet.

They went forward together then, making their way carefully through the rock field. At the mouth of the meadow, she gazed upward to where a large section had been cleaved off the highest reaches of the peak beyond them.

Maggie groaned at the sight, which was like a fresh, gaping wound on the darker granite.

"A thunderstorm can set off a landslide," he reassured her. "These hills are constantly reforming, breaking apart. It's not the end of the world, sweetheart."

"But what of the spring?" she said as she turned to him and thrust her face against his chest. "It was a wicked, *evil* thing to do."

"We'll survive," he whispered. "Somehow. But, yes, it was wicked. And vengeful. I never imagined he'd go this far."

MacGuigan told her then what had transpired by the seawall after she'd disappeared, how Matchem and Lady Fescue had conspired to trick the earl into marriage. And how he, Dorcas and the earl had defended her.

"And you never doubted my story?" she asked. "Even when everything he said sounded so logical?"

"Not for an instant," he declared stoutly.

Her heart soared. He finally trusted her, which in some ways was even better—and more enduring—than being loved.

"The upshot of everything," he said as they started walking again, "was that the earl dismissed Matchem. He sailed off in the gunship, after threatening everyone within earshot. He must have come about beyond the harbor and put in at Withy Cove, determined to make more mischief."

She put out a hand to halt him. "I don't understand. First, all the lies he told, turning the earl against you. And then this terrible retribution. Why did Matchem hate you so much, Gulliver?"

He looked away for a moment. "I suppose I can tell you, since you're going to be part of the family one day soon. He attacked Dorcas when she was fourteen—tried to force himself on her in a barn."

Maggie drew in a sharp breath.

"We had a rather public fist fight, Matchem and I, and I humiliated him. Broke that great ugly jaw of his."

"I'm sorry he's dead," she muttered. "I wish he were still alive and suffering somewhere."

"I'd forgot how bloodthirsty you can be." He gazed down at her through his dark brows. "Are you sure you don't have any Scots blood?"

"Not a drop," she said. "Anyway, I didn't kill him. It was Dorcas's pony did the job. And what a very pleasing symmetry that has."

He didn't want her to follow him up to the glen, but she insisted. Once they cleared the span of the landslide, which had scattered a thirty-foot-wide swath of rubble down the side of the hill, they hiked up through the gorse to the scree level. The entrance to the glen was full of debris but passable. Maggie clutched MacGuigan's hand tightly as they neared the bottom. Once they reached it, they halted there, shoulder to shoulder, and looked on in silence.

The pool was gone. The ledge above it had broken apart into great craggy monoliths, which had collapsed down into the once-magical spring and been strewn across the entire floor of the glen. Matchem's body was under there somewhere—or perhaps it had been blown into the chasm by the force of the blast.

"We can bring water from the mainland," Gulliver whispered raggedly, barely able to speak. "And set up cisterns at the base of the hills to catch the run-off from rainstorms. We'll find ways to irrigate the crops and water the livestock."

But Maggie wasn't thinking about crops or livestock. She was thinking about a dying young man whom she had been convinced would regain his health with the water from that lost spring.

She pushed away from MacGuigan, climbing recklessly over the large, dangerously jagged blocks that littered the floor of the glen. When she reached the drop-off, she knelt and peered over the edge. Only a trickle of water was running into the chasm—the remnants of what was left in the buried pool. Soon the great river under the hills would dry up, and then all the streams of St. Columba would be no more than dusty ditches.

"We need to get back," she called out to MacGuigan. "We need to gather as much of the spring water as we can. Guy needs it, Fingal needs it." Lord help her, her father needed it. That would have to be enough for her now, aiding those few. There would be no more plans for a grand hotel and dozens of ailing—and wealthy—visitors.

The earl would see to the islanders, which was some consolation. But MacGuigan's face was grim as she made her way back toward him.

"It's over," he said while she was still ten feet away.

"What about the cisterns . . . the rainwater? What about the earl helping you?"

He shook his head. "I was just trying to put a brave face on things, Maggie. The farms will fail, the villages will have no commerce . . . the island will die."

"You can blast the rocks away," she cried, refusing to give in. "The source of the spring is under there somewhere."

"Aye, we can try," he said. "But who is to say that the explosion didn't shift the layers below the surface and close up the narrow opening where the spring emanated."

He sat down on the nearest boulder, the back of one hand pressed to his mouth. When he finally looked up, his eyes were bleak. "I fear St. Columba is all out of miracles. I . . . I had so little to give you, Maggie, yet all that I possessed I would have gladly shared with you. But now, well, it's very difficult to share nothing."

"I only wanted you, Gulliver, not your worldly goods. We can make a start somewhere new . . . on Quintay, on the mainland."

He stood up, his expression as stony as the ground they stood on. "You don't understand. What I've lost here is not just possessions. . . . It's my history, my heritage. . . . It's my life."

"And so you don't want me any longer?" She was glad there was a space between them so he could not see how she trembled.

He smiled swiftly. "I will want you till I die, Maggie Bonner. But that's hardly the point, now, is it? Wanting and getting are rarely the same thing."

He had turned away and was starting wearily up the passage, when she called out, "What about me, Gulliver MacGuigan? You say you've lost your life. . . . Well, I found mine on this island. For years I kept looking forward, moving forward, because there was no pleasure or brightness in the here and now. I always told myself it would get better, that it simply had to get better. But as the years passed, I began to fear I was wrong. That I would get nothing more—no home, no friends, no husband or family of my own. Just toiling for strangers who remained aloof from me."

He'd swung back to face her, his eyes still clouded.

"Then I came here, and I felt as though I'd found a true home—*and* my sense of joy. At first I credited the island, but before long, I saw that it was you, Gulliver, who'd brought me back to life." She held out her hand to him, her fingers curled in entreaty. "Neither of us deserves to face the world alone. Not when we can do it together." Her fingers clenched. "So let me warn you, sir, I will not go on from here without you. And if you don't like it, then you can just go . . . soak your head."

A grin flashed across his face. "Such fire," he drawled. "A pity it's to be wasted on this puling whelp." He met her eyes across the gulf, and she had never felt less alone. "Together, you say? Aye, then, we'll fight back together, you and I . . . and the devil take anyone who stands in our way."

She moved eagerly toward him, heedless of the uneven footing—and went sprawling forward. Her palms and knees were wet when she rose. She looked down. Water was seeping up around her boot soles. The ground had been dry a moment ago; she'd have sworn it.

"Gul-li-ver," she whispered tentatively, still staring down. Then she turned slowly and studied the high pile of rocks on her left, all that remained of the great ledge. The freshly hewn edges of the gray granite were now darker in some places, dark and shining sleek. As she watched, water began to cascade from the top of the pile, running over and between the tumbled blocks.

"*Gulliver!*" she shouted jubilantly.

He had also seen it—and was scrambling across the space

that separated them. Maggie pitched forward into his arms, giddy beyond words, and he raised her up, right off her feet. He was laughing, his eyes silver-bright now, all scowls and grimness fled away.

"I don't know how many more miracles I can take," he said breathlessly as he lowered her and folded her in his arms.

The water was washing around their ankles, but they paid it no mind. The great spring of St. Columba had risen up, against all odds and in spite of the tampering hands of man; it seemed a sure portent that the island they loved would also rise up— out of its poverty and despair—and prosper anew.

Chapter Fifteen

Maggie and Gulliver made their way down from the hills in a sort of weary but exultant stupor. When they reached the level pastureland and she started off in the direction of the village, he caught her by the hand.

"Let's put off all the explanations for a while, shall we?" he said, gazing at his distant cottage with open longing. "You wanted to give Dorcas and Guy some time to themselves, and I say we deserve no less."

"Won't everyone be wondering about the explosion?" she said. She'd half expected to be met on the trail by a horde of alarmed villagers.

"There's often thunder off in those hills," he said. "Even on clear days. I doubt anyone noted it. Besides, I expect by now Fingal's got half the population busy planning a ceilidh—that's a party—to celebrate the end of the feud."

"I certainly don't want to miss a party," Maggie stated.

He regarded her with fond skepticism. "You look as though you're going to fall down any minute. Rather as you did the first day I brought you here."

"You said I looked at the end of my rope."

"At least you're a tiny bit cleaner than you were last time," he remarked as he started off toward the cottage. "Still, I'm going to have to dunk you in the cistern before I allow you into my bed."

"Gulliver!"

He turned to her with a cockeyed leer. "Unless you'd rather cavort in the sea. That raises some interesting possibilities."

Maggie mustered a severe frown. "So now you're back to acting the cad?"

"No," he said, "no, I'm not. I see you grinning beneath that frosty facade, Miss Bonner."

"You see too much," she muttered.

"Which makes up for me not listening half the time. And speaking of listening, I don't recall you ever telling me why you disappeared from the village." He made a noise of distaste. "Matchem implied you'd run off with the emeralds."

"I didn't run off with them, I ran off *after* them. They'd fallen out of my pocket while we were . . . um, kissing on the rock, but I didn't realize they were gone until we were back in St. Columba."

"And where are they now?"

Maggie hadn't given them a thought since the moment Matchem appeared. She smiled smugly now and put her hand to her throat. Her smile faded. Plucking frantically at the edge of her tucker, she stretched her chin up. "Please tell me they're still there," she moaned. "Around my neck."

He observed her bared throat with something akin to hunger but then shook his head. "No emeralds."

Maggie's face contorted into a terrible grimace. *"A-a-a-h, n-o-o,"* she groaned. "Not again."

She stalked forward toward the edge of the bog, her hands fisted at her sides. "I hate that infernal necklace. It's likely under ten feet of shattered rock." She sighed audibly. "And now I'll have to work for fifty years, at least, before I can repay its worth to the earl."

MacGuigan hurried to catch up with her. "I wager the rightful owner of that necklace won't mind having the next fifty years of your life."

She halted and shot him a stricken look. "You really think the earl would be that harsh?"

His eyes were devilish. "I can't answer for the earl . . . since he's not the rightful owner. I am."

Her mouth fell open. "What?"

He caressed her jaw with his knuckle. "So . . . what can you offer me, Maggie Bonner, to make up for the loss of such a valuable item?"

Maggie gripped him by his lapels. "Are you telling me you stole a necklace that belonged to you in the first place?"

"Hardly stealing," he said. "It was part of my mother's dowry."

Maggie thought she was going to pitch into the quagmire, her head was spinning so madly.

"But they're called the *Barkin* emeralds." She formed a box with her hands and shifted it from side to side. "Lord Barkin . . . the Barkin emeralds."

He was still laughing at her, the wretch. Maybe she should throw *him* into the bog. Except that he was such a bonny man—even if he did make her brain boil.

"I have to commend Dorcas," he was saying. "In spite of revealing my unfortunate name to you, she did manage to keep my greatest secret safe. And I must say, it's allowed me some lovely sparring with you."

"Lovely," she echoed darkly. "And how did Guy come to be in possession of *your* necklace?"

"It was willed to my mother by her paternal grandmother, Henrietta, Countess of Barkin. Guy's mother had borrowed it for an affair on the mainland . . . she still had it when the rift between our families occurred. It ended up in the earl's bank vault in London."

"Until the earl removed it last month."

"So have you figured it out then?" He was beaming at her like an over-eager puppy.

"Your mother was a Barkin?"

"Lady Katherine Barkin, to be precise."

"Lady Katherine? That was the woman's name in the portrait in the castle."

His own mouth fell open. "When were you inside Whitesands?"

"You're not the only one with secrets, MacGuigan," she said primly. "Now, let me think. If she was the daughter of the Earl of Barkin . . ." Maggie calculated rapidly in her head and then exclaimed, "That makes Guy your first cousin!"

"Yes, it does."

She rounded on him and thumped him once on the chest. *"Ooh!* And when I think of all the time I wasted worrying about your sorry neck and fretting over how casually you treated the abduction of an earl's bride—and now it turns out you were never at any risk."

He caught her gently by the wrists. "More than I knew, actually. After years of Matchem's insinuation, Guy might just have set the law on me. Still, I don't imagine he'd have welcomed another family scandal." His mouth twisted. "Though I thank you for all your worry, *mignonne*."

Her eyes flashed; she still thought it was beastly of him to withhold the explanation for so long. "And you couldn't simply have told me all this that night by the fire, when I asked about your family?"

He shrugged. "I suppose I was flattered that you were concerned over me risking in my . . . sorry neck. So I indulged myself in a bit of prevarication." He looked away for an instant. "And there was something else. Even then, I wanted you to . . . to admire me, Maggie, for who I was, not for my illustrious connections."

"I don't give a fig for any of that," she declared. "I'm quite satisfied to have found myself an . . . honest laborer."

"There's a relief."

"And you're truly not angry about the necklace?"

"An hour ago we just missed being flattened by a landslide. A half hour ago, we thought we'd lost the water that sustains this island. Let's just say the Barkin emeralds were the tribute we paid for everything turning out right in the end. After all, emeralds and gold come from the earth, and now they've returned to their source."

He squeezed her arm. "Perhaps I wasn't meant to have those emeralds, Maggie. Maybe they were only the lure that led me to you. I sailed off to steal them and came away with something much more valuable."

She tried to smile. "A butter-fingered shrew, do you mean?"

"A woman who can see beyond the tip of her nose—which is more than I've ever done. I'm not scoffing at your plans for this island any longer. If your scheme works, we won't need the earl's gold or the Barkin emeralds."

She was starting to feel a bit less guilty. It wasn't as though the necklace had fallen into the sea. Who was to say that some hunter might not find it among the detritus from the landslide?

He slung his arm over her shoulder, and together they made

their way to the cottage. They managed to get most of the grime off their hands and faces at the cistern—and with a minimum of foolish horseplay. He was just opening the front door for her, when Maggie turned to him with a sharp cry.

"Hold a minute, MacGuigan. I've finally put it all together. If Lady Katherine was your mother, then the man in that portrait was your father—which makes *you* the laird."

His cheeks narrowed. "No, I'm not."

She nearly gritted her teeth. "That's exactly what Dorcas and Fingal said when I asked them."

"You asked the wrong question," he uttered. "I am the laird's son, but not the laird. I never took the title after my father died. I'm still not sure I deserve it. Every woe that's befallen this island can be laid at my door."

"Oh, pooh," she said. "You hardly control the harvest or the abundance of fish."

He shot her a rueful grin. "I do tell myself that from time to time." He tugged at one of her stray curls. "But are you now saying you want me to take the title, Miss I-Don't-Give-A-Fig?"

"Not for me," she said quickly. "For the islanders. They've obviously needed a rallying point for ages. Can't you give them that, Gulliver? Quintay has a belted earl . . . couldn't you let St. Columba have her own head of state?"

"Well, if you put it that way. I've always fancied being a benevolent despot."

She prodded him in the ribs. "And *I* fancy you acquiring a whole population to bully, in lieu of one solitary female."

"Who gives as good as she gets," he reminded her, as he ushered her through the door.

Maggie felt as though she had returned to a safe haven—the humble, rustic dwelling had begun to feel so much like home to her. When Gulliver took her into his arms, she knew she really had come home.

His wry amusement had been replaced by an expression of simmering heat. He tipped her head back, his pale eyes burning into hers. She felt her stomach begin to pitch and roll—rather like sailing with Captain Og.

"Come lie with me, Maggie," he said gruffly.

She was about to offer up a maidenly protest, when Marguerite came to the fore.

"Yes," she said, simply and naturally, because it was what she wanted beyond anything.

"Just that and no more," he promised as he drew her into the bedroom. "After all we've been through, I think I could sleep round the clock."

"What, and miss the ceilidh?"

"Never that," he said as he plucked the featherbed from before the hearth and spread it over the mattress. "We'll hear the sound of fiddles and drums come drifting across the bay. But it won't be for hours yet."

He tugged off his greatcoat and boots, then stretched out on his back on the bed. Maggie kicked off her half boots and curled up beside him, thinking she'd never felt so tired—or so marvelously keyed up. She sighed and nestled closer when he slid one arm around her waist.

This is what my life will be for all my days, she realized with a deep-seated thrill. Sleeping beside him, waking beside him . . . laughing with him, being teased by him . . . comforting and being comforted in turn.

Something her mother once told her came back to her now—that real love wasn't a fair-weather emotion. No, it not only survived the lean times but also grew richer and stronger. Just like MacGuigan, she thought. Adversity and loss had tempered him and brought out the finest parts of his nature.

Maggie could have sworn he was asleep when she leaned over him and whispered, "I love you, Gulliver."

He opened his eyes; they were smiling up at her. "I heard that." His hand drifted to her throat. "Why aren't you sleeping, sweetheart? Don't tell me you're still fretting over that necklace."

"Maybe a little."

He leaned up on one elbow. "My only regret is that I'll never get to see you wear it. There's something particularly taking about a green-eyed woman in emeralds. For now, at least, you'll have to make do with the ring from your departed grandmama and the cherished brooch from your father."

"I gave the brooch to Barry MacNeill's wife," she said, and then winced. She hadn't meant to tell him.

He tipped his head to one side. "How so?"

"To buy feed . . . for her pet cow who was ailing."

"Ach, Maggie," he said raggedly. "I'd put off selling the *Kestrel* because I could not bear to part with my fine ship. And there you were, giving away one of the only two valuables you possessed."

"Cora needed it," she said simply. "And I wanted to do something."

His eyes moved over her face like a caress.

"You've completely undone me now," he murmured. "Right here on this bed where you struck the first blow."

Her eyes widened. "You know I'd never have hurt you like that if—"

"Hush! It served its purpose, made me start to see that you were not like any woman I'd met before. Remember, that night . . . when you told me you knew how to use a knife? On a man's throat, you said." His fingers traced across the column of her neck. "Or in his belly." His hand splayed on her stomach.

Maggie thought she was going to melt.

"Ah, but do you know the surest way to best a stubborn, headstrong man?" He lowered his mouth to her ear, then whispered intently as he pressed his hand above her breast, "Aim for his heart, Maggie. Always aim for his heart."

Epilogue

Og MacNeill tipped his chair back, took a swallow of ale and then handed the jug to his father. Fingal took a hearty swig and then waved to the man standing at the edge of the cliff. "Have a drink, Monsoor?"

The tall, gray-haired gentleman with the olive complexion and the air of a courtier acknowledged the offer and turned away from observing the view below him—which consisted of two couples strolling arm in arm along the beach and two infants toddling doggedly after a large, tawny hound. He came toward them slowly but moved with easy grace. He barely required the use of his cane now, Og was pleased to note. Quite a difference from the day, two years ago, when he'd been carried from the *Charles Stuart* in a litter, his limbs cruelly bent with arthritics.

Edmund Bonheur settled himself in a chair beside the two men and took a hearty swallow from the jug. Og swore they'd make an islander of him yet.

The row of wrought-iron chairs, with their spectacular view of the sea, was usually reserved for guests of the hotel, but Bridie had taken most of them on a stroll through the bustling village. She was in her element, cooking elaborate meals, arranging bouquets of flowers, ordering the housemaids about like a major general. Fingal was likewise busy, organizing cross-country walks and cruises to the seal rocks to amuse the guests. As for the monsoor, he was in the thick of things these days—overseeing all the entertainments in the castle. Why, only yesterday Og had overheard Lady Rathbone telling her husband that the theatricals here rivaled Drury Lane.